Dear Reader,

Well, we all know *how* babies are made. But the *what, where, when* and *why* that bring an infant into the world nine months later are a different story altogether. And Silhouette Books has three of those stories in this very special collection.

Jill Marie Landis, Debbie Macomber and Gina Ferris Wilkins have written heartwarming romances that tell how that "twinkle in the eye" began. What's more, their stories are connected. One heirloom cradle appears in each tale, carrying on a priceless tradition—waiting for a brand-new bundle of joy.

And that's exactly what *Three Mothers & a Cradle* is, a little bundle of joy for you—minus the crying, the diaper changing, the 3:00 a.m. feedings....

Enjoy!
The Editors
Silhouette Books

Three Mothers & a Cradle

Jill Marie Landis
Debbie Macomber
Gina Ferris Wilkins

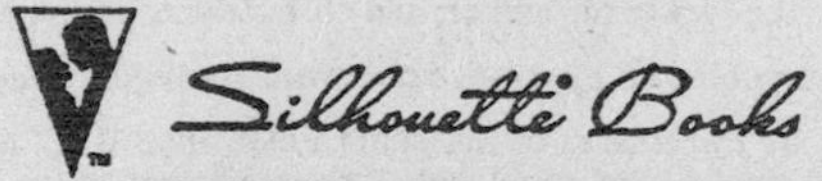

Published by Silhouette Books
America's Publisher of Contemporary Romance

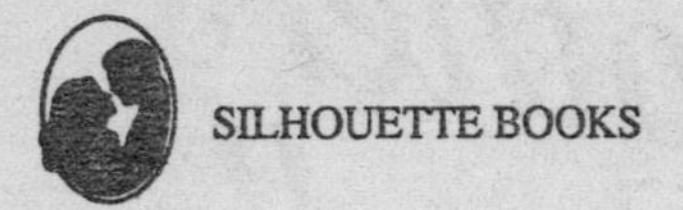

THREE MOTHERS & A CRADLE

ISBN 0-373-48335-X

CRADLE SONG

ROCK-A-BYE BABY

BEGINNINGS

This edition published by arrangement with Harlequin Enterprises B.V.

Printed in U.S.A.

CONTENTS

CRADLE SONG 11
by Jill Marie Landis

ROCK-A-BYE BABY 153
by Debbie Macomber

BEGINNINGS 287
by Gina Ferris Wilkins

CRADLE SONG

Jill Marie Landis

A Note from Jill Marie Landis

When Silhouette called to ask if I would write a Mother's Day story for this anthology, I was thrilled and excited for the opportunity to work with my friend Debbie Macomber, as well as fellow writer Gina Ferris Wilkins. Then came the challenge of *what* to write and how to begin the legend of the cradle that would figure in all three stories.

Now, you may think it a bit unusual to read a Mother's Day story about a woman who can't remember whether or not she has had a child or, if she did, what happened to her baby. This is the dilemma that Sarah, the heroine, faces, but fortunately she has the help of the hero, Adam Stroud, to see her through. When Adam discovers Sarah in a Nez Percé camp at a trading rendezvous, he pays an exorbitant price for the amnesiac white captive and then sets out to help her rediscover her past. Along the way, they experience the healing power of love and the miracle of a new beginning.

I hope you enjoy the story and wish all of you happy reading! I always enjoy hearing from readers at P.O. 3533, Long Beach, CA 90803.

Jill Marie Landis

Part One

The Washington Plateau
1857

Stick in hand, the boy child stood before her, but she refused to look up and give him the satisfaction of knowing she had felt the sharp bite of the pointed end of his makeshift weapon. She looked away from the bright flowers beaded on the little moccasins he wore and continued to stare at the ground, studying the dirt in which she sat and then the jagged edge of the hem of the calico rag that barely covered her calves. The little menace prodded her again, twice as hard as before. This time she could not help but flinch away from the pain. Still, she did not look at him.

To look into his dark eyes would make him real.

Instinctively, she knew that in time he would tire of the game and move on. Withdrawing further into the protective cloak of insanity that had begun to fit so well, the woman began to slowly rock to-and-fro where she sat. Her fingers, with their cracked and broken nails, scratched the earth as she clawed the dusty ground. A frown creased her forehead. She would not allow herself to remember anything that would give her hope, a glimmer of light. Her mind had dwelt in the safety of darkness far too long.

Her stomach rumbled. She touched it and felt only emptiness beneath the ragged fabric. Her hand lingered there for a moment, waiting for some long-missing sign of life, but nothing happened. There was no longer any quickening inside her. Hunger was her only companion now, bone-gnawing hunger that forced her to eat anything her captors threw at her—remnants of smoked meat and fish, roots and berries, even insects. Along with the emptiness and hunger, she experienced an incessant hum that droned in her head, an off-key rambling song of mourning that never seemed to end. She rocked steadily to the beat of the tune that wandered aimlessly up and down the scale.

Eventually the boy ran off, his sturdy brown legs carrying him quickly over the uneven ground. The woman leaned back against the wall of reed mats woven together and smiled a sly, secret smile to herself. Her expression was hidden from the world by the curtain of her matted hair. Soon the smile faded. She continued to sway where she sat and stared at nothing.

* * *

Adam Stroud moved easily through the rendezvous encampment at the Dalles, a village of temporary lodgings spread out beneath the bluffs along the Columbia River. One of a handful of white traders present, he nodded often in greeting, for he recognized many acquaintances among the Nez Percé.

With his shoulder-length raven hair and his skin deeply bronzed from long hours in the sun, he might have been mistaken for one of them if not for the sky blue eyes that gave him away.

His clothing was a combination of native dress and sturdy woolen wear. His fringed buckskin coat was three-quarter length and heavily decorated with beadwork across the yolk. He had been lucky to make a good trade for it three years ago. Unlike many of the other white trappers and traders he knew, he had not yet taken to wearing soft-soled moccasins. Adam Stroud was still willing to pay the price for a good pair of boots.

He could detect an eagerness to trade this year as he moved among the participants of the rendezvous. The winter hunt had been a good one. Quantity would drive the price of a good pelt down, but he could always guarantee the quality of the furs he obtained at the Dalles.

He smiled when he recognized a formidable figure approaching him from the opposite side of the camp. Runs-With-The-Wind had been his friend for six years now, ever since the winter they had found themselves trapped together in a blizzard that had swept down from the north and stranded the two strangers in a mountain cave.

Throughout the tedious days until the snow thawed enough to permit travel, the two had not only learned to communicate in each other's language, but had discovered they shared more similarities than differences.

Adam smiled, reached out and grasped his friend's forearm. After they exchanged swift greetings, Runs-With-The-Wind led him toward the communal longhouse the tribe used as a gathering place during the trade sessions.

"The hunt was good," Adam commented. They paused while a passel of children and puppies, appearing as nothing more than a jumble of arms and legs and lithe brown bodies, ran squealing past.

"It was good," Runs-With agreed. "You'll be forced to pay high prices for the finest of pelts this year, my friend."

Adam laughed, the boisterous sound drawing smiles from those gathered near one of the entrances to the longhouse. He lifted his felt hat and ran his splayed fingers through his hair, then shoved his hat back on. Squinting against the sun, he shook his head, unwilling to be baited by his friend.

"A good hunt means too many fine furs. You'll be lucky to sell them all," he said. He thought of the trade goods he had loaded upon his pack mules—copper kettles, blankets, coffeepots, bolts of cotton, wire, knives, beads and bells—and hoped he had judged rightly and brought enough.

Someone called out to Runs-With, and together they paused beside one of the doors at the side of the longhouse. Adam eyed his companion with some jealousy and knew it was no wonder Runs-With-The-Wind had found himself four wealthy wives. The man was tall and broad shouldered. His long, midnight hair, worn in the style of the Nez Percé, was cut short in front, stiffened and brushed upward. Long braids were plaited alongside his face, and the rest was left to hang past his shoulders in back. He wore intricately decorated leggings and a breechcloth, a finely tanned shirt and soft-soled moccasins that his wives had spent many hours beading. Nearly even in height with Adam, at well over six feet, Runs-With-The-Wind was a commanding figure with a ready sense of humor and was well respected among his people.

Adam Stroud counted himself lucky to call the man his friend.

As he stood waiting for Runs-With to barter with a Yakima trader that his second wife had brought over to him, Adam's gaze fell upon a lone figure seated on the ground not far away.

The creature appeared to be a woman. Her long tanned legs were shapely, but coated with streaked dirt. She was ill-kept, her clothing torn, her hair matted and tangled. As he watched her rock slowly back and forth, he was suddenly arrested by the sight of such an unkempt stranger in the midst of these people. It came to him suddenly that her filthy hair was very light in color, and that her skin, although tanned by the sun, was far too pale for her to be anything but a half-breed at the very least.

Runs-With continued to argue, first with his wife and then with a trader trying to drive a hard bargain for a horse collar worked in porcupine quills. Ignored for the moment, and still curious, Adam moved closer to the woman seated in the dirt.

She was resting on her folded legs, protectively hunched into herself, rocking to the sound of an eerie, off-key humming she produced. Her hair was definitely tangled and matted together in rats' nests in more places than not. Her arms, legs, hands and face were covered with a coating of dirt. She didn't stop humming, even when he walked over to stand directly in front of her. In fact, she didn't even break rhythm.

His feet were just inches away from her knees. Surely she realized he was there.

Adam cleared his throat. "Ma'am?"

There was no response.

He tried twice more and then hunkered down in front of her. Half-afraid she might strike him, he reached out slowly and placed his forefinger and thumb beneath her chin and tilted her face up to his.

Radiant liquid blue eyes, the color of the sea on a sunny day, stared back at him. Neither the coat of dust and dirt nor the threadbare calico gown could hide her perfect features—full lips, a slightly flared, tapered nose, the delicate line of her throat. She was painfully thin, younger than he'd first thought, and in need of a long hot bath and a haircut. She seemed to have lost her wits.

"Walking-Dead-Woman."

The sound of Runs-With-The-Wind's voice startled him. Adam let go of the woman's chin, and she immediately lowered her head, effectively shielding her eyes from him. Frowning, Adam stood up and found his friend beside him. The humming increased in volume.

"Do you know her real name?" Adam asked.

"I know of no other."

"She's white. Where did she come from?"

Runs-With paused. He glanced around so casually that it almost appeared as if he was not disturbed by the question, but Adam knew his friend better than that. He could see the slight frown that marred the other man's features. Finally the Nez Percé admitted, "She was a captive of the Crow. River-Walker traded two of his best horses for her, thinking she would make a good slave for his first wife, who needed to be appeased when he brought a second wife into his lodge. The slave has proved to be good for nothing. She is alive, but no longer living." He touched his temple. "Her mind is gone."

Adam tried to look away from the woman, but couldn't. "Where was she captured? Do you know?"

Runs-With shook his head. "Far across the mountains. Along the trail that is now filled with whites. The Crow claim they traded for her, that they did not take her from her people." He shrugged. "Who knows where she is from? She hasn't spoken." The man paused and glanced toward the center of the encampment. "We should go to the trading area. Everyone is waiting to see what you have to trade, Adam Stroud."

It was dusk along the river before the day's trading ended. With the weather being unseasonably warm for fall, the people encamped along the Columbia lingered outdoors before open fires. Single log canoes, hollowed out by fire and shaped to ply the river currents, were lined up along the banks. The bobbing light from pitch torches used to attract salmon for night spearfishing flickered like huge fireflies through the trees as Adam packed up his remaining trade goods.

All in all, he counted it a fine day's work. The beaver pelts he had acquired, along with the beautifully cured buffalo robe he'd bartered from a Plains tribesman, would bring him good money at the white settlement not far from his cabin in the Cascade Mountains.

As he moved toward the longhouse to share a meal with Runs-With-The-Wind, and his friend's wives and numerous children, Adam found himself searching for some sign of the white slave he had seen earlier that afternoon. It was not all that uncommon for the various peoples who inhabited the Plateau to own slaves. The Hupa, Karok and Yurok often made indentured slaves of those who owed them a great debt. Others, who were captured in raids by the Plains tribes, became sought after as part of a thriving east-west exchange for horses. Adam reckoned that was how the girl that his friend called "Walking-Dead-Woman" came to be with the Nez Percé.

When he reached the longhouse, he found her sitting in exactly the same place she had been earlier in the day. He wondered if she had eaten or if anyone had even bothered to see that she had been fed.

It's not your concern, Stroud. Let it be.

He lingered a moment longer, watching the girl intently before he entered the lodge. Unlike the usual conical lodges the Nez Percé had adopted from Plains tribes and so often used, the communal longhouse was built for the trade fair. The walls and roof were constructed of tightly woven mats of cattail and tule reeds.

As he stepped into the side door, the smoky scent of the interior assailed him. Even though his eyes stung, Adam could see down the length of the huge structure and noted the many families gathered together. Each family had kindled a fire within the center aisle of the structure, the center of the ceiling having been left open for ventilation. Through the firelight and shadows, Adam quickly located Runs-With and his family amid the other inhabitants.

When he arrived at the cook fire, Adam watched Runs-With, who laughed with one of his older children. The boy, Two Feathers, was nearly sixteen. While Adam stood by, the youth announced that he was going night fishing with his friends and would return later. Adam was soon seated and served a generous portion of smoked salmon. As he stared down at the food on his lap, he couldn't help but think of the white slave sitting in the dark outside the walls of the shelter. Unless she was seen to, she would slowly weaken. Once unable to keep up with the others, she would be left to her own fate.

He waited until the meal was over and Runs-With had offered to share a pipe of rich tobacco before he brought up the subject foremost on his mind.

"Does River-Walker value his worthless slave?" Adam finally asked.

Runs-With-The-Wind suddenly became preoccupied with the long-stemmed pipe in his hands. When he looked back up at Adam, there was no denying the speculative expression in his eye. "You have never taken a wife, Adam. Do you want this one for yourself?"

Adam set aside the wooden trencher that had held his meal. He met his friend's eyes and answered honestly, "I was married long ago, when I was very young."

The moment he said the words aloud, a familiar sadness washed through him. Instantly a vision of Katherine came to mind. They had grown up together, were virtually children themselves when they married. She had followed him west with enough enthusiasm for both of them. They had built the cabin together, and then, when he was certain that nothing but the future stretched before them, she had died carrying his child.

His friend was awaiting an answer. "I am not looking for a wife. I hunt, trap, move around all winter. There aren't many women who would be willing to live like that."

"No white woman, you mean," Runs-With said.

Adam nodded. "You're right. No white woman."

They sat in silence for a time, passing the pipe back and forth while the women talked softly among themselves and the younger children crawled onto their beds of thick buffalo hides and fell asleep. Adam watched them. He had lived his solitary life in his one-room cabin for so long that he could not imagine changing his life to accommodate a woman, let alone children. He had his work and his memories. He never considered himself lonely, merely alone.

But today, somehow without uttering a sound, the captive woman had appealed to something deep inside him. Physically, she was nothing like Katherine, but he couldn't help being reminded of his own wife every time he looked at her. What if Katherine had been taken from him while he was out trapping? What if she had been stranded in the same situation?

He would have wanted someone to save her. He was the only white man at the trade fair. Adam knew he could not leave the girl behind without trying to save her from her present situation.

"Why do you ask after the white woman?"

Runs-With's words startled him out of his thoughts. Adam answered immediately. "She needs care. I would take her to the missionary settlement near my home, try to find out where she's from. Surely her family is searching for her."

His friend seemed to lose interest after Adam admitted he did not want the woman for his wife.

Adam persisted. "So, do you think River-Walker would sell her to me?"

Winter would be on them in a few weeks' time. If he took the girl now and didn't get her to the mission before long, he would be stuck with her for months. How could he be sure she would even be able to travel with him? What if she tried to run away?

Adam wanted to call back his question and felt his stomach sink to his toes when Runs-With stood and walked away in search of River-Walker.

What in the hell are you thinking about, Stroud? His inquiry had surprised even himself. *That's all you need. A crazy woman to drag home with you. What have you gotten yourself into now?*

* * *

It was dark. She loved the nights, for they left her alone when the sun fell from the sky. Slowly, in case anyone was watching, she raised her head and stared across the clearing at the river. Through the pine boughs of the forest she could see what appeared to be firelight darting back and forth. Perhaps the stars were falling.

Would the earth burst into flame if they did?

She was cold. So cold now that the sun had disappeared beyond the bend in the river. The tempo of her rocking increased, but it failed to warm her. Her mouth was dry, but the effort to rise and go to the river for water was too great, the path too long. What difference did it make, anyway? She would die soon; she could feel it down to the depths of her soul.

She would die, and if she were lucky, it would be without remembering.

"Why are you laughing?" Adam knew the answer to his question, but he thought perhaps confronting his friend would get the man to stop chortling. He was irritated enough at himself for both of them.

"You paid too much, Stroud. Everyone knows that. Far too much for a Walking-Dead-Woman." Runs-With laughed, a loud barking sound that just now irritated Adam more than he would ever admit. "River-Walker is happy, at least."

"I'm sure he is. That was one of my best horses."

Runs-With laughed again. "*And* five blankets."

Adam mumbled, "*And* a set of pots and pans."

Nearly doubled over now, the Nez Percé hunter slapped his knees. "*And* two hundred trade beads . . . of all colors."

"I'm glad to see I've provided the night's entertainment for you," Adam groused.

Runs-With shook his long hair back over his shoulders, his dark eyes cutting in Adam's direction. "For everyone," he added. "What will you do now? I want to watch you go claim your prize."

Adam wished he could avoid any more of the relentless teasing he had endured since the bargain with Walking-Dead-Woman's owner had been struck, but there was no way he could ignore the plight of the girl he had paid a king's ransom for.

"I'm not going to let her starve any longer, if that's what you mean. It wouldn't be a very good business move."

"For what you paid for her, friend, you had best see to keeping her alive as long as you can."

Adam found the girl in the dark shadows that ran along the side of the longhouse. She had not moved an inch. He paused before her and stared down at the top of her head. The humming had stopped, but she was still rocking back and forth. The motion irritated him. He squatted directly in front of her and reached out, placing his hands on her shoulders to stop the repetitive motion. She paused, but the humming commenced again.

"Stop it," Adam demanded sharply and gave her shoulders a slight shake, hoping his harsh tone would cut through her withdrawal.

The humming trailed to an off-key end. She didn't look up.

He stood, pulling her up with him, half expecting her knees to buckle and cause her to melt back down into a sitting position, but although the girl trembled, she remained on her feet. Still, he didn't dare let go of her shoulders.

"I'm Adam Stroud," he told her, speaking slowly, enunciating each syllable carefully. She made no response, but behind him, Runs-With laughed.

"It would be better to talk to the trees, Stroud."

Adam sighed, sorry to admit his friend was probably right. As if in answer, the breeze set the pine boughs whispering around them.

"Come on." He let go of her shoulders and clamped his hand around her slender wrist. Intent on taking her to his own campsite, set off from the others, he walked away from the sound of laughter.

When they reached his camp, Adam settled the girl on a pile of trade blankets and then slipped a buffalo robe over her shoulders. The weight of the heavy robe forced it down off one shoulder. He righted the robe, started a fire and then began to rummage through his supplies to find her something to eat.

Figuring she was no doubt used to pemmican, the native staple eaten on the trail, he found some in his parfleche, an all-purpose bag made of tanned hide. When she didn't respond as he held the food out to her, Adam knelt down, lifted her hand and laid the food in her palm. He closed her fingers over the handful of dried meat ground with berries and stepped away, thinking that if he ignored her, she might eat when she thought he was not watching. If she thought anything at all, he reminded himself.

He made a mental note of his remaining trade goods and shook his head in the darkness. With what little supplies he had left, his trading would end by late morning. Glancing over at the girl, he discovered with some satisfaction that she was shoving the entire handful of pemmican into her mouth. He couldn't help but wonder how she would fare on the long trail back to his cabin. At least she had come this far without balking.

Adam gave her water, and then, silently calling himself every kind of a fool, he sat down not far away and merely watched her. It seemed she knew what to do with the water bag. In fact, she raised it to her lips and drank as if she were dying of thirst. When she was finished, she remained oblivious to his presence and for the moment was still. He was wondering if she had fallen asleep sitting upright, but then she slowly turned her head to stare at him with vacant eyes. The firelight bathed her features with an eerie glow. Her face was smudged with dirt and ashes; her hair straggled down across most of her face and partially over one eye.

He returned her stare, wondering what, if anything, was going through her mind.

"I'm Adam Stroud," he said softly. "Who are you? Can you tell me your name?"

She cocked her head in a way that reminded him of a curious puppy, and for a moment he held his breath, certain she was about to answer him. Perhaps his words had triggered her memory; perhaps she could tell him who she was and how she'd come to be handed off from tribe to tribe across vast, unsettled territories. He would help her find her family, and then, relieved of the burden he had managed to shoulder so easily, he would be on his way.

She was staring at his mouth. He spoke again. With a little more prodding, he hoped to hear her answer his questions. "Your name is . . . ?"

The girl lifted her hand and reached toward him. Adam was struck by the sorrowful emptiness in her eyes. Her hand never wavered as she lightly touched her forefinger to his lips. Tempted to pull away, he remained still and watched her as she stared back at him. She was beyond comprehension, but his words, or at least the sound of them, had intrigued her somehow.

"I am Adam Stroud." He formed each word slowly.

She withdrew her hand and clasped the buffalo robe.

"Can you understand me?" As he sat there wondering how to reach her, it occurred to him that it was possible she might not speak English at all. Many of the travelers on the Oregon Trail were from foreign countries. He tried what little German he knew and then French. Her expression never wavered, nor did she show any sign of understanding.

Adam sighed. It was late. The dampness that came with nightfall was heavily upon them. He glanced around, wondering if he should tie her to a nearby tree to prevent her from wandering away while he slept. Deciding that since she had shown no inclination to move away from the longhouse earlier, he was probably safe in leaving her unfettered. Adam unrolled his own bedroll and placed it near the fire. Before he crawled beneath his blankets, he commanded, "Lie down."

She didn't move.

Adam returned to her and squatted there before her, reached out and shoved her into a resting position on top of the blankets. He pulled the heavy robe over her, making certain she was protected from the cold.

"Sleep," he said softly and then whispered, "And for the love of God, don't run off."

With what he had invested in her, he would hate to lose the girl before he could find her family, hoping they would be so overjoyed that they would generously reward him. If so, he might be able to recoup the losses that had come from this idiot notion.

He could see her across the campsite. The firelight played off the features of her dirt-streaked face and every so often highlighted her eyes, which remained open and staring. As far as he knew, she never closed them. For once the fire had burned down to glowing embers, she was still awake as he was finally able to get to sleep.

* * *

Uncomfortable with the thought that he was about to start on the trail home with the strange woman trailing along behind him, Adam tried to concentrate on what Runs-With-The-Wind was saying. The Nez Percé warrior stood beside his third wife, who was holding a four-year-old boy on her hip even though she wore a carrier with a much younger child on her back.

"My wives want you to have this," Runs-With told him, indicating an oversize parfleche of woven hemp. He extended the bag with its geometric designs and Adam accepted it as Runs-With added, "There is something inside for your woman."

"She's not *my* woman," Adam grumbled. Awkwardly, he held the bag, wishing he were on the trail, wishing he'd never stopped to pay one bit of attention to the white slave who stood mute as stone behind him, clutching the heavy buffalo hide around her shoulders.

Adam opened the parfleche and withdrew a woman's gown, which had been tanned to a buttery softness. It was made of two deerskins, the yoke covered with the intricate floral beadwork that was typical of the Nez Percé. There was a pair of calf-length leggings, as well, and a pair of moccasins.

"Thank you," he said to Runs-With's young wife. "These are fine pieces." As he folded the items and slipped them back into the bag he added beneath his breath, "She won't be wearing them until I can get her cleaned up."

"Safe journey to you, my friend," Runs-With-The-Wind bade Adam.

"And you," Adam returned. "You know where I'll be, if you need me."

Runs-With nodded.

Adam turned around and took his new companion's wrist to lead her out of the camp. He supposed he should be thankful that this morning she had still been right where he'd bedded her down last night and that just now she was following him so willingly—but he could only concentrate on the acute embarrassment he felt as he lead the girl away.

The New One was different.

The New One had not hurt her, yet. The beating, slapping, pinching and tormenting had stopped. So had the hair pulling. Perhaps now she was safe. They kept moving away from the others, away from the place where the little ones had taken such delight in tormenting her.

They had been traveling all day, walking with an even pace across the open land and then up into the mountains and through the forest. She stumbled once, expecting to feel the blows and hear the shouts and insults she did not understand, but when her feet faltered, the New One merely reached out for her arm and helped her to her feet.

After she tripped, they walked slower. The New One had stopped speaking to her.

She chanced once to glance up, just to see if she could tell how the sun had somehow pulled itself up to hang in the sky again. She frowned, staring at the back of the New One. The size of him, the long dark hair, reminded her of something she could not place, but she would not let the pictures in her mind surface. Thankfully, she still remembered nothing of the past.

They walked all that day and the next, the New One leading the horse covered with bundles. He gave her food. The hunger had subsided, but not the eternal emptiness that filled her. When it was dark, he pushed her down on the blankets, but she was afraid to sleep. Sleep was a luxury she could not afford. The visions would come if she slept, visions of blood and death, and she knew if she saw too much in her dreams, that what little awareness she had salvaged would be shattered.

Rolled up in the warmth of the heavy fur he had draped around her, she watched the New One through the flickering flames of the campfire as he slept. The firelight danced over his relaxed features, highlighting pulsating pieces of the whole. A long rifle lay on the ground close beside him. She smiled at the weapon. No gun would help if anyone seriously wanted to harm them. Nothing would save them if they were overwhelmed. She didn't know how she knew; she just did.

Let him sleep. She would watch and wait. Death had been chasing her for a long time now.

Adam sighed with relief when they finally reached his cabin. With the girl along, it had taken him four full days of travel, twice the normal time, to get home. He led her to the low porch that fronted the hip-roof cabin he had built himself and urged her to a sitting position by placing a hand on her shoulder.

She had taken to staring at him lately, watching him through the tangled strands of blond hair that hung over her eyes. He found her unblinking blue gaze far more disturbing than her former vacant stare. She seemed to be trying to place him, or at the very least to decide who he was and why he had taken her away from the others.

It took him awhile to unpack his horse and then feed and water the animal. On his way back from the lean-to stable built against one end of the cabin, he paused to pick up a half barrel tipped up on end.

Adam carried it back to the porch. There was no way he was taking the girl into the cabin as filthy as she was now.

"Bathtub," he said, pointing to the half barrel. "Wait here." He didn't know whether she understood him or not, but decided that he would go right on talking as if she did. Sooner or later she just might catch on.

He lit a fire in the fireplace, and from the rain barrel at one corner of the house, he filled the largest pot he had and hung it up to boil. While he waited, he carried his trade goods inside and stacked them along one wall, took the clothes Runs-With's wives had given the girl and laid them out on the bed, and then hunted down a piece of strong lye soap.

A glance at the girl told him she had not moved. No longer watching him, she sat on the edge of the porch, legs dangling, bare toes tracing lines in the dirt. Adam paused long enough to survey the dense woods surrounding his home. It was good to be back, to stand on the mountainside amid the lodgepole pines and aspen and stare down at the golden valley stretched out below.

Dusk had crept up on him by the time the makeshift tub was filled with water. Until the lukewarm bath was ready, he hadn't put much thought into how to proceed. With a shrug, he turned to the girl, hoping her instincts would take over or that she would relish feeling clean again, so much so that she would take the initiative and bathe herself.

He wasn't that lucky.

Adam took her hand and led her to the side of the tub.

"Water," he said, pointing halfheartedly.

She stared at the wall of the cabin.

"You need a bath." He laughed at his own understatement. "You need to soak for a month of Sundays." He pantomimed scrubbing his arms and shoulders. "In the bath. Now."

She started humming.

Adam sighed and ran his fingers through his hair. He was in need of a bath himself, tired, hungry and in no mood for this.

"Get in," he said a little louder than before. *"Get in now."*

She simply stood and stared at nothing.

Something inside him snapped. He grabbed her, pulled the buffalo robe out of her hands and tossed it aside. Adam lifted her arms out to her sides until she stood like a scarecrow. Amazingly enough, she left her arms extended, just as he had placed them. He unbuttoned the two buttons left of the dozen or more that had once closed the front of her ragged calico gown. After studying her dress for a moment, Adam bent down and grabbed it by the hem and began to draw it up the length of her. He had the dress off her and had tossed it over her head before he paused long enough to realize she was nude beneath the thin fabric.

"Oh, Lord," he whispered. He scanned the forest before his eyes locked on the tub at their feet as he fought for control and tried to avoid looking at her body.

"*Please,* lady. Please get in the damn tub."

He led her forward, took her by the arms and made her step into the tepid water, worn moccasins and all. When she was standing in the tub, he gently pressed on her shoulders, and she obediently sank down, folded her legs and submerged up to her breasts. Adam gave a sigh of thanks.

Kneeling behind her, he found the soap and tried to ignore the fact that his hands were shaking as he dipped the bar into the water and lathered it between his palms. Figuring it would be safer to start at the top, Adam began to wet and soap her hair with his two hands. He was hard pressed not to catch his fingers in the many tangles and knots.

"Time to rinse out the soap," he warned as he pushed her head down and then scooped up great handfuls of water and let it pour out of his cupped hands. Adam steeled himself to remain impervious as he set about to complete his task. He pulled off her sodden moccasins and set them on the porch.

Even in the dim light, he could see the fading scars of beatings long past that crisscrossed her back. Her upper arms and shoulders were bruised. He gently traced the marks across her back with his soapy fingertips, wishing his touch could remove them. Here and there she bore new, angry red scratches. He had noticed on the trail that her fingertips appeared to have been scarred from burning, but had had no idea her injuries were so extensive. Some of her nails were jagged and torn to the quick.

Gently, seething inwardly over all she had endured at the hands of her earlier captors, he lathered one of the girl's arms—one of her long, finely tapered, delicately shaped arms. As he turned it over, he couldn't help but note the fine blue veins that showed through the translucent ivory skin on the vulnerable underside of her wrist. An overwhelming urge to kiss her wrist swept through him, but he would not allow himself to follow the forbidden thought to completion.

Beads of sweat broke out on his forehead and along his upper lip. He swiped at the moisture with the back of his hand and tried to concentrate on anything but what he was doing. He had spent so many years alone that the simple task was like enduring torture.

Think of something else.

Trying to picture his wife, Katherine, failed. The sight of the naked girl crouched in the barrel was too impossible to dismiss. She remained impassive as he lifted her arm by the elbow and began to soap it.

An arm is just an arm.

He held fast to the thought and repeated it to himself as he continued to bathe her.

A leg is just a leg. Just like any other leg.

A neck is just a neck. A long, slender neck.

A breast is just . . .

He swallowed.

A breast . . .

A hip is just . . .

When he broke into a full, cold sweat, Adam decided it would be for the best if he left some of her most private areas unscrubbed. Finally, satisfied that she was as clean as she was going to get for the time being and that the water was too dirty now to do much good, Adam stood up, stretched his cramped legs and reached down to pull her up out of the water.

She didn't resist his touch, even though he noticed the goose bumps that peppered her skin and the shivers that had begun to set her slender frame trembling.

"Damn."

He had forgotten the towel and had to leave her alone as he went inside to grab one. By the time he returned, she was shaking uncontrollably, her arms wrapped futilely across the front of her body as she stood alone in the dark. Adam wrapped her in the towel, took her hand and led her into the cabin.

"Welcome," he whispered. He placed his hand beneath her chin and forced her to look up at him.

Physically, he knew her now. Knew the intimate curves and lines of her body, knew some of what she had suffered along the path that had led her to him. The intimacy of the act he had just performed frightened him, for it had moved him in a way that he had not allowed himself to be moved in a long, long time. Not since Katherine's death.

He hurried to finish the work he had started, to find something for her to wear, to get her fed and bedded down so that he wouldn't have to touch her intimately again.

He turned away from the sight of her sky blue eyes and rifled through a pile of his own clothing until he found a long-sleeved flannel nightshirt. After pulling it over her head and down to her knees, he reached up beneath it and whipped the damp towel off of the girl and then hung it on a chair in front of the fire. Adam led her to a hand-carved chair he had finished that past winter, sat her down and then reached out to shove her hair back off her face. It would be impossible to try to run a comb or brush through the tangles.

"I'll have to cut it off," he muttered half to himself as he left her there while he warmed some beans and coffee for dinner.

The walls were closing in on her. Where were the dark, looming shadows of the trees, the night wind that made the pine needles whisper their secrets, the canopy of stars that had become an essential part of her nights outdoors?

She felt trapped here, entombed inside with the New One, the one with gentle hands who had washed her as if she were a babe, disturbing the dark, forbidden memories lurking at the edges of her mind.

The water had renewed her, brought her from the inky depths to a murky shadowland where forbidden images leapt just out of focus. They frightened her, those haunting scenes that her mind held at bay. Despite the fact that the New One had left her beside the fire, wrapped in soft blankets that smelled of the welcome scent of fresh air and sunlight, she could not still the racking shivers that quaked through her.

Not even rocking would hold the fear of her memories at bay.

She sensed him across the room from her, could hear him tossing and turning where he lay alone on the big bed in the center of the room. In some secret compartment of her mind she knew he meant her no harm.

It had been so long since she was certain of her physical safety, on any level, that the concept was nothing more than a ghost of a thought. Even though it was a mere wisp of an idea of security, it drew her thoughts to the New One again and again.

She tried to burrow down into the blankets, seeking warmth and comfort, but a continuous draft blew in beneath the door, a whispering escapee of the fierce wind that had begun to moan through the treetops. The sound grew louder as the fire died, and soon the mournful wailing outside forced her to press her open palms over her ears. She began to hum to drown out the sounds.

He was too tired to sleep.

Adam lay awake, his fingers locked behind his head as he stared through the darkness at the ceiling above him. Across the room, the girl was in her bedroll, once more humming the endless, monotonous tune that set his nerves on edge. Even over the drone of her voice he could hear the split pine pop and hiss in the fireplace and the wind as it howled around the eaves of the cabin.

His mind was made up. Tomorrow morning he would pack up a few supplies, take the girl and head for the mission that was a two-day ride away. Somewhere, someone had to be looking for her, and Adam knew that if he didn't pass her on soon, in a few weeks' time he would become just as crazy as she was.

She didn't eat unless he fed her, and he didn't know if she ever slept, and worrying about her was already taking its toll on him. He was dead tired but couldn't sleep. After hammering his pillow into submission, Adam rolled away from the fire and faced the wall. He closed his eyes and tried to force himself to relax. Then, just as he lay on the edge of consciousness, he felt the edge of the bed dip.

Adam lunged to a sitting position and turned, all in one motion, reaching out, half expecting to find the crazy woman standing over him with any number of things she could use as a weapon. He caught her unawares as she crouched over him, one of her knees on the lumpy mattress filled with pine needles.

He grabbed her by the shoulders. Driven by the fear that had startled him into action, he shouted into her face, "What in the hell are you doing?"

In the back of his mind, he expected no reaction, but before he could complete his question, she started screaming—bloodcurdling, one-upon-another ear-splitting screams that shook the rafters.

He didn't know who was more frightened—the girl or himself. Adam did the first thing that came to mind to silence her—he clapped his hand across her mouth and jerked her up against him, imprisoning her tight against his shirtfront. He held her there while he silently prayed that she would soon stop.

After a moment or two, she fell silent.

Adam waited to catch his breath. His violent heartbeat subsided while he pressed her cheek against his heart and rocked her gently, hoping that the familiar motion would calm her further. He sat frowning into the darkness, wondering what she had intended to do to him. More determined than ever, he knew he had to pack up and take her down to the mission as soon as first light dawned.

The wind rattled the windows and moaned around the cabin. Adam lifted his hand to brush her hair back off her face and then cupped his palm over her ear to keep out the sound of the storm. He had cut off most of her hair rather than fight the mass of tangles with a comb, and now he discovered that it had gently curled as it dried. The ringlets teased his fingers, and he gave in to the urge to run them through her hair.

Her arms slipped around his waist in response to his touch. Adam didn't breathe. He didn't move—he couldn't—not with her leaning so trustingly against him, her head and shoulders on his chest, her arms locked about his waist. She was breathing softly, evenly, which was more than he could say for himself. Holding her so near had set his own heart pounding against his ribs.

She sighed and snuggled closer. He wondered over the change in her. Had the fright she experienced when he grabbed her somehow brought her to her senses?

Finally, he took a deep breath and dared to whisper, "Ma'am?"

She looked up into his eyes.

He couldn't see the brilliant blue of her eyes in the darkness, nor could he tell if she was lucid. He ran his hand over her cheek, then straightened the neckline of the collarless nightshirt he had dressed her in.

"Who are you?" he asked.

She didn't answer. As if she were mimicking his motions, she reached up and traced the line of his jaw with her fingertips, then let her fingers move over his temple and through his hair, down the column of his neck and along the front of his shirt, until her hand rested over his heartbeat.

Her fingers clutched his shirtfront as she pulled herself closer. Her lips were just inches from his. He expected her to whisper her name.

Instead, she tugged on his shirtfront until he lowered his head, and then, unable to resist temptation any longer, Adam slowly, tenderly, tentatively, touched his lips to hers. After what she might have endured, he expected her to react violently, to cry out, to begin screaming again.

Instead her lips opened, warm and welcoming, and moved beneath his as naturally as if they had been fated to be together. He heard her moan low in her throat as she held him tighter. Surprised that his shirt did not rip from the strain of her intense grasp on the fabric, he shifted and wrapped his arms around her.

The kiss deepened. Adam felt himself harden as the blood surged through him. The heady scent of soap and the soft warmth of the flannel nightshirt that protected her from the night's chill aroused him. It had been forever since he had held a woman in his arms, since he had taken pure pleasure in lovemaking.

Even as they held one another close, their lips and tongues teasing and savoring, Adam knew that if he didn't pull back, soon there would be no stopping the inevitable. It wasn't fair, he knew, to take advantage of this nameless girl. She was a lost soul, unaware of what she was doing, where she was, even *who* she was.

It would definitely be wrong to let things progress any further.

Adam ended the kiss and held her at arm's length. His need was so great he was shaking, but he managed to get out of bed and drag her with him as he did.

"Back to bed," he said firmly.

She followed him docilely to the pallet until he tried to get her to lie down again. "Here you go." Adam let out a pent-up sigh of frustration. He shoved his fingers through his hair. "Now stay put."

Almost violently, the girl shook her head in response. She moaned in wordless complaint, fighting to grab hold of him as he sought to push her away. She protested until he gave up and took her in his arms again and let her rest her head against his chest.

"This isn't such a good idea," he whispered against the curls on the crown of her head. Shifting, he tried to ignore the fact that she had begun to wrestle with the buttons down the front of his shirt.

She might be out of her mind, but he wasn't.

He grabbed her wrists and tried to stop her.

She fought him, jerked out of his hold and grasped his shirtfront. This time she didn't pause. She held tight to both sides of his shirtfront and tugged until the buttons strained and ripped off.

Speechless, Adam could only stare down at her in amazement.

Outside the trees were still crying, screaming terrible screams that set her nerve endings on edge. The idea that he was trying to disengage her hold soon broke through the cobwebs of her mind. Even though he was trying to shove her away, the New One would not hurt her. She knew that as certainly as she knew that instead of despair, he offered hope. Instead of hunger, food. Instead of pain, pleasure. Maybe he would be capable of banishing the demons that raged deep inside her. She had to try, and so she had climbed into the low, wide bed with him so that he might comfort her and keep her from harm.

When he surprised her by lunging up from the bed and looming over her, an instant of fright had plunged her back toward her dark memories and forced her to scream—for how long she couldn't guess—but quickly, as his hands moved over her face and hair, she forgot her fear again.

He was warm and alive. The scent of pine and woodsmoke clung to him. She wanted to feel the familiar heat of human contact again and to take comfort from him. She wanted the New One to reach deep into the core of her and touch her where she was the most hollow, the most injured and afraid.

She had to have him, for on an elemental level she knew his touch might bring her out of the shadows and into the light.

He was making sounds again, but no matter how hard she tried, she couldn't understand him. The words merely vibrated in her ears and confused her more than ever.

Perhaps if she touched her lips to his she would understand, somehow take the words inside herself. She leaned forward and pressed her lips against his and felt an immediate flush of comforting pleasure, but it was short-lived. He continued to try to push her away.

No.

She wanted to cry out in protest, but the words wouldn't come. Instead, a jumbled protest of sound was all she could manage. She grabbed for his shirt and ripped it open, the urgent need to feel his warm, comforting flesh against hers becoming all-consuming.

He went perfectly still. She ran her hands up and down his chest, over the smooth contours of his ribs and waist, then up again, to his shoulders. She pressed against him, frantic to feel his flesh against hers, so afraid that he would set her aside, that he would refuse the human contact she craved.

It had been so long, so very long, since she felt a part of anything, since she had wanted, needed, longed for, anything except the darkness, the shadows and an end to the pain.

He made one last futile attempt to set her aside. She could hear his words again, and this time she struggled to comprehend. The sounds came to her in jumbled bits and pieces. She absorbed the parts, but not the whole.

"Not right . . . can't . . . this . . . lady, please... crazy..." Even though his sounds were words of protest, he whispered them almost tenderly against her lips. She welcomed his touch. Finally his arms closed around her and drew her up tight against him. Somehow, some way, she had to make him understand how much she needed his warmth and healing touch. Frustrated that she was unable to express herself in words, she drew away until she was out of his arms. She walked away and then stood alone beside the bed.

Firelight danced across his features. He was watching her intently. She discovered that she did not mind returning his gaze. Afraid the remnants of her soul might be stolen if the wrong person gazed too deeply inside her, it had been forever since she had looked into another's eyes. Now she dared and saw that his deep blue eyes were dark, shining pieces of the midnight sky that shimmered with light. His gaze told her that he didn't understand what she wanted, what she needed so desperately. Unable to communicate in any other way, she quickly reached down for the hem of the garment she wore and pulled it up over her head, then tossed it to the floor.

His eyes widened. Unabashed, she ran her hands over her body, pausing for the briefest moment as her fingertips lingered at her abdomen, then trailed up to her breasts. Fighting to remember how to communicate with words, she frowned at him as she strained to think, to form one word that would tell him all she could not say.

"Please..."

Her plea came out as a rasping, unintelligible sigh. She clasped her fists at her sides and waited for some sign that the man had understood. She desperately ached for solace.

Adam heard what might have been her attempt to plead with him. The pitiful sound broke his heart. The sight of the woman standing there clothed in nothing but the firelight that gilded her ivory skin demolished his resistance.

"I must be as crazy as you are," he whispered beneath his breath.

He crossed the room and enfolded her in his arms. Adam held her close for a while and rocked her gently, more than aware of the feel of her soft, lush breasts pressed against his chest. Finally he slowly lowered himself to the bed and slid over, making room for her beside him.

Adam kept hold of her wrist as he drew her down into his arms and held her close, giving himself permission to let his hands and fingers explore the curves and hollows of her cool flesh. She seemed content to lie beside him and imitate his movements. Her madly wanton act of throwing off her nightshirt had inflamed him. Her pitifully voiced plea and the struggle she had gone through to beg him to take her into his bed nearly broke his heart even as they inflamed his loins.

She had not consciously meant to be sultry or seductive. Her need was born of a hunger for the contact of flesh upon flesh, a need as raw and carnal as his own. For a moment, as she had stood beside the bed staring down at him, he could have sworn she had been as sane as he—if he could call himself sane at the moment. There had been an almost lucid determination in her eyes.

Adam put all thought aside as he began to gentle and calm her with his hands. If it was his touch she craved, that was what he planned to deliver. But he would go slow, ensure that they each savored the moment. Perhaps making love would have a healing effect on her, maybe pleasure after so much pain would bring her to her senses again.

He pressed her onto her back, and she followed his lead without protest. Except for the scars along her back and the calluses on her palms, her skin was smooth and supple. He lay over her and kissed her deeply, aligning his body alongside hers, breast to breast, hip to hip, thigh to thigh.

As he kissed, he stroked his hand over her shoulder, down her arm to her breast. He cupped the fullness there, teased her nipple until it budded for him, then leaned over and took the rosebud peak into his mouth.

She cried out as he suckled her, clasped his face between her palms and held him there, to be certain he had his fill. He teased both breasts, laving them with his tongue, drawing on them until he elicited a shuddering response from her.

There were many ways to pleasure her, and he meant to try them all. He kissed her again, long and hard, as he slid his hand along her waist and hip. She sighed and pressed closer. His fingertips traced a line from her hip to her belly. His touch wandered lower, and he paused just above the nest of curls at the juncture of her thighs.

She moaned against his mouth and nudged him with her hip. Her hands were clinging to his bare shoulders. His hair had come free from the thong that held it tied back. It brushed his shoulders, falling forward to sweep alongside his cheek and brush hers.

He pressed closer and let his hand cup her mound. Slowly, gently, he explored her soft, moist, inner folds and then carefully eased his finger inside her.

She gasped, and he froze, but there was no protest from her, rather a silent desperation that urged him on. He began to stroke her until she writhed beneath him. Her fingers pressed into his shoulders, communicating her need. She was panting now, her head thrashing from side to side, her hips undulating in response to his touch.

Adam buried his face against her neck and gently teased her soft flesh with his teeth. He laved her ear with his tongue, and she moaned and thrust against him. When he slipped his finger out of her and took his hand from her mound, she whimpered in protest until he rose over her, carefully spread her legs and moved between them.

Uncertain, he hovered at the slickened entrance to her inner core and then slowly, gently began to slide his shaft inside her. She tilted her hips to welcome him, and he found her tight, but without any hindrance to his passage. She was no virgin.

Still, he meant to linger, to take and yet give as much pleasure as he could before he reached his own climax. He could feel her around him, tight, hot, pulsing. He could not hold back the groan of ecstasy that escaped him.

She urged him on again with her hips, and then, when he had sheathed himself fully inside her, she wrapped her legs around his waist and clung to him, writhing, sobbing, begging over and over with the only word she seemed able to utter.

"Please..."

He began to thrust harder, to pull back and plunge again, driving himself to the brink and then willing himself to hold, to pause, to quiver in readiness as taut as a bowstring on the edge of release.

She gave a wordless cry, moving along his length as she reached fulfillment. Intoxicated by the feel of her throbbing around him, Adam was unable to hold back any longer. He buried himself inside her and cried out, his shout mingling with the cries of the windstorm that raged outside the cabin.

Wave after wave of passion washed over him as he poured himself into the woman beneath him. She arched against him, willing to take all he could offer. Finally, still shuddering beneath him, she relaxed against the bed but continued to cling to him.

As Adam dropped his head to her breasts, his ragged breath slowly eased. Still shaken by the depth of the emotional exchange, he pulled back in order to see her face. At last she lay tranquil, her eyes closed. Her breathing had slowed. Her bright halo of curls caught the firelight. Adam reached up and smoothed them, watching them spring back into a beguiling disarray kissed with light.

Unwilling just yet to unravel the mystery of what had just passed between them, he carefully moved off her without disturbing her and then drew the covers up over them. For a long while, Adam simply lay staring at her in the darkness.

Morning dawned. Light gilded the floorboards beneath the windows and draped itself across the rumpled blankets and thick buffalo hide that covered Adam Stroud's bed. He awoke before the girl and found her still clinging to him, one arm around his waist, one leg entwined between his. Her golden ringlets were shining in the sunlight, a bright contrast against his own sun-bronzed skin. The scars across her back and shoulders were faded, but very visible. He wondered if the scars in her mind would ever fade.

Tempted to kiss her awake, he dismissed the thought, uncertain of what frame of mind she might be in by the light of day. Maybe insanity was contagious. Maybe he had imagined everything that had transpired between them last night. He was probably as crazy as she was and didn't even know it.

She sighed in her sleep and shifted against him, and the feel of her long bare thigh where it brushed against his fully erect manhood told him the events of the night past had not been conjured out of his imagination.

Adam began to close his eyes, determined to control himself, yet content to laze away a few more minutes holding her close before he climbed out of the warm cocoon to light the fire. He felt the girl stir. She rose on her elbow and met his gaze straight on. He was startled by the iridescence of her azure eyes. Her lips were lush, inviting and, as he knew so well, very kissable.

"Good morning," he whispered, his gut churning as he awaited some reaction.

She lifted her hand and tenderly traced his lips with her fingertip.

Adam smiled.

Although it was tremulous and wavering, she smiled back.

"Who are you? Where have you come from?" he asked her softly, voicing aloud what he had wondered a thousand times since he'd first laid eyes on her.

As he stared down into her fathomless eyes, Adam couldn't help but think of Adam in the Bible and how the first man must have felt when he woke up to find the new wife of his flesh lying beside him. And what of Eve? Had she gazed up at her new mate in the same far-off, bewildered way?

"I'm Adam," he told her softly and touched his chest. "Adam. Say it."

"Adam."

He lay speechless for half a second and then caught her up in a bear hug. "You did it!" He pulled back to look down at her and found her just as startled as he by her accomplishment.

"Say it again. Adam."

"Adam."

"Again."

"Adam."

He reached down and tipped her chin up until he was nearly nose to nose with her. "Do you remember *your* name?"

She sighed. And simply whispered, "Adam," before she fell silent.

He could read the disappointment in her eyes, but even that was better than the wild, crazed expression he was used to seeing there.

"We can't both be Adam. If you can't think of your name, I'm going to have to start calling you something."

Adam pulled out of her grasp, and found his pants on the floor near her nightshirt. He slipped on his wool trousers and fastened them before he turned around again and handed her the makeshift gown.

"Put this on and stay in bed until I get the room warm. Understand?"

She didn't make any sign that she had comprehended, but she balled the nightshirt protectively against her breasts and watched him as he backed away.

Circumstances being as uncertain as they were, Adam wished he could keep the hint of a smile off his face, but he couldn't do that any more than he could stop whistling as he placed the logs on the embers of the fire and coaxed it to life. He hung a pot of coffee over the fire and then threw some handfuls of cornmeal into a pot of water and prepared to make mush.

When he turned around, half expecting his mysterious companion to be asleep, he found her standing beside the bed, once again dressed in his nightshirt.

Adam looked her over from head to toe, knowing far too well what was hidden beneath the shapeless nightshirt. He had committed to memory every curve of her body, every turn of her long, luscious legs, the swell of her breasts with their rosy tips, the soft velvety feel of her skin. Even the sight of her bare toes curled away from the cold earthen floor warmed his heart.

"Get hold of yourself," he mumbled as he turned away, forcing his attention on finding a pair of woolen socks for her to wear.

"Adam?"

He whirled at the sound of his name on her lips, instantly touched by the bewilderment on her face. His heart went out to her in that moment as she stood alone in the center of the room, her gaze darting to every item, every nook and cranny of the place, before it fled back to him. Fright and confusion had replaced the look of insanity. She was quaking like a leaf.

She stood there as if waiting for him to explain, to help her understand how she'd come to be alone in a strange cabin with a man she had never seen before. Adam crossed the room, then hesitated but a second. When she did not flinch away from him, he slipped his arm around her shoulders and led her over to the bed.

He sat on the edge of the mattress and pulled her down onto his lap, cradling her in his arms, hoping to still the tremors that racked her slender frame.

"I don't know who you are," he began softly, stroking her back, her arm, "where you're from, or who your people might be. I found you living with—"

He stopped abruptly, afraid that any mention of her captivity might send her reeling back into the dark corners of her mind. Adam cleared his throat and collected his thoughts.

"I brought you here to keep you safe—"

And then made love to you.

He took another deep breath. "Until we can contact your family."

She seemed to have calmed some. Adam felt her gaze upon him and looked down. Sure enough, she was watching him carefully, as if weighing every word. Something in her eyes scared the hell out of him.

You begged me to make love to you. He wanted to voice the thought aloud, but what if she had forgotten? What if the events of last night had fled with the rest of her nightmares? The loving look in her eyes told him different, almost as if their love-making had driven the terror from her mind, as if she had been reborn, with no memory of anything or anyone before this moment.

Sarah. The name came into his mind unbidden. Sarah. He had to call her something until he found out about her past. Sarah had been his great-grandmother's name, and it was as good a name as any.

Deciding he definitely liked the look of her tousled, short curls, he ran his fingers through them, brushing them back away from her temples. He smiled down at her and then straightened the hem of her too-short gown. "I'm going to call you Sarah."

She merely blinked, wide-eyed.

He touched his chest. "Adam." Then he reached out and touched a spot above her heart. "Sarah."

Relief washed over him when she slowly nodded in understanding.

"Say it," he demanded quietly.

"Sarah," she whispered. "Adam. Sarah."

Part Two

Her name was Sarah.

For so long there had been only nightmares where her memory once dwelt, then the blessed, blissful void. Now, after a tranquil week of care and tenderness, she had begun to replace missing memories with new ones.

She watched the big man across the room as he moved about, intent on his tasks.

Adam. His name was Adam. He was the center of her world now, this blue-eyed man with the slow smile and gentle ways. He was all she knew for the moment, Adam and the four walls that surrounded them.

As had become their morning custom, he left her sitting on the bed after he arose, pulled the covers up around her neck and told her to stay warm. He would bring breakfast to her. With wondrous clarity, she now understood his words. As she watched him move around the room, she no longer felt panicked by her lack of memories.

It was enough for now that she felt warm and safe.

Yes, it was enough for now.

She watched him lift a coffeepot from the fireplace and carry it to a waist-high shelf that ran along a wall. He took two cups off some nails on the wall, filled them, then carried one over to her.

"Your coffee," he said, slowly holding it out to her.

She smiled up at him and carefully took the steaming brew in her hands, then savored the warmth before she brought it close to her lips.

"It's hot," he warned.

She blew on the dark liquid and tasted it, then she grimaced.

He looked so disappointed. "You don't like coffee very much, do you?"

"Tea." She looked up quickly, startled at her own spontaneous admission. "I like tea," she said softly, amazed. Sarah frowned and shook her head. "I like to drink tea."

As if he understood her confusion and where it came from, he reached out to take the cup of coffee back. "I don't have any tea," he told her.

She did not let him take the cup. "I'll drink this. I'm growing used to it."

He looked far too uncomfortable. Sarah smiled and nodded. "It's smells good. It's warm. I'll drink it."

"You don't have to."

"I want to."

“I never buy tea.” He sounded disturbed.

“You’re angry?”

He turned away from her, and she wondered what she had done to upset him.

“No.” He was suddenly staring at her again, studying her intently, his forehead marred by a frown. “I’m not angry.”

“What is it, then?”

Adam moved toward the bed and stood over her, his hands jammed in his pockets. “You’re starting to remember.”

Fear, an emotion she had never seen in his eyes before, startled her. “Adam, what are you holding back? Please, don’t you think it’s time you told me how I came to be here?” It was the first time she had felt brave enough to push him to answer the question she had been asking herself for days.

Slowly, he lowered himself to the side of the bed and sat next to her. Thoughtfully, as if weighing every word he said, “I found you two weeks ago along the Columbia River when I went to a trade fair.”

“Was I alone?”

Again he thought over his response before he spoke. “None of your people were with you.” After a pause he asked, “You’re sure nothing has come back to you?”

Adam appeared so upset that she forgot her own concerns in order to reassure him. Although she felt a blush creep across her cheeks, she held his gaze as she admitted, "I recall nothing before the night I awoke in your arms."

Obviously uncomfortable, Adam stood up again and paced across the room. He fingered his own coffee cup. The contents were growing cold. Finally he turned to face her again.

"Sarah, I didn't bring you here intending to...seduce you."

"Adam—"

"No, let me finish." He held up his hand to stop her. "I was going to try to find someone who knows you. The Redemption Mission is a two-day ride from here. I thought I would put out word that I'd found you. Your family must be searching...." His expression darkened as his thoughts trailed off.

"But you don't want to go?"

He walked across the room until he stood before the fire, stared into it for a few seconds and finally spoke without turning around.

He answered her question with another. "Do you remember anything before that first night you slept here?"

Sarah recalled nothing but the moment when she reached fulfillment and awoke from her nightmares in this man's arms. She knew her cheeks were flaming. She answered as honestly as she could. "As I said before, I remember . . . you. I felt safe. I felt protected."

Even from across the room she sensed her answer had disturbed him deeply.

"What will we do now?" she asked.

"About you?"

"About me."

He ran his hand over the night's growth of dark beard that shadowed the lower half of his face. It was a while before he responded with another question. "What would you like me to do?"

She held the cup in one hand and lifted the covers. After swinging her legs over the side of the bed, ignoring the cold floor, she hurried to him on bare feet and stood staring up at him.

The heat from the burning pine in the fireplace warmed her as much as the sense of relief she experienced just standing near him once again.

"I don't want you to leave."

"I'll take you with me."

Sarah shook her head and reached out in protest, then let her hand fall before she touched him. "I mean, I don't want to find out yet. I don't . . . I can't."

She tried to fight the tears that welled up in her eyes, but the biting sting would not be denied no matter how hard she tried to blink them back.

"Maybe in time I'll remember on my own." Fighting back a sense of panic, Sarah set the cup down on the nearby table and twined her fingers together in order to keep her hands from shaking. "It's just that right now, I can't... face the darkness again. Not yet."

"What do you mean?"

"I'm afraid of what I'll find out. I'm afraid that this will all come to an end, and if it does, the darkness and the pain and the emptiness will come back."

He didn't move, didn't speak. She sensed he was fighting some inner battle of his own.

"Is it too much to ask... that you... let me feel safe here for a while?" She pressed him to respond.

"I—"

"Maybe, given time, I'll remember something, but please, Adam, give me time."

Adam stared at her, clenching and unclenching his fists at his sides. He guessed that in *her* mind she wasn't asking all that much, but from where he stood, she was asking for the moon. To keep her here, to be alone with her night after night, to know how she felt in his arms... If he fell in love with her only to lose her when she regained her memories—he would know the pain he had felt when Katherine died.

"Adam?"

She was awaiting his decision. He knew he should tell her it was best for them both to pack up and head out right away. She could very well be back in the arms of her family in no time. At the very least, at the mission she would be surrounded by womenfolk who could cosset and tend to her, chaperon her. Yes, that would be the best thing for Sarah.

But he had already come to think of her as *his* Sarah. He'd found her. It was true that he had bought and paid for her, but they were held together by stronger bonds now. For a week they had shared the most intimate act a man and woman could ever know.

He had named her. She needed him.

Why not let her stay as long as she wanted? As long as *he* wanted, for that matter?

"You don't want me here," she said in a voice so low he barely heard it.

Adam sighed and walked over to the table. He pulled out a chair and sat down, ran his hand along the edge of the yellow pine plank surface and tried to explain.

"It's not that I don't want you here." He glanced up at her and found her listening intently. He couldn't tell her that he was afraid he couldn't bear to lose her once he came to love her, so he used the same excuse he had given Runs-With. "It's just that I've lived alone for so long, it might be hard for me to get along with someone day and night."

He cleared his throat. "Besides, it's not proper, you know. You and me living alone out here like this."

She glanced toward the window. Outside, acres of green pine grew thick along the mountainside and dotted the fertile valley below. "You said this place is called the Oregon Territory."

He watched her try the name on her tongue. "Mean anything to you?"

She shook her head. "No."

"I was afraid not. I have a feeling you came from miles away."

"I don't want to talk about that."

Sarah rubbed her upper arms as if to ward off a chill. He jumped up immediately and took his buckskin jacket down off the peg near the door. "Here, put this on."

She slipped into it as he held the jacket for her. When she looked over her shoulder at him, Adam's heart sank to his toes at the sight of her sparkling, sky blue eyes. He had the overwhelming urge to bolt out the door and run until his legs dropped off or his heart burst from the effort, but he knew he could no more abandon this woman than he could deny her request.

"Listen, Sarah, I'll forget about going to the mission for now, but—"

He was about to add that it was only for a while and that he would give her his own bed and make a pallet for himself on the floor, but the words died on his lips when she threw her arms around his neck and held him tight.

"Thank you, Adam," she whispered against his throat. "Thank you for giving me time."

Adam lost the war with his conscience, slipped his arms around her protectively and held her tight. He closed his eyes against a sudden wave of guilt. Sarah had not been a virgin when she climbed into bed with him that first night. He didn't know what she had suffered or if she had been ill-used by her captors—and it made no difference to him where his feelings for her were concerned even if she had been. But the fact that she had sought comfort in his arms led him to believe she must have known more of physical love than rape.

As he stood there with his arms locked around her, not only was he betraying Katherine's memory and putting his heart at risk again, but he was haunted by the nagging suspicion that he was more than likely holding another man's wife in his arms.

Sarah stopped to survey the world outside the cabin. It had become a wonderland of white, the sunlight sparkling off snow crystals and the icicles that hung from the edge of the porch roof. She had convinced him not to go to the mission, not to court trouble. Like the snow, her time here had built up gradually, until the days with Adam soon slipped into weeks, the weeks into nearly two months now. Her memories were still as blank as the unbroken field of snow outside the window, and yet there had been glimmers of light, flashes of remembrance that she could not bring herself to speak of to Adam.

Adam. He was still her entire world; she had no memory of a time before she had come to life in his arms. Sarah could not envision life without him. She found herself lost on days like this when he left her alone while he emptied the traps he had set around the area. She counted the seconds until he returned.

She reached out to touch the freezing windowpane, felt the icy bite of the cold and shivered. The assortment of garments he had given her to wear were odd, but they kept her warm. Beneath a native dress of soft buckskin, she wore a set of Adam's long underwear, the quilted cotton arms and legs warming places the buckskin didn't reach. He had donated a pair of wool socks that thankfully filled out the extra room in the beaded moccasins she wore on her feet. When she had asked him how he'd come by the buckskin clothing, he'd explained that it had been part of a trade.

She had found over the past weeks that Adam Stroud was a man of few words. She knew little more about his past than she did her own. He had told her that he was originally from Philadelphia, that he had five brothers and three sisters, and that he had left home at an early age. His great-grandmother's name had been Sarah.

She did know the name Sarah suited her. If she'd ever had another, she still had no idea what it might have been.

A kettle of stew was simmering over the fire. Adam was teaching her to cook, and in his rare moments of levity he loved to tease that she no doubt possessed the skill but was keeping the knowledge to herself so that he would be forced to do all the work.

She smiled in remembrance, then turned away from the window and crossed the room to stand before the fire and give the stew a stir. Intent upon trying her hand at baking apples, she left the stew to simmer and found the bag of apples beneath the sideboard he had built against one wall. As she tugged on the bag, the drawstring on top gave way, and the apples spilled out and bounced to the floor, rolling in every direction.

On her hands and knees, Sarah collected them all and knelt with them in her lap as she put all but three back into the bag. It was not until she bent down to shove the sack in place that she noticed an ornately tooled leather trunk that was covered with dust and shoved back against the wall. The initials KES were engraved on a brass plate near the lock.

She set the apples aside, and reached down to pull the trunk toward her. It was heavier than she'd thought it would be, so she set her back to the task and yanked until it gave way and sent her toppling back into a sitting position with a sharp smack.

Sitting cross-legged, she ignored her throbbing tailbone and lifted the lid, pleased to discover the trunk was not locked. It opened to reveal a piece of carefully folded, yellowed satin. Even as she gently lifted the fabric out of the trunk, she felt a knot tighten in her throat.

She could tell before she shook out the fabric that it was a special gown, carefully stitched and beaded, the bodice dripping with crumpled lace. Smoothing out the delicately worked lace, she let her fingers drift over the rich material and wondered at how it had come to be here. Glancing up at the door, she realized she did not want Adam to find her searching through what must be his most precious, secret possessions.

Quickly she folded the dress, refusing to contemplate its meaning until she was rid of it. But as she went to put the dress away, she couldn't help but notice the pieces lying beneath it. Small and just as yellowed with age, tiny baby gowns that had been hand stitched and decorated with embroidered flowers and smocking were neatly folded in a pile. Sometime, not so very long ago, someone had been preparing for the birth of a child.

Adam's child.

She knew it as surely as she knew there was snow outside the cabin. As Sarah continued to stare down at the baby clothes in her trembling hands, her heart began to pound. The tattoo roared in her ears until she was forced to close her eyes, afraid she might faint. By the time she was able to open her eyes again, her hands were shaking so badly that she dropped the tiny clothes on the floor.

What is happening to me?

An overwhelming feeling of helplessness and loss came over her, so great that she began to rock back and forth and sob, her arms curled protectively, instinctively, around her middle.

She felt herself slipping back, losing her grip on the light, on her surroundings, on her place in the universe again. Almost as if she were dreaming and yet awake at the same time, she recalled being so exhausted she could not move. An incessant pain radiated up her spine. In her mind's eye she saw herself in a filthy, ragged dress, her feet bare and bleeding, her abdomen distended.

As if the pain of the dream were a part of her now, Sarah continued to rock back and forth, her hand on her stomach as she moaned over and over again, "My baby, my baby." She vividly recalled lying on her back, staring up at a cerulean sky as pain ripped her apart. Then, a wash of warm blood, intense pain and then blessed, dark release followed by a feeling of emptiness so deep and hollow it felt as if it went on forever.

"No! Not again." She cried out aloud in protest and forced herself to open her eyes. Terror filled her, terror spawned by the fear that the nightmarish vision would force her back to the abyss. She could not let her mind grow dark or she would fall into the void, and this new Sarah, like her old, lost self, would be gone forever.

By sheer will alone, she forced herself to calm down, then made herself pick up each precious, yet terrifying piece of Adam's past. Folding them as carefully as she could, even while she sat shaking like a leaf, she reached out to place them back in the trunk. She raised herself onto her knees and looked into the bottom of the trunk. Lying on the faded striped lining was an ivory-backed hand mirror. She tucked the baby clothes into the trunk and lifted out the mirror, raised it with both hands and stared at her own reflection.

The face staring back at her was unfamiliar, but the sorrow in the tear-filled eyes arrested her. Sarah gazed at herself in confusion. She reached up and touched the springy curls that barely reached her shoulders, and frowned.

Something about the reflected image was all wrong. She knew intuitively that something was missing. She had a sudden vision of the same face surrounded by long blond hair done up in bouncing ringlets and ribbons. Shaken, she shoved the mirror back under the baby garments and then replaced the satin dress. Sarah slammed the lid back down on the trunk and then, shoving with all the strength she could marshal, she pushed it back into place beneath the sideboard.

As she fought to collect herself, she wished she had never touched the cursed trunk. Finding the wedding gown had been painful in that she now knew Adam had not trusted her enough to speak of a wife. But when she had touched the lovingly stitched baby clothing, overwhelming emotion had welled up inside her and cried out from her very soul. Somewhere she had a child of her own.

Gathering up the apples, Sarah had no sooner pushed herself to her feet than she heard a knock at the door. Without thinking that it could be anyone but Adam, she set the apples down, wiped the tears from her cheeks and tried to collect herself.

She didn't have any idea what she was going to say to him. Try as she might, there was no possible way to put a smile on her face before she took a deep breath and opened the door.

It was not Adam. Standing there, not an arm's length away, nearly blocking out the light with his height and his broad shoulders covered by the great buffalo robe he wore, stood a towering Indian with an assortment of feathers, shells and trade bells tied in his long black hair. He took a step forward, his hand extended toward her.

For the second time in less than an hour, her heart raced uncontrollably. Scenes flashed in her mind, one upon another, bursts of memory that made no sense to her at all. An involuntary scream escaped her, and she struggled through the pain, intent on slamming the door in the native's face. Before she could shut out the sight of him, and without warning, the world went black.

"What in the hell happened?"

Staring up at Runs-With-The-Wind, Adam sat on the floor just inside the cabin door. He cradled an unconscious Sarah in his arms.

The Nez Percé shrugged. "I knocked. She opened the door, saw me and screamed. Then she..." He gestured to Sarah to explain her faint.

Adam bent over her, gently running his hand over her cheek. "Sarah? Sarah, honey, wake up." He glanced over at his friend. "What if she wakes up the way she was before?"

"Before?"

"She's not crazy anymore. She hasn't been since I brought her here. She still can't remember her past, but she's been fine, talking, lucid." *Laughing, smiling, making love, making my life complete.* "What if she slips back?"

"I'm sorry, Adam Stroud."

Shifting Sarah's weight in his arms, Adam stood up and started to carry her toward the bed. "It's not your fault. I shouldn't have left her alone."

As he was about to lay Sarah on the bed, she moaned and began to struggle in his arms.

"Sarah?" He put her down gently and sat beside her.

She opened her eyes, glanced up at him and then frantically searched the room. When her gaze fell on Runs-With, she cried "No!" and gripped Adam's hand so tightly that he winced.

"It's all right," he whispered. "He's my friend." Sarah continued to stare warily at Runs-With as

Adam held her hands in his and tried to get her attention.

"Sarah, say something. Are you all right?"

She nodded. "Yes, but..." Struggling to sit up, she grabbed hold of his shoulders. He helped her to a sitting position, relieved to find that she had not slipped back into insanity.

"Sarah, this is my friend, Runs-With-The-Wind. He is a Nez Percé, one of the tribes that moves about the area." Adam paused and then asked, "Do you recognize him at all?"

She stared at the other man, watching him warily, then met Adam's gaze. "No, but he frightens me. I saw visions of terrible things when I looked at him. Horrible scenes I don't understand."

Hoping beyond hope that his revelation would not be too hard on her, Adam began to speak slowly, watching her carefully as he explained, "When I found you, you were a captive owned by one of this man's people."

She frowned. "A *captive?*" she whispered.

He nodded. "A slave. A member of Runs-With's tribe had traded for you somewhere east of here. It's not known how you came to be taken captive... that's what I was hoping to find out, why I had planned to go to the mission, to put out the word that I had found a white woman at the rendezvous."

"Rendezvous . . ."

"A big trading session."

"You bought me?"

Adam nodded. "To get you out of there."

She closed her eyes and shuddered. He held his breath for a moment, then touched her shoulder. "Sarah?"

"I think I'm all right," she said hesitantly. "It's all so confusing and so very frightening."

"That's why I haven't wanted to tell you before now. You just rest, and I'll put some food on the table for all of us. The stew smells great. You didn't let it burn, I see."

"I was going to bake apples," she began absently, and then glanced over at Runs-With.

"It's all right." He leaned forward and touched his lips to hers in a quick, reassuring gesture, then, mindful of the man watching him, he stood and went to collect some bowls from the sideboard.

Sarah watched Adam closely, afraid to be caught staring at the exotic native standing in the center of the room. While he and Adam talked softly, she closed her eyes and tried to collect her shattered nerves. A white captive. A slave. More bits and pieces of the crazy quilt her life had become.

She held tight to her own secret discovery. If the strange vision was to be believed, at one time she had carried a child, given birth to a child. Somewhere there was a baby who even now might be crying out for her. And if there was a child, who was the man in her past? And where was he now?

There was so much she didn't know, so much she could only guess. And what of Adam? Why had he never mentioned the woman who had worn the satin gown, the woman who had made the baby clothes he still kept hidden in the old trunk?

She reached up and rubbed her temples, fighting against the headache pounding behind her shuttered eyelids.

"Are you hungry?" Adam was beside the bed again. The table was set with three steaming bowls of stew, and his friend was waiting for her to join them.

She pulled herself together and, with Adam's help, stood up. It wouldn't do to worry him. She would eat a little, then excuse herself to go outdoors to the privy. A short walk in the cold air would do her good, settle her nerves. She was determined to be calm and collected when she asked Adam the questions that were burning in her heart and mind.

The men gave attention to their meal, saying little. Sarah sensed that they were hesitant to speak while she was there. She ate as much of her stew as she could force past the lump in her throat and then smiled over at Adam.

"If you don't mind, I need to go outside for a minute."

"Are you all right?"

She smiled to reassure him, nodded to Runs-With, who had been watching her throughout the meal, and then stood up. "I'm fine. I'll be right back. I just need to get some air and, well, you know."

Adam walked her to the door, took his heavy coat off the coatrack fashioned of antlers and held it while she slipped it on. He gathered the heavy wool lapels in his hands and drew her close. "Be careful," he whispered.

"I will."

Adam opened the door, and she slipped outside, welcoming the biting cold as she tried to convince herself it was the reason for the rush of tears that filled her eyes.

When Adam turned around, he found Runs-With leaning back in his chair, his arms crossed over his chest. "I was surprised to find the woman still here. I see you have grown used to living with someone after all."

"It's not polite to look so smug," Adam told him as he refilled Runs-With's coffee mug.

The Nez Percé helped himself to a hearty dose of sugar and then sipped at the steaming brew. "Have you changed her name to Woman-Who-Cost-Too-Much?"

Leaning his hip against the table, Adam eyed his friend with a skeptical expression. "Did you come to insult me, or was there a reason for your visit?"

The Indian laughed heartily and set his mug down on the table. "It is good to see you, Stroud. I came to tell you we are camped beyond the river for winter. I also came to see if you turned the woman over to her people."

Adam slipped into his chair again. He glanced at the door. There was no sound from outside. "She didn't want to go to the mission, yet. Sarah was hoping she would remember something."

"Sarah?"

"It's what I call her. She's accepted the name until she can recall her own."

Runs-With sobered again, and Adam's heart skipped a beat. "You know something," he said.

"It may be nothing. Maybe the news is not even about this woman, but another," Runs-With said.

Adam shifted, rested his forearms on the table and leaned forward. "What is it?"

"Last spring a band of Kiowa was attacked by whites. Women, children were killed. The warriors wanted blood, revenge. They were hungry for it. They came upon a small wagon train. Many whites were killed. A few captured. Your woman might have been one of them."

"Do you know where they were attacked?"

"No."

Adam let out a long sigh of relief. Unable to sit any longer, he stood up and began to pace the room. "There are hundreds of people on the Oregon Trail. Sarah might not have been one of the members of the group you're talking about. She could have come from anywhere, a settlement, a fort. Who knows?"

"Perhaps she fell from the sky."

"Very funny."

"I can see you are not laughing. You have come to care for the woman, haven't you, Stroud?"

In that instant Adam knew he could not lie to his friend the way he had tried to lie to himself. Forced to face the truth, Adam stopped pacing and stood beside Runs-With's chair. "Yes," he said, softly at first, then louder, "Yes, I love her."

"What will you do?"

"She seems content. We've been happy. Very happy." He found out once he had voiced his feelings for Sarah that it was getting easier and easier to admit how much he cared for her. "I'm not going to do anything. Besides, who could find her way out here?"

Runs-With appeared thoughtful. He finished his coffee, pushed back the chair and stood up to face Adam. "No one. Besides, she is yours, bought and paid for. No man has the right to claim her now—at least, that is our way. But it is not the way of your people. Is it, Stroud?"

"No, it isn't."

"I wonder how long you can go against your own ways?"

Sarah took a deep breath of fresh air and then opened the cabin door. The close warmth ebbed out to meet her, and she shivered as she stepped inside. Adam's friend was wearing his buffalo robe again, standing in the center of the room, obviously ready to take his leave. She shrugged off Adam's coat, hung it up and then crossed the room to stand beside him. Sarah slipped her hand into Adam's as he bade his guest farewell.

"Come again," Adam invited. "Before spring."

"Please do," Sarah added. "I promise not to make a scene again."

The Nez Percé nodded. The men were of the same height and build. They both had near blue-black hair. The native's eyes were black, Adam's blue. Adam's complexion, although still somewhat bronzed from his hours in the sun reflected by the snow, was not as dark as Runs-With-The-

Wind's. She felt her cheeks heat up when she recalled that he was not tanned all over, just above the waist.

As Runs-With left the cabin, Sarah let go of Adam's hand and turned to the task of clearing the table. She heard the door close, heard Adam moving about behind her, collecting his gun and the implements he used to clean the firearm.

As she scraped the bowls and crossed the room to start the kettle with water simmering on the fire, she started to tell him what she had experienced when she saw the baby clothes. But the admission would lead to telling him about her invasion of his trunk, and she feared his reaction. He had guarded the secret so carefully, she had no idea how he might respond.

She had the bowls and mugs washed and put away before he looked up from where he sat at the table oiling the wooden gunstock. Sarah turned and found that he had set aside his work and was waiting for her to look at him.

"What's wrong, Sarah? Are you still upset about Runs-With's sudden appearance?"

"What makes you think something's wrong?" If she could hear the tremor in her own voice, how could he not?

Adam stood up and came to her, wrapped his arms about her and held her close. She could hear his voice reverberating through the hard wall of his chest. "I know you so well, Sarah. I can see it in the way you hold your shoulders, in the way your smile has dimmed and your eyes have lost their shine."

He lifted her chin, forcing her to gaze up at him. She knew he was about to kiss her and was powerless to look away. Their lips met, and she felt the rush of longing she always experienced in his arms. Adam was her strength, her rock, the center of her universe. How could she think of leading another life? There was no life before him.

But what of the visions?

Sarah couldn't stop the shudder that shook her.

"Sarah? What is it? Tell me."

She squeezed him tight and then moved out of the shelter of his arms. "While you were out I spilled the bag of apples, and as I was cleaning them up, I found the trunk beneath the—"

"I know damn well where it is," he said, his brows knitting, suspicion and hurt mingled in his eyes.

Shaken by his immediate, angry response, Sarah was afraid to go on but knew that at this point, there was no going back. "I opened it," she said quickly, "and found the beautiful gown."

He turned away from her. She reached out to him, then let her arm fall to her side. Staring at his rigid shoulders, she pressed her palms to her abdomen and took a deep breath. Before she could explain further, he cut her off.

"It was my wife's wedding gown. I married when I was seventeen." His voice held a far-off note, as if he had to strain to utter every word. "Katherine was her name. She was a year younger than I. We headed west, to California, but I didn't want to settle there. She was willing, so willing, to go wherever I asked, to keep moving. Finally we chose this place."

He turned to face her, his eyes ravaged with the pain he had held inside for far too long. "She died ten years ago."

Briefly, Sarah closed her eyes. When she opened them, she said, "I found the baby clothes, too."

His hands clenched into tight, white-knuckled fists he held at his sides. She prayed he would not break down entirely. She didn't think she could bear it if he did. All she had ever known of Adam was his strength. Deep in her heart she had come to believe that nothing could hurt him, now she found herself clinging to the belief that he was invincible. That belief was keeping her sane.

His shoulders bowed. He turned away again. It was a moment more before she heard him whisper, "She died with the child still inside her. I buried them in a meadow not far away."

Sarah couldn't hold back a sob. She ran to him, tried to get him to look at her, and when he wouldn't, she put her arms around him and pressed her cheek against his rigid back. It was as if he had turned to stone.

"I'm so sorry, Adam. I never meant to hurt you like this."

"Why couldn't you leave it alone, Sarah?"

"Because something happened when I saw those baby things in the trunk, something happened that I can't explain. Admitting that I had trespassed into your things was the only way I could talk about this with you."

He broke the embrace and stepped away. He didn't pause until he stood before the fireplace, resting his fist on the thick log that formed the mantelpiece. His blue eyes were unusually bright, his lashes spiked by unshed tears. "You remember—"

She couldn't bear the space that yawned between them. Sarah crossed the room, and, although he did not open his arms to welcome her, she refused to let his emotions erect a barrier between them. Not now. Not when she knew that what she was about to say might shatter what they had built in their short time together.

"When I saw the baby clothes I felt like I was coming apart. I saw myself giving birth. I felt the pain. I felt the child slip from my body. Then there was only emptiness and loss.

"The sight of those little gowns triggered what can only be memories that moved me so deeply I felt everything. I thought for a moment that I was going to faint. Adam, in that instant I knew for certain that I must have had a child of my own. I don't know where or when. All I know is that I'm certain it's true.

"I shoved the gown and the baby clothes back in the trunk, but before I closed the lid, I found the ivory mirror and saw my reflection." Her hand trailed up to her hair, and she touched her short curls. "The image I saw there didn't match the picture that flashed through my mind. I had long hair once. Long ringlets that I wore tied up in bows and ribbons."

"*I* cut your hair off," he said. Finally, thankfully, he reached out for her and cupped her face in his hands. "Your hair was matted. So tangled that I couldn't get a brush through it, Sarah. I had to cut it off because it had been neglected for so long."

It wasn't until he smoothed her cheek with his thumbs to wipe away the tears streaming down her face that she realized she was crying.

"You loved Katherine so much you couldn't bear to tell me about her," she whispered, acknowledging the truth aloud.

"I did," he said. "And in a corner of my heart, I'll always love her, Sarah, but you must know—you have to know—how much I love you."

She wrapped her arms around him again and held on tight, afraid that if she let go she would shatter into a thousand and one pieces. "And I love you. But I'm so scared. What will I do? What if there's a baby out there somewhere who needs me? Surely I have to find out."

"If you have a child..." He left the rest unspoken.

"Then I must have a husband." She pulled back to look up at him. The pain in his eyes reached her, pierced her heart. "How can I love you so much if there is someone else waiting for me? How can it be that I don't feel some knowledge of him deep in my heart? Wouldn't I remember *something?*"

Sarah pulled away from him, openly crying now, and walked over to the bed. She sat down, unwilling to look up at Adam, not when she knew her words were hitting him like physical blows. She covered her face with her hands. "What am I going to do?"

It was awhile before he answered, and when he did, there was no inflection in his tone. "I've lived with this since I found you and brought you home. I can't stand it anymore, Sarah. I'm going to have to go find out."

Trembling, she didn't trust herself to go to him. Instead she held out her hand, urging him to cross the room, sit beside her and take her in his arms again. "What if it means . . . ?"

"I have to do it. We can't go on like this forever. What if someone is grieving over you the way I grieved for Katherine? I've tried to be selfish and keep you here as my own, but I can't hide from it any longer, and neither can you. You're starting to remember things. Today proved that. Will you still love me when you remember it all, or will you hate me for refusing to help you discover the truth?"

Suddenly terrified, she glanced around the small cabin, the only world she knew. The thought of what might lie beyond these four walls frightened her to the marrow. "I'm so scared."

"We can only pray we don't learn anything, but I can't sit here and do nothing any longer. I have to do this for your sake, for your child's, if there is one out there somewhere."

She buried her face against his shoulder. "I can't leave you, Adam."

"We will do what we have to do," he said, fighting to keep his own sorrow out of his voice.

In his heart, he'd known this day was coming, he had hoped it never would, but finally he was faced with it. Sarah had remembered a few details of her past, minute details at best, but she had remembered, nonetheless. As his mind raced ahead, planning his departure to the mission, he felt her press closer, burrowing into him, seeking comfort much the way she had on their first night together in the cabin.

He hesitated for a second, debating with himself. This might be their last night together.

Pulling her closer, he kissed her temple, her cheek, then her lips. Sarah closed her eyes with a sigh and settled against him with familiarity. They moved as one as he laid her down on the bed and stretched out beside her. It was growing dark outside, the daylight shortened to a few hours.

In the back of his mind, Adam knew he should put another log on the fire, but he could not bear to let her go long enough to perform the mundane task. There would be time for that later. Not since they'd made love that first night had he felt such desperation in her touch, and he knew his own matched hers.

Sarah clung to him, relished the feel of Adam's strong limbs entwined with hers. He was her world, and yet, as she felt his hands move over her possessively, she realized that they would never be free until they knew the truth. She stared up into the depths of Adam's sky blue eyes and watched as he lowered his head, bringing his lips close to hers. The kiss he gave her was slow and lingering, as if he wanted it to last forever. She returned his kiss in kind, tasting him, reveling in the heady sensations that pulsed through her as their tongues met and dallied.

As his hand slipped up along her rib cage and teased her breast through the buttery soft gown she wore, Sarah gasped and arched against him.

"I need you," she whispered, the words escaping her before she could stop them.

"I need you, Sarah," he whispered back. "I never thought I would let myself feel this way about anyone again."

She couldn't help but hear the sorrow in his tone. Sarah reached up and ran her fingers through his hair, closed her eyes and sighed. "I'm so sorry, Adam. I never meant to hurt you."

"I know." He kissed her throat, gently teasing the soft, vulnerable flesh with his teeth. "You haven't asked for anything I wasn't willing to give."

Desperate to feel his skin against hers, Sarah began to tug his shirt from beneath his waistband. He groaned, a low growl of a sound, and pulled away from her. Sarah raised herself up on an elbow.

"What is it?" She studied his profile in the firelight.

"We can't do this."

She felt tears of frustration and sorrow fill her eyes as she sat there so close and yet so far away from this man she had come to love. "I'm not as honorable as you are," she whispered.

His hands were shaking as he shoved his shirt back into his pants; he tried to hide it from her, but he couldn't. She felt as if her new world was slowly dissolving around her.

"What if you don't find out anything? What if there is no one searching for me? Maybe I was wrong about what I felt today."

"When I get back, we'll decide what to do next."

"But—"

"Sarah, please." He took her in his arms and held her close against his heart. "I want you. I want you so bad it hurts, but I don't have the right."

"You must think I'm shameless."

Shaken, she suddenly realized what her demands must be doing to him. How could she beg him to make love to her knowing that on the morrow he would be leaving in search of her former life, a life that might include another man, a child, a family she did not remember but who needed her and would insist upon her return?

"Forgive me, Adam."

"There's nothing to forgive."

He reached out and pulled her close against his side. They sat there staring at the dying embers of the fire. Frost clung to the outside of the windowpane, pressing minute crystals into a mottled pattern. She prayed he would come back with news that would set her free. He wondered how he would find the strength to give her up if he had to.

"Do you have your extra socks?" Sarah fussed with his belongings, closed the saddlebags he would sling over his horse and avoided meeting Adam's eyes.

"You'll be all right? You remember how to use the rifle if you have to?"

"Don't worry. Besides, you promised to send your friend to look after me."

"I did. Runs-With will be here before sundown. His encampment is fairly close by. I should reach it in an hour or two at the most, and he'll be here a few hours after."

She walked to the window, not knowing what to say, fighting the urge to beg him not to go to the mission, to bar the door and damn the consequences, but then she recalled the earth-shattering emotion that had swept through her when she'd held the baby clothes, and knew she had to let him go at any cost.

"I'm ready."

Sarah's breath caught in her throat, but she forced herself to move, to walk toward Adam, to take his hand and go with him to the door.

He was smiling down at her, but the smile was forced. She realized he was trying to appear confident for her sake, but the smile didn't reach his eyes. He was bundled up to the ears in his heavy, fur-lined coat, his eyes overly bright. With one hand on the door handle, he told her, "Don't stand in the draft."

"I'll be fine."

He bent to kiss her on the cheek. Sarah closed her eyes, unwilling to face the sorrow she was putting him through.

"I hate this," he whispered after he kissed her goodbye.

"Me too."

They clung to each other in the open doorway until Sarah shivered from more than just cold. "Go," she told him softly, "before I beg you not to."

He turned away quickly, but not before she caught a glimpse of unshed tears in his eyes.

Adam ducked as he entered the low door to the trading post that stood alongside the Redemption Mission house. The place was as close as civilization had dared encroach upon the vast wilderness of the Plateau. The smoky warmth in the log structure stung his eyes, and he swiped at them before he pulled off his gloves and shoved them into his coat pocket.

"Adam Stroud!" A short, balding man nearly concealed by a stack of blankets called out in greeting from behind a long counter. "I didn't think to see you around here until spring. What brings you down the mountain this time of year? Did you come to trade or just to hear the sound of a voice besides your own?"

Adam wound his way past sacks of sugar and flour, boxes of fish hooks and awls, and leaned against the counter. "Howdy, Tom. I guess you might say I just stopped in for a visit."

"A lame excuse if I ever heard one. Preacher Whittier caught sight of you, yet?" The clerk pulled up a high stool and perched atop it, obviously eager to ignore the inventory he was counting to chat with the only customer in the place. "He finds out you're here, he'll be over makin' an attempt to bring your wayward soul into the fold."

Adam knew that if the good Reverend Harmond Whittier knew the life he'd been leading or the thoughts he'd been thinking lately, he would give up converting him without a fight.

"Everything going all right down here?" he asked, choosing not to comment on the subject of his salvation.

"Right as can be with December comin' on. Bound to see deep snow anytime soon."

Adam said, "All the more reason I can't waste time jawing with you, Tom Anderson."

The trader laughed. "Take off your coat and sit a spell. The alternative is goin' up to the mission house to be accosted by the preacher's daughters. Besides, I've got coffee on and no hope of anyone else comin' by all day."

Setting his rifle on the counter first, Adam shrugged out of his coat and tossed it beside the weapon. He took off his hat and finger combed his hair. After being outside, the room was overly warm, the close dry air an irritation rather than welcome relief. Adam accepted the tin cup of coffee. It was dark as pitch and tasted almost as bad, but mulling over it gave him something to do besides wondering if his insides would settle down long enough for him to ask the questions he had come here to ask.

Tom was more than content to carry on a one-sided conversation until Adam drained the cup and refused a second. Finally, steeling himself for whatever Tom Anderson might reply, Adam asked, "You wouldn't happen to have heard about anyone looking for a white-woman captive around here lately, would you?"

Anderson made a point of slowly perusing the empty room. "Oh, hell, Adam. Two or three times a day."

"I'm serious."

The man sobered instantly. "I can see that."

"I thought you might have heard something, maybe seen a notice or a reward out for a missing woman? Anything like that? Remember anything that came through last summer or early fall?"

Tom frowned and ran his thick, short fingers through the few strands of hair remaining on his scalp above his forehead. He remained thoughtful long enough for Adam to fear he might lose the coffee that was churning in his otherwise empty stomach. Finally Tom Anderson shook his head and said, "Nope. Nothing."

Adam wished he felt relieved.

"One of your Indian friends got hold of a white woman? I know last time I seen you, you were headed to the Dalles rendezvous. You find more than you bargained for?"

The man was closer to the truth than he knew. "I got more than I bargained for, Tom. There was a white slave at the Dalles, and I traded for her. I had hoped to find her family."

Tom appeared thoughtful for a moment more. "The Dalles was over in October. It's December, Stroud. You still got her?"

Adam felt the warmth of embarrassment stain his cheeks. "I have. Not that it's any of your business." He wished to heaven he'd never come, wished he had tried to talk Sarah out of the idea that she had dredged up memories of having a child of her own. Angry at himself more than at the curious clerk, he picked up his coat, intent on slipping it on to leave. The door opened, and a draft of cold air swept the room.

Tom called out, "Howdy, Preacher. Look what the cat dragged in."

Adam shoved his arms into the sleeves of his coat and began to button it up. Given the least encouragement, Harmond Whittier could talk the legs off a buffalo. All Adam wanted was to get out of the trading post as fast as he could, but the preacher was fast closing in on him.

"Adam Stroud. Welcome, son. Welcome. What brings you down here? You must come over to the house, let Marta fix you a hot meal before you head out again. I'm sure Melinda and Maxine would enjoy some company."

The preacher's plain but abundantly tall, abundantly endowed, man-hungry daughters came to mind. Adam picked up his rifle. "Thanks for the invitation, Preacher Whittier, but I need to get back before this weather breaks."

The preacher reached out to thump Adam between the shoulder blades. "Nonsense. It looks to be clear for a week," he assured Adam.

"Stroud's found himself a white captive, been asking if we heard about one," Tom blurted out.

Adam squelched the urge to leap over the counter and strangle the man.

The Reverend Whittier pulled back in astonishment. "Is this true, Adam? You've found a lost soul and delivered her from the heathens?" He turned to look in all directions, as if expecting her to pop up from behind a crate. "Where is she?"

Adam grabbed his hat and shoved it on, but not before he glowered at Tom Anderson. "She's at my cabin," he said slowly.

Harmond Whittier appeared perplexed. "You didn't bring her to shelter? Didn't lead her back into the arms of God and civilization?"

"Nope."

"But—"

"You have any word of anyone searching for a missing woman in the last few months, Preacher?"

"Not that I recall, but surely someone must have been."

The idea made Adam's insides roil.

"Where is she from?" Whittier asked.

Adam shrugged. "I have no idea. I found her with the Nez Percé at the Dalles. They had traded with the Crow and seemed to think she came from pretty far east of here, probably ambushed along the Oregon Trail, but that's not certain."

"When did you find her?"

"End of September."

The preacher sputtered, "And...and you've been living with her—*alone*—in your cabin since then? Why, the woman must be overwrought, at the very least. She needs proper care and nurturing until we can spread the word and locate her family."

Adam's mind conjured his last sight of Sarah. Along with the love for him shining in her eyes, she had appeared worried, torn between her past and the future, but not distraught. No, not distraught. She was finally sane, happy until she had found his hidden trunk.

"I'm taking perfectly good care of her, Preacher, even though that's none of your business."

"All God's children are in my charge."

"You've got your hands full, I'd say, too full to worry about me."

"And that helpless, confused woman," Whittier added.

Adam had to get out. He had to get back to Sarah.

"Stroud, listen to me." The preacher grabbed his sleeve. Adam halted in his tracks, but he refused to turn around. "I'm sorry. I want to help, that's all.

You came here to tell me about the woman. At least give me some information. Her family must be frantic."

"She might not have any people," Adam told him, trying to keep the hopefulness out of his voice.

"That's true. Tell me anyway."

Adam closed his eyes, pictured Sarah. His Sarah. "She's blond, average height, slender. About twenty-five. She can't remember her age."

"And her name?"

"She can't remember."

"Amnesia."

Adam turned to face the older man. "She's happy. We're both happy, but we can't keep on living with the fear that someone will find her and want her back."

Harmond Whittier was watching him closely. Adam shifted uncomfortably. Finally the preacher said, "You love her."

"She loves me, too," Adam whispered.

The preacher volunteered, "I'll come back with you. Marry the two of you. At least then you won't be living in sin."

"No."

"Stroud—"

Adam sighed, the weight of the world on his shoulders. "What if she already has a husband?"

Whittier frowned, obviously perplexed and sorting out the situation. "What if she doesn't?" he countered. "Time to make a decent woman out of her."

"Could you marry us knowing she may already be married?"

"That'd be some fix." Tom Anderson stood listening behind the counter, shining his bald head with a handkerchief.

Whittier shot him a dark glance. "Most certainly. Until there is any concrete proof that she is married, I cannot condone your living in sin. And I can tell by that scowl on your face that you don't intend to give her up."

Adam knew he was right. "Let me go back and talk to her first. Ask her to marry me."

When Whittier looked about to balk, Adam eyed the man of God and bargained, "You claim we're already living in sin, Reverend, so what difference will a few more days make? Let me explain that there has been no word of anyone searching for her. If she wants to marry me, you can perform the ceremony. If not, you can bring her back to the mission."

Whittier weighed his words. Then he nodded. "I'll give you two days to get back, then I'll start out. It'll take me two days to get there. I pray the weather holds."

"So do I." Adam couldn't face the thought of having Harmond Whittier snowed in with them.

Sarah paced back to the table, eyed the tall, smiling man seated there and asked for the tenth time, "Do you think he'll be here soon?"

Runs-With shook his head. The trade beads and bells woven into his braids rattled against one another. "Soon enough. You will wear a path in the floor."

"I miss him so."

The Nez Percé man arched a brow. "I can see that."

"You really don't need to stay any longer. I'm certain Adam will be home today. That's what he promised."

"I will stay until he returns."

Sarah sat down, realized the corn bread was finished baking and jumped up again. As she hurried across the room to pull the Dutch oven away from the fire, she wished Runs-With would leave her alone. She wanted to prepare herself for Adam's return. She had so much she wanted to tell him.

As if he sensed her impatience, Runs-With-The-Wind stood up and walked to the door. "I can see you want to be alone. I will start home now. If I don't pass Stroud on the trail, I'll return before nightfall."

Feeling guilty, Sarah straightened and wiped her hands on a piece of muslin that served as a dishrag. She extended her hand to her husband's friend and offered him her thanks.

"I hope I haven't offended you, but I'd like to wash up and be ready for Adam when he returns." Just the thought of seeing him again sent a thrill of anticipation through her. Runs-With donned his buffalo robe and silently left the house. Sarah watched his silhouette through the window until he disappeared. He was such a striking figure that she had no notion of how she could have erased the memory of Runs-With-The-Wind or her time with his people.

Impatient to have everything just so when Adam returned, she bustled about the room, set the table, hovered over the venison stew and corn bread to be certain the dishes were warm but not overdone. She couldn't wait to share her secret with Adam, to tell him the wonderful revelation that had come to her the night after his departure. Even now she could recall lying alone in the big bed they had shared, hugging his pillow tight, staring into the embers of the dying fire. She had insisted Runs-With sleep inside on a pallet near the fire, and the seasoned warrior had done so without embarrassment; he'd merely stretched out, pulled his buffalo robe over him and gone to sleep, leaving Sarah to her musings.

Now, that his arrival was imminent, she became more and more anxious for Adam to walk through the door. The hours passed slowly even though she tried to stay busy. She washed her face and combed her hair. With nothing left to do, Sarah decided to sit down and wait for Adam's return.

The sun had slipped behind the distant mountains when she finally heard his footsteps outside. Although she had fallen asleep at the table with her head resting on her arms, Sarah heard him in time to jump up, run her fingers through her hair and smooth the front of her buckskin dress. Unable to wait any longer, she flung the door open.

Adam stood beside his Appaloosa. Arrested by the sight of him, she danced on tiptoe in anticipation of his approach. He dropped the reins, and came to her and she rushed headlong into his arms.

He held her close. She drew back to stare into his eyes. His expression told her nothing.

"Well? What did you find out?"

He immediately turned her toward the warmth of the cabin. "Let me unpack while you get inside. I don't want you to catch cold."

Sarah's heart tripped over itself. "Are you hiding something from me?"

He didn't answer, simply turned away and pulled his saddlebags and a sack of supplies from his horse's rump. Then Adam stepped inside and closed the door, stripped off his gloves, hat and coat and didn't speak until he had his things hanging in place on the coatrack. He opened the drawstring bag and reached deep inside for two lengths of calico and a small wooden box of tea.

"These are for you," he said, handing her the gifts.

Sarah took them in her hands, ran her palms over the smooth fabric and then opened the box and sniffed deeply of the aromatic tea. "Oh, Adam. Thank you so much." She set the items aside and took his hand. "Now tell me, please. What are you hiding?"

"I'm not hiding a thing. No one at the settlement had any word on any missing persons at all."

He'd expected her to be disappointed. He didn't know what to feel when all the way back to the cabin he'd convinced himself that his journey had been fruitless. They were still in limbo regarding her status before he'd found her. Curbing the urge to grab her up in his arms, Adam walked over to the dry sink and took a cup down off the wall. He was about to pour himself a cup of coffee when she said, "That's wonderful news."

Coffee sloshed over the rim of the cup, and he cursed under his breath when the steaming liquid hit his skin. He brought his hand to his lips and sucked the burn in the curve between thumb and forefinger, then picked up the cup again.

"Wonderful? We don't know any more than we did four days ago."

The joy in her smile lit up her features and nearly broke his heart. Adam ducked his head and took a mouthful of the coffee, hoping the shock of the hot liquid would dilute his need to touch her.

As if Sarah could read his mind, she closed the space between them and took his hand. "Adam, the night you left I was lying awake, thinking of you, worrying about what would become of us. I thought back to the moment I found the clothes Katherine had made for your child and the visions I experienced. The next morning, I pulled the trunk out again—"

"Sarah—"

"Let me finish. I wanted to experiment, so I opened the trunk and took out the baby clothes and held them again, but no horrible memories came back this time. Not at all. I had been doing a lot of thinking since that first time, and something started to nag at me. Adam, I know why the sight of those precious pieces moved me so."

"Why?"

She closed her eyes and squeezed his hand. "Because I'm certain now that I'm going to have a baby. Your baby, Adam. I'm sure of it."

He fumbled with the cup and set it down before he dropped it. "What are you talking about?" He wondered if she had gone mad again. If not, perhaps he had.

"I haven't had my monthly the whole time I've been here, have I? And then there's—" Her cheeks flamed, and she looked down at his shirtfront. She took his hand and moved it to her breast until he cupped her gently. "I ache here. There's a heavy, swollen feeling in both breasts. And besides," she looked up at him, her eyes aglow, "I just *know* it, Adam. I'm going to have your baby. Our baby. *That's* what I felt the day I found the clothes. I wasn't seeing a memory from the past. I think it was more of a revelation, a premonition of the future."

If she had blasted him with his shotgun he couldn't have been more stunned. His mind raced ahead of him, counting the days she had been here. Indeed, she had not had her monthly time. He had explained it to her, questioned her when she was able to understand, and then lost track of time. He studied her carefully. She seemed so sure, so hopeful. Was it possible? After all, she had been through an ordeal so great she had lost her mind. Why not her menses, too?

"Sit down, Adam." She laughed, dragging him to the table and depositing him in his chair. "You look as if you might swoon."

"What if..." he began slowly, thinking out loud. "What if you were already pregnant when I bought you at the rendezvous? No one knows what you've been through. It's a possibility." When she didn't answer, he glanced up at her.

Sarah shook her head, an expression of horror on her face. "No. That's impossible."

"How can you be sure?"

"I just am," she said, but she didn't sound quite as certain as before.

He wished he could be as sure; still, it did not matter to him whose child she carried. He would willingly raise it as his own if Sarah was willing to give up the shadows of her past and be his wife.

He pulled her down onto his lap and held her there. She wrapped her arm around his shoulders and held his head against her breasts. She whispered, "Are you sorry?"

"No." He raised his head and looked straight into her eyes as he said, "Never sorry."

"I want to forget about my life before you found me, Adam. I'm yours now. I'm free. The darkness is behind me, and I want to leave it there. I was born in your arms the night we made love for the first time, and I can't bear to think of a life before that moment in time."

"Reverend Whittier wants to come up here and marry us."

"What do you want, Adam?"

"You know what I want. I want you. But I don't want to be looking over my shoulder for the rest of my life, wondering when and where someone's going to show up and claim you."

"But you said there's been no word of anyone searching for someone like me. No notices, nothing. Surely we're safe."

If she was right, there was a baby to consider. A child who needed a name. There was no trace of doubt about his love for Sarah. No doubt at all.

Unwilling to admit that her past might come back to haunt them whether they wanted it to or not, Adam pushed the thoughts aside, thought of the children she would give him, and felt his heart threaten to burst with joy.

"Marry me, Sarah. Be my wife."

Sarah fought down the nervous anticipation that had unleashed a bushelful of butterflies in her stomach when Reverend Harmond Whittier had arrived to perform the wedding ceremony a good two weeks after Adam proposed, a surprise storm having kept him away. Certain by now that she was carrying a child, Sarah tried to calm down for the baby's sake.

The small cabin had been swept clean and put to rights. A tasty venison stew bubbled over the fire. The minister, a tall man with a receding hairline and beaked nose, stood before the fire mumbling to himself as he paged through the worn Bible in his hands. Small, square-lensed glasses rode the tip of his nose. Sarah noticed he had acquired the habit of peering over them every few seconds.

Runs-With, outfitted in buckskins and furs, stood beside Adam, who was quietly explaining the ceremony to his friend, who had brought along his eldest son. Adam had told her that Two Feathers was Runs-With-The-Wind's oldest son. Sarah thought him a most handsome lad and guessed him to be around sixteen years old. Like his father, the youth would stand witness, but he seemed more interested in when they would eat the stew than in the wedding.

"If you're ready, ma'am?" Harmond Whittier was gazing at her over his glasses again. His mud brown eyes held no censure, but he had watched her curiously since he'd entered the cabin and Adam introduced them.

Sarah nodded. She paused beside the table to pick up the spray of young pine boughs Adam had cut and bound for her to hold in place of a bouquet. Holding the fragrant pine arrangement, she walked over to join the men standing before the fire. Adam reached out and took her hand in his and held it against his side. His touch lent her quiet strength.

Palms up and holding the Bible, the preacher rocked back on his heels and then onto his toes before he settled himself. He looked first to Adam and then Sarah.

"You understand that this marriage is only binding so long as you are unwed? Any previous ceremony takes precedence over this one, unless of course, the other spouse has passed on to glory."

Sarah wished the earth would open up and swallow her. Adam squeezed her hand.

"We know that, Preacher. Get on with it," Adam mumbled.

As Reverend Whittier read the vows, Sarah kept her eyes on Adam, certain that it was only the love she saw mirrored there that got her through the ceremony. Half expecting someone to crash through the door and stop the proceedings at any moment, she was as nervous as a cat, and she didn't breathe any easier until it was over and Adam took the pine sprigs from her and handed them to Runs-With.

As he took her in his arms, she whispered, "What are you doing?"

"It's traditional to kiss the bride," he whispered back.

She glanced at the three men surrounding them and tried to protest. "But—"

Adam's lips met hers with a brief but soul-stirring kiss. "I promise, Sarah, to keep you safe and love you until death do us part." He whispered the quiet vow for her ears only.

She closed her eyes against a sudden rush of tears and then buried her face against his collarbone. As Adam held her close, the others congratulated them.

"Do we eat now?" Two Feathers asked.

The spontaneous burst of laughter that followed his question put everyone at ease.

After the meal was finished and Sarah sat chatting with the missionary before the fire, Runs-With signaled his son that it was time to leave.

"Sarah, I'm going to walk them to the edge of the clearing," Adam told her. "Will you be all right?"

She smiled up at him in understanding and nodded. "Reverend Whittier was just telling me about his daughters. You go right ahead. Thank you, Runs-With-The-Wind," she called out. "Please bring the rest of your family next time you come to visit."

The two men, followed by the youth, stepped out the door and crossed the porch. Where the wind had crusted the snow, it crunched beneath their moccasins. They paused where the forest began. Adam stared back at the dwelling he had built himself, warmed to his soul by the sight of the golden lamplight spilling out from the windows and the thought that Sarah was inside waiting for him.

"This ceremony makes the Woman-Who-Cost-Too-Much your wife?"

"It does," Adam affirmed, wishing he felt as sure as he sounded.

"She carries a child."

Adam's brow wrinkled as he stared hard at his friend, trying to make out his features in the darkness. "How did you know?"

Runs-With snorted. "I have eight children. One learns to see the signs."

"Sarah is carrying a child."

"It might not be yours," Runs-With said.

"I've thought of that." Screwing up his courage Adam asked, "Do you know of anyone who might have fathered the child?"

"Not of my people. She was crazed when River-Walker traded for her. He is as bad at making a decent trade as you are, my friend."

Long used to the way Runs-With liked to tease, Adam ignored the gibe.

"If another man comes to claim her now, will you have to pay for her again, or does this ceremony make her yours?"

Adam rubbed his arms and stomped his feet to ward off the chill. "If she had a husband who finds her and comes to claim her, I'll have to give her up."

"Could you challenge him and fight for her?"

Knowing he would fight to the death for her if he could, Adam forced himself to face the truth. "No. With us, it's not that simple."

"Then I wish you luck, Adam Stroud," Runs-With told him.

Adam reached out and clasped his friend's hand and shook it. "Thank you. I hope I don't need it."

Spring burst onto the hillsides in wide swaths of color and heady scents as wildflowers bloomed in abundance. Adam sat on the bank of a nearby stream, paying little attention to his fishing line and letting his mind drift as lazily as the feathered lure bobbing upon the water. His winter take of pelts combined with what he had traded for before he spent his goods on Sarah made for a good year. It was past time to head down to the trading post to strike a bargain with Tom Anderson for all the things they would need to see them through the coming year.

Any other time he would have been there and back by now, but this year he had Sarah, and he was in no hurry to leave her. Her suspicion had proved to be true, and throughout the winter she had kept apace of the child growing inside her by becoming more beautiful every day. Now, at seven months gone, she had passed the stage where Katherine had taken ill and died—but Adam still found himself worrying constantly about her. If all went well, the next few weeks would tell if the babe was his by blood or not. But whether it arrived early or late, Adam couldn't wait to claim the child as his own.

Try as he might, he couldn't recall exactly how he had felt when Katherine was expecting. He sensed he had willed away the painful memories much the way Sarah's mind had let go of her own past. He did know that he could hardly wait to hold this infant in his arms, to hear his son or daughter cry, to cradle the baby in his arms. "You've grown soft, Adam Stroud," he said to himself.

Soft and vulnerable.

Sarah had slipped into his heart and in so doing made him as defenseless against pain as he had been when Katherine was alive. There were nights when he would awaken in a cold sweat, nights when he dreamed Sarah told him she was leaving him to return to her old life. He dreamed he was standing over Katherine's grave, but it was the loss of Sarah he mourned.

In the first few months of their marriage, he'd found himself listening for footfalls, for the sound of a man's voice calling out for Sarah, but his anxiety had lessened as the weeks and months passed and no one had appeared. It didn't matter now. She was his, and her child was his, and Adam vowed to himself that no one would ever be able to take Sarah from him.

"She's mine," he whispered as his fingers tightened on his pole. "My Sarah."

Overhead, the pines chided him with wind whispers of nonsense words of their own.

He shifted position on the hard ground, pulled the line out of the water and cast it in again. Lulled by the sound of the water rushing over the stones that lined the creek bed, he leaned back, closed his eyes, and let the spring sunshine stain his cheeks.

Sarah carried the clean linens indoors, tossed them on the bed and picked up a pillowcase. She shook it until the linen snapped and then reached for one of the pillows at the head of the bed. It never ceased to amaze her how much her increased girth slowed her down as she moved through her familiar chores.

Just as she was tucking in the sheet beneath the mattress and admiring the birdsong trilling on the breeze that slipped in through the open window, something thumped at the door, and she straightened. Unable to resist a long stretch, she placed her hands on the small of her back and thrust her shoulders back. She wondered how she could possibly carry the baby two more months.

She pulled open the door, determined to tease Adam for calling her away from her work. "Did you catch so many fish you can't even open the door for yoursel—"

Sarah froze. It was not Adam who stood on the other side of the door, but a strikingly handsome man a few inches shorter and a few years younger than Adam. He stared back at her from hooded, deep green eyes as if he was seeing a ghost.

"Lucy?"

Her hand fluttered to her throat. She tried to speak but couldn't form any coherent thought. The man didn't move. He simply continued to stare through tear-filled eyes.

Please, God, no. Sarah knew that if he called her wife she would die right there on the threshold. She glanced over his shoulder, fearful of having Adam return and be shocked by the sight of this stranger at his doorstep.

A stranger who stared at her through a haze of unshed tears and called her Lucy.

She was Sarah. Sarah Stroud.

No matter what this man might have to say.

Part Three

She stared at the man on her threshold, her heart beating so frantically that she feared for the safety of the child she carried. With one hand riding protectively on her swollen abdomen, Sarah bade him enter and then stepped aside to let him pass. Watching him closely, she then glanced over her shoulder, anxious to bring the stranger inside before Adam walked up and caught sight of him standing there.

If all went well, she prayed she would somehow be able to convince this man that she was not the woman he sought and send him on his way before her husband returned.

The man took off his hat and paused just inside the cabin. He had a full head of fair hair that was neatly trimmed along his collar and hung down over his forehead. He glanced around the room while Sarah closed the door behind them. Upon closer inspection, she could see that his pants, although soiled, were of rich, textured brown wool.

Sarah was tempted to stare longer but forced herself to look away. The man appeared to be as nervous as she. Finally he cleared his throat and managed, "You don't remember me, do you, Lucy?"

"I'm sorry. I—" She watched a sad, lost expression move quickly across his face. His shoulders slumped as if he was greatly fatigued or terribly disappointed.

"May I sit down?" he asked.

She wanted to tell him no, to demand that he take his leave immediately, but even as frightened as she was, she could tell that he was so very disappointed by her reaction that she couldn't bring herself to send him away. She nodded toward a chair.

He sat down without removing his jacket. The way he continued to stare openly at her only caused her jitters to accelerate. It was easy to see he was taking note of her obvious condition as well as studying the simple, tentlike calico gown she had fashioned and stitched by hand.

She stared at him long and hard, especially at his strange, sea green eyes. He looked to be a kind man, a caring man, definitely someone too gentle for a life as rugged as the one Adam led. He was clearly out of his element here in the wilderness, which made her wonder what had driven him to come all this way to find her. Bewilderment and concern showed in his eyes, but if there was some deeper emotion there, she could not read it.

"I'm sorry," she began again. "I'm afraid I don't know you. I don't mean to be impolite," she said with a quick glance toward the door, "but I would appreciate it if you would state your business before my husband gets home."

With a heavy sigh, the man settled back into his chair and continued to look her over for a few seconds longer. Then he rubbed his hand over his eyes and forehead as if he bore the weight of the world on his shoulders.

"Your husband?"

"Yes."

His gaze went directly to her belly. "Perhaps you had better sit down," he suggested gently.

Sarah forced herself to breathe. The ache in her back agreed with him. She lowered herself into a chair across from him, wishing her lack of encouragement had sent him packing. He seemed determined to stay.

"You seem to know who I am," she said as calmly as she could.

"Better than you know yourself, it appears. I'm Lee Carrigan. I'm a banker from Philadelphia. I have corresponded with and finally met Reverend Whittier at the Redemption Mission. He told me you might be the woman I was searching for."

"Why would you be searching for me...or rather, this...Lucy?"

"We've been friends for years. Your husband was—"

The catch in her throat and a wave of her hand interrupted him. He waited in silence as Sarah took long, slow breaths and sat with her eyes closed, her hands pressed against her stomach as she tried to fight down a throatful of raw fear.

Visions of this stranger demanding she accompany him back to her rightful husband, the thought of being forced to walk out of Adam's life to return to one she no longer remembered or even longed for on any level, was more than she could bear thinking about. She pushed the nightmare images from her mind.

Finally she whispered, "My husband . . . ?"

"James Hartman. He was my best friend."

"And I'm—"

"Lucy Hartman."

Slowly she shook her head from side to side, unwilling to believe him. "I would remember if it were true, wouldn't I? I should feel something when I hear his name."

"Perhaps not. Not after everything you've been through."

"If I don't know what I've been through myself, how can you claim to?"

"I know only what I have pieced together." He leaned forward and reached out to cover the hands she held clenched in her lap with his own. His hands were warm, but the touch brought her no comfort.

As she sat staring back at him, fighting the urge to run from the room and seek the shelter of Adam's arms, there was a slight sound outside, and then the door swung inward. Sarah jumped to her feet.

Adam stood stock-still, framed in the doorway, the spring sunshine pouring in around him, highlighting the blue-black streaks in his hair, shimmering and glistening off the string of fish that dangled from one hand. His hair was coaxed into a queue tied back by a thong, but it was long enough to give him a savage, untamed look. Well built, proud and intimidating, Adam took in the scene before him without blinking an eye, but the smile on his face instantly faded when he realized she was not alone.

Staring back and forth from Sarah to Lee Carrigan, Adam didn't move. She could read the wariness in his stance, the mounting anger and then the undisguised pain in the depths of his eyes. The intensity of his stare forced Carrigan to immediately let go of her hands.

Sarah swiftly rose and went to his side, reached out to take his hand and clung to him, hoping her touch would reassure him somehow. Her husband did not respond to her, nor did he take his eyes off the stranger.

Lee Carrigan quickly rose to his feet. Extending a hand in greeting, he introduced himself. Refusing to let go of Sarah's hand, Adam didn't move to shake Carrigan's.

"This is Adam Stroud." Sarah turned to Carrigan and volunteered the name feebly before she added with more emphasis than needed, "My husband."

Adam reacted to the words the way she hoped he would. He gave her hand an intimate squeeze and then let go long enough to set the string of fish in a pan on the dry sink. He took off his hat and hung it up, carefully wiped his hands off on a towel and then helped Sarah to her chair. He left the door open and moved about the room precisely, as if going through routine motions would somehow keep the inevitable at bay.

Finally Adam turned back to the man waiting to be acknowledged. "Sit down, Mr. Carrigan. Would you like coffee?"

The man shook his head. "No, thanks. Mr. Stroud, I've already spoken to Reverend Whittier, and I'm sure you know why I'm here. I would hate to upset Lu—your wife any more than she already is."

Adam crossed the room to Sarah. He remained behind her chair, resting his hand on her shoulder. She reached up to touch his hand, to hold on to him as if to ground herself in his world.

He had always thought himself a man of honor, a man who would choose right over wrong no matter what the situation. In that instant he realized he didn't know himself at all. If this man thought he was going to take Sarah away from him, he had another think coming. It would be over his dead body.

As he stared down at his wife's nimbus of gold curls, Adam knew that he would do whatever it took to see that she stayed with him forever.

He would never give her up.

Sarah glanced up at him and explained, "Mr. Carrigan claims he knows me and that he also knows all about what happened to me. We haven't had time to speak of it, yet."

Carrigan leaned forward, concentrating on Adam as he spoke. There was no hint of fear in his eyes, only concern. "Your wife's name is Lucy Hartman. She and my best friend, James, were married six years ago in Philadelphia. He was a teacher, quite good at what he did, and he seemed to enjoy teaching, so you can imagine my surprise when he decided he wanted to move west, to Oregon. Do you recall any of it, Lucy?"

"Her name is Sarah now." Adam spoke in a tone barely above a whisper, yet he couldn't keep the underlying threat out of his words. He could barely contain his temper as he stared at the handsome, well-dressed man who sat across from Sarah. Unlike his own mix of native and frontier clothing, Lee Carrigan was outfitted from head to foot as if he had just stepped out of an Eastern haberdashery.

Carrigan didn't comment. He was still waiting for her answer. Afraid the men would come to blows, Sarah quickly told him, "I don't remember anything about my past, and although you claim I was once married to this...James Hartman, his name stirs no memory." She wanted to tell him to stop, to leave without further explanation, but a morbid sense of curiosity held her tongue.

The man went on. "The family tried to discourage James. You had just found out that you were with child at the time...."

Sarah gasped and once more placed her hand over her stomach. Her gaze once again flew to Adam, who was staring intently at Carrigan.

"Surely not this one," she protested. "This *is* Adam's child. I know it is."

Lee Carrigan frowned. "It couldn't be James's. You left Philadelphia over a year ago now. A few months later we received word that the wagon train was ambushed somewhere on the Plains. There were no male survivors, and James's body was found among the dead. His family tried to trace you for a time, but the army didn't hold much hope. One of the women had been left for dead, but she survived long enough to tell the commanding officer that you and two other women were taken captive. The consensus was that you would have been better off if the savages had killed you."

"I *was* dead," Sarah whispered. "Dead inside." Another thought troubled her. "What of my own family? Do I have parents? Anyone who is still searching for me?"

"None. Your mother and father died of consumption when you were sixteen, and you were raised by a maiden aunt who is no longer living. You and James met at a church social and were married when you were nineteen."

While he paused in his telling of the tale, Sarah tried to force herself to remember something of her past as he had described it. Married to a teacher, a home in Philadelphia, an aunt who had raised her—but nothing came back. The information he had provided, these mysterious keys to her past, had failed to unlock the doors in her mind.

A baby, he had said.

So there *had* been a baby, but she had obviously not carried it to term. Sometime between her capture and the day Adam found her, she had lost a child. Too shaken to respond, she fought back the urge to retch and looked to Adam for help.

"How did you find us?" Adam had not yet begun to relax. He wanted to know, *had* to know, everything.

"Reverend Whittier sent a letter through military channels. It was forwarded to the families of the missing. From the description he gave of your wife, I knew the woman he wrote of had to be Lucy."

"What's your stake in all this, Carrigan? Why come all this way if you're not even blood kin?"

Before answering Adam's question, Lee Carrigan continued to watch Sarah closely before his eyes met Adam's without hesitation. "As his best friend, I felt I owed it to James to find Lucy, if she was still alive. I'm sure you can understand that, Mr. Stroud."

If Lee Carrigan felt anything for Sarah other than responsibility, he kept his feelings well hidden. Adam saw nothing but respect in his eyes. He thought of Runs-With and knew that he would have gone on the same quest for his friend.

"I do understand," he told Carrigan truthfully; still, his hands tightened on Sarah's shoulders.

"Then you won't mind telling me the rest of the story and about how she came to be here?" Carrigan asked.

"I found her with the Nez Percé when I was at a rendezvous on the Columbia about two days' hard ride from here. Before that she had been traded from tribe to tribe. By the time I found her, she was out of her mind. She might have been that way since the attack." When Adam thought of the wagon-train ambush, of the unspeakable acts his wife must have witnessed, he knew why she had taken sanctuary in oblivion.

He traced a circular pattern on her collarbone with his thumb as he talked. "I traded for her with the intention of locating her kin, but at first, after she regained her senses but not her memory, Sarah was too scared to leave. She felt safe here."

"Actually, I begged him to let me stay," she broke in. "And then we fell in love." She glanced back up at Adam and smiled. "I'm sure you can understand why I have no desire to go back to my old life, Mr. Carrigan."

Unsmiling, he watched her closely, as if weighing the truth of her words. Finally, satisfied that she was indeed happy here, Lee Carrigan asked, "What should I tell James's parents?"

Sarah paused. She was perched on the threshold of the future. Beside her, Adam remained sure and strong, offering her his life, his love, his strength.

It was enough. It was more than enough.

"Tell them the army report was wrong. Tell them Lucy Hartman died with her husband."

The three remained thoughtfully silent, as if, indeed, someone's life had just come to an end in their midst. Outside the air was filled with birdsong, the sun was still bright, the land burgeoning with buds and the promise of new life. As Sarah looked out the open doorway at the radiant world beyond, the baby inside her moved, almost as if her child experienced her joy. Sarah smiled up at Adam and saw that the shadows that had been mirrored in his eyes for so long were finally gone.

At last they were free of the threat of her past.

Finally it was time to begin again.

Feeling incredibly light, as if she had been reborn, Sarah stood up. Thankful, she beamed at Lee Carrigan, the bearer of what had become good tidings. "Mr. Carrigan, we would be proud to have you stay for supper and spend the night. No sense in sending you back to the mission on an empty stomach."

After glancing at Adam to be sure the welcome she extended came from them both, Lee accepted. "I'll take that meal, but I'll head out while it's still light. Preacher Whittier assured me that his two daughters would be sorely put out if they didn't have a chance to entertain a traveler. I promised I would take him up on the invitation."

Adam thought of the man-hungry Whittier girls and merely smiled in response.

Later that afternoon, Adam and Sarah stood arm in arm in the clearing before the cabin and watched Lee Carrigan disappear into the trees as he followed the narrow woodland path through the pines. Sarah leaned against her husband's side and closed her eyes, breathing deep of the mingled scents of pine and sunshine.

"It's over," she whispered.

Like her, Adam was unwilling to break the spell that had come over them. It was a moment or two before he turned her in his arms, placed his hand beneath her chin and forced her to look up at him.

"You really don't remember?"

She shook her head. "None of it. When he told us about my past, I felt like he was talking about someone else."

He leaned close and pressed a blood-stirring kiss on her lips. When he lifted his head, he continued to hold her close as he whispered, "You don't know what I went through in that instant when I walked in and found Carrigan sitting there holding your hands."

"Yes, I do. It's the same thing I felt when I opened the door and he called me Lucy. For a moment I thought he might have been—"

"Your husband?"

She nodded, burrowing as close to him as her increased waistline would allow. "I have a terrible confession to make. I've never come so close to seriously contemplating murder."

Adam laughed out loud. "Mrs. Stroud, I'm ashamed of you."

"No more than I am of myself."

"For a flash I considered the same thing."

She pulled back to stare up into his eyes. "Oh, Adam. You're not serious?"

He shook his head. "No. It wouldn't have come to that. But if he had tried to take you, I would have thrown him out and sent him running for the authorities. That would have given us time to get away."

"We might have been running for the rest of our lives. You'd do that for me?"

Adam brushed her curls back off her face. Her hair had grown longer and fuller. It hung almost to her shoulders now. He ran his hands through her hair as he considered her question and then finally said, "I lost one wife. I never thought I would come to love anyone again. You brought light and love into my life again, Sarah. I would go to the ends of the earth to keep you."

"I'll never leave you, Adam," she told him as her arms slipped up around his neck. "Never."

"I'll be here to see that you don't."

* * *

In late July the mountain air was clear and warm, the buds that had held such promise in spring had opened into full bloom. Sarah sat propped against a mound of pelts and pillows on the bed and smiled down at the infant nestled in the crook of her arm, ever amazed at her newborn daughter's beauty. Only two days old, the babe, who was still unnamed, was blessed with her father's coloring, his dark hair and serious blue eyes. Her raven brows were shaped to mimic his exactly. Her appearance in the world so far into the summer months left no doubt as to her parentage—although as far as Adam and Sarah were concerned, that would have mattered little.

As the babe slept comfortably within Sarah's arms, she watched Runs-With's second wife, Mountain Spring, as she bustled efficiently about the room. Sarah would be ever grateful that Adam's friend had moved his wives and children nearby until Sarah's time came. Indeed, she felt blessed to have had such expert hands there to assist at her daughter's birth.

At first she had been shocked at the notion that Runs-With was married to not one but four women and had children by each, but she soon became used to the notion, especially after she teasingly obtained a promise from Adam guaranteeing that he was not about to bring home any more wives.

He assured her with a hearty laugh that one was all he could afford.

Mountain Spring, a short, stocky woman with a brilliantly radiant smile, was watching Sarah carefully from across the room. Occasionally she would glance over at the door and then fight to hide a smile. Although they could not speak each other's languages, they could communicate with signs and gestures. For the last hour, not only Mountain Spring but Runs-With, Adam and all the children had been acting unusually secretive, which led Sarah to believe that they had a surprise in store.

She smoothed her finger down the baby's cheek and touched her rosebud lips, then looked up when she heard a loud thump on the porch outside, followed by hushed whispers and giggles.

Trying to project a serious demeanor, Sarah waited until Runs-With walked through the door, and then she asked him, "What's all that noise outside?"

Adam's friend folded his arms across his chest and said, "Your husband is a clumsy man. Maybe you would like to leave him and come with us on our summer journey over the high passes to hunt buffalo and trade horses with our brothers to the east?"

Sarah joined in the teasing banter. Nothing could dampen her mood of late. "I think not. What kind of a wife would I be if I left my husband simply because he was clumsy?"

Before Runs-With could respond, two of his children came through the door and rushed over to the side of Sarah's bed. A doe-eyed, shy ten-year-old girl stood beside her father, while a boy of four carrying a child-size bow rested his elbows on the edge of the bed and studied Sarah closely.

Mountain Spring joined them. Although she had grown used to having the extended families around, Sarah felt as if she and the new baby were on exhibit and wondered if the other three wives and children were about to join the growing audience gathered around her bedside.

Just then Adam entered the room, his arms spread wide. He was carrying a bulky object completely covered by a striped blanket. He crossed the room and set it on the floor beside the bed.

Sarah began, "What in the world...?"

The children giggled in anticipation. The youngest boy ran across the room and spoke to Adam in the language of the Nez Percé. After a quick exchange, Adam cleared his throat and bowed as if to make a grand announcement. Mountain Spring hid her smile behind her hand. Runs-With-the-Wind tried to appear stoic and unconcerned but failed when his eyes flashed brightly.

Adam looked into Sarah's eyes. "My little friend, Laughing Jay, would like to help me present this small token of my affection for you, since it is from all of us."

He nodded to the little boy, who grinned knowingly at Sarah and hopped up and down, nearly bursting with anticipation. With a flourish, Laughing Jay took a corner of the blanket and whipped it off the gift to reveal a hand-carved cradle set on rockers made of a rich wood of a yellow hue.

As she held her child in her arms, Sarah stared at the beautiful cradle and then let her gaze move around the room as she took in everyone gathered there. She bit her lips to keep them from trembling and signaled to Adam to come closer. She handed his daughter to him and then slowly slid over to the edge of the bed and swung her legs over the side.

Through tear-filled eyes she glanced over at the cradle and then looked up at her husband. "Oh, Adam, it's beautiful. You made it yourself?"

He nodded, his own eyes shining bright. "Runs-With brought the wood as a gift for the baby. It's yellow pine."

Since Adam had the child in his arms, Runs-With stepped forward and took Sarah's elbow, guiding her over to the cradle as he explained, "The pine is used to build canoes to carry trade goods up and down the rivers. It is a symbol of life and prosperity. Our children's cradle boards are often made of the same wood, for the pine is a symbol of life. The pine trees live through winter, when all others seem to die."

His smile warmed Sarah's heart as he said, "You have beat death, a great coup, and now you have brought a new life into the world. This is a time of beginnings. The gift is a reminder of this day we celebrate."

Gingerly Sarah knelt beside the cradle and ran her hands over the smooth, well-oiled wood. She gave the cradle a gentle push to set it rocking.

"It's perfect," she whispered. "A wonderful, wonderful gift."

"Don't go all teary eyed on us," Adam warned, his own voice suspiciously tight. Then he said something she couldn't understand to the children, and they ran to stand at both ends of the cradle.

"I want you to read what I carved in the bottom," Adam explained. At his signal, Runs-With's children tipped the cradle over far enough to reveal the script carved into the bottom.

Made By Adam Stroud For His Wife, Sarah
Washington Territory—1857
"For a new life and new beginnings."

Sarah didn't move to brush away her tears of joy. Instead she stood up and held out her arms for the baby.

"I have some blankets ready," she told him, indicating a pile of child-size quilts and blankets she had made with the leftover scraps of the calico material he had brought her from the mission. "I want to put her in her new cradle before our friends leave."

"They're not leaving yet," he assured her as he collected the items she needed. "We have one thing left to do."

Runs-With stepped forward and held his arms out for the babe. Sarah placed her daughter in his arms without hesitation. "The custom of some of my people is that an elder names the child. I have spoken with Adam, and he agrees that since you have no people here, I will act in their stead."

Sarah's eyes flashed to Adam. She would not insult Runs-With-The-Wind for the world, but she didn't know if she could agree to naming her child Born-In-A-Cabin or Cries-Like-A-Wren or whatever the Nez Percé warrior might choose for a name.

The tender, sincere expression in Adam's eyes begged her to trust him. Still, she couldn't help but feel a bit anxious. Runs-With smiled at Sarah and then looked to Adam.

"I name this child of my friends Adam and Sarah Stroud . . . Vivian. A name which he tells me comes from a word meaning life."

Sarah breathed a silent sigh of relief. Vivian had been Adam's mother's name. She nodded her head, and smiled across the room at him, realizing she should never have worried.

"And—" it seemed that since Runs-With held the floor, he was not finished "—she will also be known as Daughter-Who-Is-Worth-Much."

He laughed so loud he woke the sleeping infant. Vivian began to cry in protest. "My friend Adam knows why," he said over the ever increasing cries. Quickly he handed Vivian back to her mother. The impromptu ceremony ended and Runs-With walked over to speak with Adam as Sarah gently laid the baby in the new cradle and set it rocking.

Adam walked his friend to the door and then out to the edge of the porch. Behind them, Mountain Spring and the children were bidding Sarah a noisy farewell over the baby's protests. Soon they hurried out of the cabin. After a few quiet words to her husband, Mountain Spring bade Adam goodbye and then joined her children on the walk through the woods to the place where the rest of the family was camped nearby.

"I will see you in the fall, my friend," Runs-With-The-Wind told Adam. "We will have much to talk of and many things to trade."

Adam reached out to take his friend's hand. "Go carefully as you travel over the mountains to the east and don't make any bad bargains."

Runs-With laughed. "Maybe I will buy a slave and sell her to you. Would you like another wife?"

"I can't afford another one." Adam laughed in return. "Besides, Sarah is all I need."

"What are you two laughing about?" Sarah asked as she moved outside to join them. She walked to the edge of the porch and turned her face up to the sun.

"Just saying goodbye," Adam interjected before Runs-With could explain. As he slipped his arm around his wife's shoulders, Adam realized that even if he had paid ten times the amount it had taken to gain her freedom, he would still have made a fine bargain.

They wished their friend a good journey and walked back into the house. Sarah paused beside the cradle to fuss with the blankets and rearrange them over the sleeping babe. Then, content that Vivian was sleeping comfortably, she straightened and turned to find Adam standing close behind her. He opened his arms to her, and she stepped into his embrace.

"I'm the luckiest woman alive," she told him as she smoothed her hands down the back of his cambric shirt.

"That makes me the luckiest man. Have I thanked you for Vivian lately?"

"Not for at least two hours."

He pulled back far enough to look down into her eyes. The love she saw reflected in his made her heart sing.

"We never know what lies ahead, do we?" she asked him.

"What do you mean?"

"Oh, just that when things appear to be at their worst, when we seem to be the most hopeless, how often do we pause to wonder what might lie in store for us beyond the darkness? If I could have foreseen this, my life with you..."

"If we could see the future, you would never have started along the trail west...and I would never have found you."

She hugged him close and sighed. "I suppose you're right."

"It's life's lessons and hidden surprises that make it worth living—" He was interrupted by Vivian, who had begun to wail from her cradle.

"One of life's little surprises happens to be hungry." Sarah laughed as she slipped out of his arms and went to pick up the baby.

Adam smiled at his wife as she began to open the buttons that ran along the bodice of her gown as she carried his daughter over to the bed.

In the middle of the room, the empty cradle stood waiting.

* * * * *

ROCK-A-BYE BABY

Debbie Macomber

A Note from Debbie Macomber

When my hardworking editor invited me to participate in this year's Mother's Day anthology, I was surprised. I'd been honored and pleased to be in the 1993 edition. My first thought was "Again?" But that's the way it is with motherhood in general, isn't it? Just when we think we're finished and the children have grown and begun to forge their own paths in the world—bingo, they're back again.

As my children have grown into adulthood, the questions have become more difficult and the answers less clear. I remember when my four were toddlers and I was running myself ragged keeping up with them. My mother told me to cherish these moments because they would be the very best times of my life. I can remember thinking, "You mean it gets worse?" Not worse, exactly, just more involved.

In the two years since I last penned a letter for a Mother's Day short-story collection, Ted, my son the Airborne Ranger, married his high school sweetheart. If everything goes according to schedule, by the time you read this he'll be out of the service and a full-time college student. Dale will be in college, as well, with his sights on a career in sports medicine or teaching, or both—or neither.

Despite bribes and subtle pressures, Jenny and Kevin refuse to make Wayne and me grandparents, but they assure us the time is coming soon enough. I can hardly wait.

As for Jody, my oldest daughter... She's survived a disastrous relationship and walked away stronger because of it. The most difficult task I've found in being a mother is allowing my children to make their own mistakes. I'm writing "Rock-A-Bye Baby" for Jody, and for the promise of the future. My heroine has been badly hurt, as well, but she rebounds and learns that love's right around the corner. I'm confident my daughter will soon discover the same lesson.

And so the tricky business of being a mother continues. Of holding on and letting go, of stepping aside and holding my breath.

I hope you enjoy "Rock-A-Bye Baby" and the special connection it has with the stories by Jill Marie Landis and Gina Ferris Wilkins.

Debbie Macomber

Chapter One

"You did what?" John Osborn demanded of his mother.

"I hired you an assistant," Mamie explained in low tones. She glanced nervously toward the woman working unobtrusively in the far corner of the store. "She's wonderful, John, really. In addition to working the floor, she does light bookkeeping. You know as well as I do that you've been needing someone for months. You can't help liking Dani."

"Dani? What kind of name is that for a woman?"

"Dani Beckman," his mother responded. "She's a sweet thing and I won't have you upsetting her."

"Upsetting her? What about upsetting me?" The minute his back was turned his mother took it upon herself to involve herself in his business affairs. This was what he got for asking her to watch the store while he was away on a buying trip. John studied this woman his mother had hired and groaned inwardly. One glance told him Dani was entirely unsuitable for the antiques store.

First off, he didn't approve of the way she dressed. She had on an outfit that looked like something a rock star would wear. Her black skin-tight pants weren't pants at all—they resembled leotards. And if her flowery top was supposed to be a dress, then it was by far the shortest one he'd ever laid eyes on. No one wore hats these days, especially black velvet ones with big yellow daisies.

"Mother, what were you thinking?" he muttered under his breath.

"That you could use the help," Mamie reminded him.

That was true enough. The antiques business had thrived the last several years, even in the "off" season. John had worked hard to build a clientele in the small seaside community of Ocean Shores.

"I prefer to hire my own help."

"I know," his mother said contritely, "but Dani is such a dear. I liked her the minute she inquired about a job. You will, too, once you get to know her. It was either hire her then or let someone else snap her up."

That was exactly what John wanted. He had no intention of keeping Dani around for more than the next five minutes.

He'd never been comfortable around women like Dani Beckman. She was too pretty, too bright, too gregarious. Mostly too damn young. When he was with someone like her for more than a few hours, John came away feeling dull and witless. This was Patricia's legacy, he supposed. He hadn't been clever enough, charming enough, romantic enough to hold on to the only woman he'd ever loved. She'd said he was dead boring when she'd left him, and John strongly suspected she was right.

"Introduce yourself," Mamie urged. "And John, please, be cordial."

John supposed that was the proper thing to do, seeing that he'd be laying her off before the end of the day. For everyone concerned, the sooner Dani Beckman was gone the better.

John walked over to where his new assistant was sitting at a desk. From the looks of it, she was tallying a list of figures. "Hello," he said stiffly, "I'm John Osborn, the owner." He stressed the last bit of information, hoping she'd realize his mother had only been tending the store as a favor to him.

"Hi. I'm pleased to meet you." Dani's face brightened with a smile that outdazzled the lights of Las Vegas. He should have known firing her would be like aiming a rifle barrel at Bambi.

The sensible thing to do would be to explain there'd been a simple misunderstanding. He'd tell her his mother had no business hiring an employee on his behalf. He'd make it as painless as possible and be done with it.

He would have, too, if she hadn't looked so damn vulnerable, sitting there with those round, dark eyes of hers gazing up at him as if anticipating the worst. For the life of him, John couldn't make himself say the words.

"I understand Mother hired you for sales and bookkeeping," he muttered instead.

"Yes." The woman was no dummy, she must have known what he intended. He noticed the way her fingers tightened around the pencil.

"How much sales experience do you have?" he asked.

She sighed audibly. "None."

"None," he repeated slowly and cocked his eyebrows as he assimilated the information.

"I worked for Murphy's Department Store for nearly seven years," she was quick to add.

"Seven years?" He didn't think department stores were into child labor these days. If she'd been employed that long, she had to have been hired while still in junior high school.

"I'm twenty-seven," she said as if reading his thoughts.

It would have been impolite to check her identification, but frankly John had a hard time believing she was a day over twenty-one.

"I know I look younger," she said quickly, the words rushed and raised, "but it's true."

"And what exactly did you do at Murphy's?"

"A little of this and that, but mostly I did the window displays."

His mother certainly knew how to pick them. The woman knew absolutely nothing about the antiques business. Nothing about sales or bookkeeping, either, he'd wager.

"What about your bookkeeping skills?"

"Your mother said the job entailed *light* bookkeeping."

"Then you've had some experience in this area?" Maybe he was being unfair to prejudge the woman.

"Not real experience," she admitted reluctantly, "but I routinely balance my checkbook and I'm a fast learner."

She was batting those big brown eyes at him again. John didn't doubt for an instant that she'd turned many a man's mind by fluttering those long lashes of hers. He, however, was immune. It would take a whole lot more than Bambi eyes to change his mind.

"I hope you'll give me a chance to prove myself."

She regarded him, and John felt a grudging respect. It was a shame, really. The situation was unfortunate. But he wasn't going to be blackmailed into working with someone his softhearted mother had hired on a whim.

In addition to everything else, John sincerely doubted that Dani would last more than a couple of weeks, if that long. He'd seen plenty just like her who arrived at the ocean resort for the summer, looking for a good time and a little romance. Once she'd had her fun, that would be the last of her. By that time, he'd have wasted months training her, and would need to start the process all over again with someone new.

The bell above the door chimed and a customer walked inside. John immediately recognized Mrs. Oliver. She was a looker. He'd lost count of the number of times she'd wandered into his store, eyed several items and asked a variety of educated questions. Her routine was always the same and John grew accustomed to her visits. She came because she liked the atmosphere, he suspected, and because she wanted someone to visit. John couldn't remember her ever buying anything.

"Hello," Dani said eagerly, and moved toward the front of the store and Mrs. Oliver. "It's lovely weather we're having for April, isn't it?"

"Why, yes." Mrs. Oliver glanced from Dani to John and then back again.

Apparently Dani wanted to prove her sales prowess with the widow Oliver. John almost pitied her. He left the two alone and walked into the back room where his mother was assembling a pot of coffee.

"Well, dear," she said when he joined her. "What do you think of Dani?"

"She'll have to go."

"Go?" Mamie sounded shocked. "What do you mean?"

"Mother, the woman's completely unsuitable. She knows nothing about antiques. As for the bookkeeping part...that's a joke. She doesn't know any more about that than she does sales. For the love of heaven, she dressed mannequins for a Seattle department store."

"She'll learn." Mamie stared at the measuring cup over the rim of her granny glasses, then poured the grounds into a container and inserted it into the coffeemaker.

"I'm sorry to disappoint you," John muttered, "but I have no choice."

"Really?" Mamie turned on the water faucet. Distracted as she was with the task at hand, she seemed not to be listening. "I do hope you'll reconsider."

"Give me one reason why I should."

"A reason?" she repeated. "Actually I could give you several. You need to lighten up a bit, son.

Now I don't want you to take this the wrong way, but ever since Patricia—"

"Mother, please, I don't want to talk about her. Patricia and I are finished, and have been for a good long while. Please, just drop it."

"I'm not talking about her, dear. It's you we're discussing. It's time for you to realize not every woman in the world is like... her."

John's spine stiffened. "You're doing it again."

Mamie looked up and sighed expressively. "I am, aren't I? I apologize. It's just that I worry about you and the way you've thrown all your energy into this business. It's as though... the shop is your whole life."

John cleared his throat. He found this conversation uncomfortable. His mother was right, his life did revolve around the antiques store, his collection of books and an occasional game of chess. But he was content and if it was a crime, then he was guilty. He certainly didn't need or want someone cute like Dani Beckman messing with his mind, reminding him of all the might-have-beens.

"You're playing the role of matchmaker again, aren't you?" he asked, making sure the disapproval was thick in his voice. Not that he would consider dating Dani. It was clear to anyone looking at them how different they were. To be perfectly frank, he wasn't interested in becoming involved with a woman who dressed like a fruitcake. He'd had his fill of feminine games, and a woman's wiles.

"Matchmaking? Heavens, no," Mamie answered, laughing softly. "It's just that, well, you could use a bit of fun and laughter in your life, and Dani's just the person to brighten things up around here. It's fine to care about the past the way you do. But John, really, there's no need to bury yourself in a time long since gone."

John blinked, miffed by the way his mother involved herself in his affairs.

"Of course, you can let Dani go, if you wish," she persisted. "Osborn Antiques belongs to you, but I do hope you'll reconsider."

The coffee brewed noisily behind him as John mulled over his mother's words. He pulled aside the drape that separated the office and small kitchen from the main part of the store.

Dani Beckman stood beside Mrs. Oliver. She'd smoothed out the fragile blades of the antique lace fan and fluttered it daintily in front of her face, her lashes lowered.

John had shown the identical fan to this customer no less than ten, possibly fifteen times. He watched, mesmerized as Dani closed the fan and balanced it in the palm of her hand. The distance was too great for him to hear what she was saying, but whatever it was had Mrs. Oliver's rapt attention.

To his utter amazement, the matronly client nodded sharply and opened her purse. John stood back with his mouth gaping open as Mrs. Oliver wrote out the check.

He waited until the woman had left the store before approaching Dani.

"What did you say to her?"

Dani looked up at him innocently. "About what?"

"She bought the fan, didn't she?" he asked brusquely.

"Yes."

"I want to know what you said that convinced her to make the purchase."

"Nothing special," Dani said, looking mildly surprised by his reaction. "We chatted a bit about who might have owned this lovely fan at one time, and the places it could have been. I read a historical novel recently in which the woman cleverly used a fan to reveal her love for a certain young man." She hesitated, as if she wasn't sure she should continue. "I did suggest this very one might have brought lovers together in ages past."

"I see," John said with a frown. Frankly, he didn't understand it. The fan was pricey. He'd had it for several months and had been wanting to sell it, but didn't think he would get his asking price. Yet Dani had sold it, with ease, to a woman who'd never bought a thing from him.

"Are you going to keep me on or not?" she challenged, her shoulders squared.

John scratched the side of his head while he mulled over the situation. Five minutes ago he'd known exactly what he intended to do. Not anymore.

"You're going to have to look more like a..." He stopped, not knowing how to say it.

"Go on," she urged.

"I'd prefer it if you dressed... differently."

Her eyes revealed her surprise as she looked down on her leotards and top. "What's wrong with what I have on now?"

"You resemble a teenager. If you work for me, I want you to look like an adult. How old did you say you were? Twenty-seven?" He was probably breaking some employment code that would cause the state to close him down if she ever reported him. But he didn't care. She wanted honesty and that was what she was going to get.

"All right."

She seemed eager enough to please, and that suited John, although he didn't suspect it would last long. "I own the shop, not my mother. She occasionally works for me, but that's about all."

"Understood."

John rubbed his hand along the side of his face, still of two minds. If he kept her on, he was asking for trouble. There were plenty of people from the community who'd welcome the opportunity to work for him. By keeping Dani he was depriving someone else of employment.

"I'll give it a month," he decided.

"A month," she echoed, then grinned. "No problem, I'll have proven myself by then."

John suspected she wouldn't stay on more than a couple of weeks. "Frankly, I expect you to be long gone by then."

"Really?" His assessment of her staying power appeared to nettle her.

"I've seen it before. You're here for the sun and the fun."

The line about her mouth became thin and white. Her lips relaxed after a moment. "We'll just have to see about that, won't we?"

John Osborn didn't like her. Well, that was fine with Dani, because she didn't think much of him, either. He scowled at her as if she'd done something terrible by selling Mrs. Oliver the fan. One would think he'd be pleased.

As for the rude comment about the way she dressed, well, she could make a few remarks of her own about his wardrobe.

Mamie had said her son was thirty-five, but John looked older. . . in attitude, if not in fact. It was as if he'd purposely set out to discourage her. The guy probably didn't know what a pair of jeans and running shoes looked like. It wasn't just her he didn't like, she suspected, it was women in general.

No wonder he wasn't married. It seemed to Dani that he'd settled comfortably into bachelorhood, which was perfectly fine with her. At the moment, a relationship was the last thing on her mind.

Frankly, Dani mused, she didn't care what Mr. John Osborn thought. She was keeping this job. She needed it. Desperately. Working at the antiques shop meant she didn't have to return to Seattle. It meant she didn't have to see Bob Adams again for a very long time, if ever, which at the moment suited her just great.

The shop closed at five and after bidding everyone a good evening, Dani headed out the front door.

"I'll see you in the morning," she said to John, who looked none too pleased at the reminder.

He nodded without comment.

"Have a good evening."

"You, too," Mamie called after her.

Dani heard John mumble something. At first she couldn't make out what he said, but as she walked across the street and headed for the beach, the words made sense. John had insinuated she'd probably spend the night partying. He made it sound as if she was some kind of party animal, simply because he didn't approve of the way she dressed. The man had a low opinion of women, and she wondered who had hurt him so terribly to cause him to distrust all womankind.

Dani had been hurt, too. She considered this time, these days, a period of recuperation. She'd moved to Ocean Shores to rebuild her shattered dreams, to repair the damage to her heart.

Her, a party animal? Not likely. It was an effort not to traipse home each night and give in to bouts of self-pity. It demanded energy to count her blessings, instead of remembering what a complete idiot she'd been over Bob.

It had been by accident that Dani had ended up at the ocean the day she'd discovered Bob was involved with Pamela. The pain of finding the man she'd loved with another woman had been so overwhelming, so powerful that she'd gotten in her car and started driving, with no destination in mind.

Her thoughts had been dulled with such intense pain that she was all the way to Olympia, the state capital, before she realized she'd left the Seattle city limits.

A freeway sign directed her toward the ocean beaches, and Dani had driven until she arrived in the resort community of Ocean Shores. She'd parked on the beach, left her vehicle and taken a long, brisk walk barefoot in the sand. A vigorous wind had buffeted her, and the salty spray mingled with her tears.

Something about the surf pounding relentlessly against the shoreline had eventually quieted her spirit. The wind, wild and free, had blown hard against her while the sea gulls called overhead. With her hands buried deep inside her coat pockets, Dani had walked and walked, and let the tears flow, cleansing her.

It had been that fateful afternoon, two months ago, that Dani had found her peace. It had come grudgingly, after a deep inner struggle, and at a price.

But it had come.

Those were the last tears she'd shed over Bob Adams. It still hurt to think about him, to acknowledge how easily he'd managed to dupe her.

He was every woman's dream. Tall, handsome, wealthy and fun. When Dani was with Bob she felt like the luckiest woman alive to have this man love her.

It had taken that afternoon at the beach to swallow her pain, admit how incredibly naive she'd been and decide what had to be done.

Breaking off the relationship with Bob hadn't been easy. But it was necessary for her sanity and her self-worth. Bob, however, was determined to do what he could to repair the damage. But as far as Dani was concerned, everything they'd shared was over. She returned the engagement ring, gave her two weeks' notice at Murphy's and packed up her belongings. She knew automatically where she wanted to live.

The ocean.

The key to her plan was finding employment. She had been about to despair when she wandered into Osborn Antiques and met Mamie. The two had struck up a conversation and before long they were sipping tea and chatting like long-lost friends.

Mamie had hired her, but she'd also given Dani adequate warning. "Be patient with John," she'd advised. "He means well, he really does, but he's got his own way of doing things." She paused as if she'd already said too much.

"I'm sure we'll get along just fine," Dani assured Mamie. She genuinely liked people. There wasn't anyone Dani actively disliked, and she figured that with a little effort she'd learn to get along with Mamie's son.

That, however, was before she met John Osborn. He might prove to be the exception, but if that was the case, she was going to go down in flames.

"It's a beautiful morning," Dani said when she arrived for work the following day.

John glanced up from the morning edition of the Seattle newspaper and sipped from his mug of coffee. It looked as if he was going to ignore Dani, then said, "It's raining."

"Yes, but that's liquid sunshine." Weather didn't determine what kind of day it was going to be for Dani. Every day was a new adventure.

John glared at her. "Are you always this happy so early in the morning?"

She hated for her enthusiasm to be a blight on his grumpiness. It amazed her that his business thrived if he greeted his customers the way he did her. "Is my good mood going to be a problem?"

"No," he grumbled, without looking at her.

"Is there anything you'd like me to do?" she asked and removed her jacket. She hung it in the back room and stored her purse where Mamie had showed her.

"Pour yourself a cup of coffee," he instructed.

Dani hesitated.

"What now?" he barked.

What a disagreeable sort, Dani mused. "I don't drink coffee. Do you want me to learn?"

He grinned at that, or at least it was the hint of a smile, but Dani was encouraged. Perhaps he wasn't such an ogre, after all.

"No," he said, without revealing any of his amusement, "that won't be necessary."

"I drink tea," she told him.

"Great. Make yourself a cuppa."

His mother had used the same term and it had seemed friendly and inviting. She didn't feel the same warmth from John, but then, she didn't expect she would.

She brewed herself a cup of herbal tea and, holding the mug in both hands, wandered back out to where her employer sat reading the newspaper.

She waited a couple of moments until he raised his eyes expectantly to hers. "You wanted something?"

"Does what I'm wearing meet with your approval?"

She'd carefully scrutinized her wardrobe and purposely chosen one of her less flamboyant outfits. She set off the blue-and-white striped bib overalls and huge silver snaps with a red kerchief at her neck. A long-sleeved white turtleneck was a perfect contrast.

"You look like a train engineer," he muttered. "Don't you own a dress, like other women?"

"Yes," she admitted reluctantly, "but I don't think you'd approve of it."

"Why not?"

"It's made of green sequins."

John set his coffee aside and folded back the front page of the newspaper. "I should have guessed." His gaze didn't waver from the print. "I didn't finish up the paperwork last night. There's some *light* bookkeeping, if you think you can handle it."

"I'm sure I can," she replied optimistically, eager to prove herself. She'd gone to the community library after work the night before and checked out a couple of books on this very subject. From the little bit she'd read, bookkeeping didn't look all that complicated.

She headed for the desk and chair across from him. He lowered the newspaper long enough to give her a dubious look.

Dani found the paperwork he mentioned and went about making entries in the ledger. She felt downright proud of herself until John casually strolled past and read over her shoulder. She felt him stiffen behind her.

"Is something wrong?" she asked.

"You're entering those as debits instead of credits."

"Oh."

The door opened just then and a retired couple walked inside. "Morning, John."

Her employer's face relaxed. "Howdy, Ron. Darlene. What can I do for you?"

"We're looking for a new dining room set," the man explained with a tired expression. "Darlene's been to every furniture store between here and Seattle and she just hasn't found anything that appeals to her. I have a feeling we'll find what we want here instead of those fancy showrooms we've been visiting." Ron looked flustered and frustrated with his wife, and more than willing to call it quits.

"They just don't make furniture the way they used to," the woman explained.

"They certainly don't," John agreed. "I've got a couple of dining room sets here. They both date from the early forties. The first one's made of polished cherrywood and the other's mahogany."

John led them to a far corner of the store, while Dani erased everything she'd entered into the ledger and started anew. She was so intent on her task that she didn't notice when John and the couple returned.

"This is Dani Beckman," John said, interrupting her thoughts. "She'll be working for me over the summer months."

Dani looked up from the ledger and smiled warmly, in spite of John's insinuation she would only be with him for a few short months. "Hello."

"The Freemans bought the cherrywood table with the matching shield-back chairs."

"Congratulations," Dani said. The table was beautiful and would grace any dining room.

"I'm thrilled," Darlene told her. "And to think we've been searching for months for just the right set and we were able to find something practically in our own backyard."

While her employer and Ron arranged to have the table and chairs delivered, Dani stood and chatted with Darlene.

"You're new around here, aren't you?" the older woman asked. "I don't mean to be nosy, but Ocean Shores is a friendly town and we generally know just about everyone."

"I moved here last month. I'm renting a duplex off Geoduck Avenue." It was only two blocks away from the beach and with her bedroom window open at night, Dani could hear the ocean as clearly as if she were sitting on the beach. She didn't keep her window open long; it wasn't warm enough yet, but it would be soon.

"So how do you like working with one of our most eligible bachelors?"

Dani studied John a second time. She hadn't thought of him as an eligible bachelor. True, he was good-looking enough, she supposed. He was six feet, maybe an inch above that. He had a nice face, gentle eyes—sometimes. At other times, he could frown on her like a curmudgeon, but then she'd seen him smile, too. John wasn't any Bob Adams, that was for sure, but Dani had learned the hard way that looks were a poor estimate of a man's worth.

"This is only my second day on the job," Dani explained.

"Oh, you'll like John, once you get to know him. He's a sweetheart."

"I'm sure that's true," Dani agreed, but personally she had her doubts. Her reservations stemmed from the fact he seemed to be looking for an excuse to fire her at the earliest opportunity. He certainly anticipated her quitting on him. The fact she'd worked for Murphy's Department Store for all those years apparently meant nothing.

The Freemans left soon afterward, and John walked over and examined the ledgers, while Dani dealt with the next customer. She was pleased when she sold a lovely porcelain vase, and waited for John to praise her efforts.

He did, but what he had to say didn't have anything to do with her salesmanship.

His brow was knit in a look of dissatisfaction. "It might be a good idea if you didn't do anything more with the ledger."

"But I can learn," she insisted. "All I need is a bit of instruction."

"I didn't hire someone to teach them what they claimed they already knew," he muttered.

Dani stiffened her shoulders. "I didn't misrepresent myself, if that's what you're implying."

John didn't respond, but she had the distinct feeling there was plenty on his mind.

Thinking it might be a good idea to acquaint herself with the shop's inventory, she made a point of inspecting the furniture and other antiques scattered about the room.

On the far side of the building, she unexpectedly found a door behind a dresser with a tall mirror. She opened it a crack and found another small room filled with furniture. "What's in here?" she asked John, who seemed to be doing his best to avoid her.

"Items I've picked up over the years that need repairs or one thing or another."

"May I take a look?"

He shrugged, indicating he didn't care.

Dani let herself into the room, and found the light switch. The musty scent assailed her and she wrinkled her nose. The room was crammed full of odds and ends. A mahogany captain's chair with a broken arm was propped against a rocker with a missing spindle.

It was then that Dani saw the cradle. It was sitting on top of a scarred cedar chest. She walked over to the chest and ran her hand over the gentle curve at the top. It was handmade and old, far older than many of the other pieces in the store. She guessed that it came out of the eighteen hundreds. She didn't recognize the type of wood.

Her heart constricted, and Dani bit into her lower lip as a flash of unexpected longing swept through her. When she'd broken her engagement, she'd relinquished the dream of her and Bob someday having a family. She'd let go of the fantasy family she'd created in her mind.

She didn't mind the broken engagement. As far as Dani was concerned, she was pleased she'd discovered Bob's philandering ways long before the wedding. But she so did want to marry and have children.

Without warning, this beautiful cradle suddenly reminded her of all that she'd lost.

"I see you found the cradle." John's voice came from behind her. "What do you think of it?"

"It's lovely," she answered, and her voice cracked.

"Dani?" he asked, surprising her with his gentleness. "Are you all right?"

Chapter Two

"I'm fine," Dani lied, recovering quickly. "What's wrong with the cradle?" Once again she ran her hand over the smooth surface of the curved top, enjoying the feel of it against her palm.

If anything, the feelings of loss she'd experienced earlier had intensified. Her throat momentarily closed up and she struggled with herself, unable to explain the strength of the emotion. Explaining her feelings to John was out of the question. Dani couldn't believe John Osborn was a man who'd allow himself to be hurt the way she'd been. He didn't know a whit about shattered dreams and broken promises.

"I can't remember exactly what's wrong with it," John answered, moving around her. He picked up the cradle and examined it. "Ah, yes, there're several scratches on one end. I thought I'd give it a good polishing someday. The fact is, I'd completely forgotten about it. I've put off several repair projects like this one lately." It went without saying that the reason for the delays had been his need for additional help, although Dani guessed he'd do almost anything rather than admit as much to her.

"You can't refinish the cradle," Dani said, seeing the underside.

John tossed her an odd look. "Why can't I?"

"Because there's something carved on it."

John examined the bottom of the handcrafted piece more carefully. "You're right, there is something there. What does it say?" He squinted at the words deeply embedded in the wood.

Dani moved closer in an effort to make out the words, as well. Their heads were close as she whispered the words. "'Made By Adam Stroud For His Wife, Sarah. Washington Territory—1857. *For a new life and new beginnings.*'" Her hand lightly touched the smooth wood. "He loved her very much."

"You can't know that," John replied skeptically.

"You're right, of course," she said, stiffly stepping away from him. "I can't possibly know that, but in my heart I feel that it's true. He must have built the cradle for their child. Wherever did you find it?"

"At an auction, several months back, now that I think about it. Let's bring it out front." John carried the cradle into the main part of the store and set it down on top of the desk where Dani had been working earlier. The light was much better and the scratches on the cradle more visible.

"What kind of wood is this?" she asked.

"Yellow pine," John answered absently.

Dani couldn't stop looking at the cradle. After reading the inscription, she understood far better what it was about this piece of furniture that had struck her so profoundly. It was the love she felt that had gone into it. The tender care with which the piece had been constructed, and the commitment it represented between two people all those years ago. She couldn't keep her mind from wondering about the hardships they'd faced, the struggles they endured and the hope they must have experienced with the birth of their child.

A child.

Dani bit into her lower lip and waited for the surge of pain and bitter heartache to pass. She'd discussed her desire for children with Bob numerous times, and he'd seemed as eager to start a family as she was.

Or so it had seemed. Like so many other things with Bob, Dani learned it had all been empty talk.

"You said you did window displays for Murphy's?" John asked, breaking into her thoughts.

"Yes . . . quite a few as a matter of fact."

"Great. Go ahead and do one up using the cradle. That should attract some interest, don't you think?"

"Yes...yes, it would," she said, but her heart sank. If she put the cradle on display it was sure to sell quickly, and for reasons she didn't care to examine, Dani didn't want that to happen.

"I'll clear out the window for you," John offered.

"I can do it." She didn't want her employer doing anything she could do herself for fear he would use it as an excuse to let her go. Dani wanted to keep this job.

John frowned, which was something he did on a regular basis, it seemed. "You can't lift that chest of drawers."

"No, but I can scoot it aside and use it as part of the display."

His frown deepened. "All right, have at it, but I don't want you doing anything too strenuous, understand?"

"Of course," she said, her mind eagerly assembling ideas. "You don't need to worry, I've done quite of bit of this type of work."

John looked as if he wasn't sure he should believe her. He walked away mumbling under his breath. Dani wished she knew what he'd said, but on second thought, it was probably best that she didn't.

Feeling she had something to prove, Dani went about setting up the window display with a flair and talent that were natural to her. When she buried her mind in her work, she didn't have to think about all that she'd left behind in Seattle or the reasons why.

She set a rocking chair next to the cradle with a patchwork quilt casually draped over the arms and back. A kerosene lamp rested atop the chest of drawers. She added small odds and ends from the past, creating a scene out of yesteryear. She left the impression that all one needed was to step over the threshold and they'd walk into another world, one long passed.

Several people stopped and stared as she worked on the display, but Dani was accustomed to that.

"It's lunchtime," John said interrupting her.

"Already?" She stood and rubbed the small of her back. The morning was gone before she knew it.

"You have an hour."

That was more than fair. She agilely leapt down from the window and dusted her hands. "I brought a sandwich. I thought I'd eat in the back room." It probably wasn't necessary to announce her plans, and she felt foolish afterward.

"That'll be fine." John sounded distracted. Unconcerned. Dani had been so involved in her own project that she hadn't noticed if he'd been busy with customers or not.

She poured herself a cup of tea and set it on the table. It felt good to sit down and relax. She stretched her legs out in front of her and rotated her shoulders a couple of times before opening the brown paper sack.

Fifteen minutes later, she carried her tea into the main part of the store. John was working on the ledgers she'd made a mess of that morning. He glanced up when she appeared.

"I hope I didn't do too much damage."

He almost grinned. A smile came to his eyes first before reaching his mouth, but for no reason she could name he wouldn't allow himself the luxury of revealing his amusement.

A couple strolling down the sidewalk stopped and stared at the window. Dani felt like she should step outside and explain that she wasn't finished with the window display, yet. When it came to her work she was something of a perfectionist, and there were a number of things to add, small touches that would complete the picture.

"It looks like they're coming inside," John said, rising from the table. "Good. Business has been slow all morning."

"Good afternoon," he greeted as the two moved inside the store.

"Hello," the tall, distinguished-looking woman returned. "We're not really in the market for antiques, but I couldn't help admiring the window display with the cradle. It's lovely."

"Thank you," John said, accepting full credit.

"Years ago, my grandmother sewed patchwork quilts," the woman continued in a wistful tone. "Every stitch was done by hand. Most folks prefer to use a machine these days, not that I blame them, mind you."

"The quilt is the genuine thing," John said. "It's been well preserved over the years, and from what I understand was hand stitched more than sixty years ago."

"About the same time as my grandmother."

"Perhaps you'd like to see it," Dani offered eagerly, noting the customer's wistful look. She set the teacup onto the desk, leapt back into the window and removed the blanket from the rocking chair. She'd draped it in a way that best displayed the starburst design, and at the same time left the impression that whoever had gone from the rocking chair would return momentarily.

"Oh, Thomas, look," she said softly when Dani showed her the quilt. Dani noticed the tears gather in the corners of the other woman's eyes.

"We'll take it," Thomas said emphatically. "Now, Mary, I don't want you arguing with me. I can see how much this would mean to you. I've been looking for something special for our anniversary gift and this quilt is perfect."

Mary blinked back the tears. "It's just that I remember my grandmother so clearly. I have grandchildren of my own, and yet it only seems like yesterday when I sat with my own grammy and she read to me by the fireplace."

"How much?" Thomas asked, reaching into his hip pocket for his checkbook.

John named a price that seemed reasonable to Dani. While he wrote up the slip, she returned the teacup to the back room and searched the store for something to replace the blanket in the display.

She heard the door close and risked a look in John's direction.

"I suppose you're looking for me to thank you," he said gruffly.

"Thank me for what?"

"That sale. If you hadn't placed the quilt in the window, it would never have sold."

"That's true, but then, that's the reason shop owners do displays," Dani returned without emotion. One would think he'd be pleased. It was all too clear that he was looking for a reason to fire her. Every time a customer made a purchase due to her efforts, he had less of an excuse.

Dani gathered together the items she needed and returned to the window. She wanted this job, and given half a chance would prove herself, but it would be difficult with John's current attitude.

John wasn't fond of eating crow, but if matters progressed as they had the first two weeks since his mother hired his assistant, then he'd be forced to admit Dani Beckman was worth her weight in gold.

She wouldn't last.

John would be a fool if he let himself think she'd stay longer than the summer tourist season. He'd seen her type before. True, he couldn't fault her work. Yet, he almost wished she'd give him a reason to lay her off, and not for any of the arguments he'd given his mother.

Against his better judgment, John was beginning to like her. Dani was warm and gracious and attracted people the way ants head for honey.

When it came to sales, she was a natural. It didn't take him long to discover she could sell just about anything to just about anyone. And really, that was all that should concern him. The less personal contact between them the better. John found himself doing less and less of the selling and more and more of the bookkeeping, which worked out well.

But John didn't dare trust Dani to stay with him past the adventure-filled summer months. And why should she? She was pretty and bright and fun. He couldn't think of a single reason why she would want to settle down in an out-of-the-way tourist town. Not when the bright lights of the city beckoned her back to everything she'd left behind.

When the rainy season hit and the days grew long and dreary, he fully expected Dani to hustle back to Seattle. His problem, as he saw it, was lowering his guard and coming to rely on her. Coming to enjoy her company. Coming to think of her as someone more than an employee.

If he did, he'd be setting himself up for a major disappointment. The best thing he could do, John decided, was to keep his distance. That, however, was proving to be more difficult than he had assumed it would be.

Keeping his guard raised was something John had been doing with the opposite sex for a good long while. It wasn't difficult to remain standoffish with women. It had become second nature to him over the years. Since Patricia.

He realized that he could think of Patricia now and not experience a crushing sense of loss. In actuality, he was better off without her. That was what he'd been told by those he respected and loved. But it wasn't what his heart had said, and their words of comfort had offered damn little solace.

What had frightened him in all this was that he probably would have taken Patricia back, had she come. In the beginning. His complete lack of pride brought a bitter taste to his mouth. He'd made a mistake and he wasn't about to make another.

Later, he'd have rather died than admit he'd ever loved Patricia. Died, rather than let anyone know how dreadfully he missed her.

In time, John had steeled himself not only against Patricia, but all women. They weren't to be trusted. Only a fool would allow another one to muddle up his life.

John was no fool, and the last thing he wanted, needed, would allow, was Dani messing with his life. Dani messing with his heart. Dani messing with all the empty spaces he faced each and every day.

And so, he ignored her as much as possible. Ignored the fact that an exotic flower bloomed in the shadows of his antiques store.

John tallied the receipts for the end of Dani's first two weeks. Once he'd finished, he added them up a second time. She'd been with him only a short while and already this had been his most profitable month of the year.

The phone rang and John reached across the desk for the receiver. He groaned inwardly when he recognized his mother's voice.

"How's Dani working out?" Mamie wanted to know first thing. She sounded as if she'd been looking over his shoulder the whole time he'd been figuring out his profit margin. Almost as if she'd known Dani was the best thing to happen to the business since he opened his front door.

John's hand tightened around the telephone receiver. "Fine."

"Fine? I bet she's terrific."

John couldn't very well argue. Reluctantly his gaze followed Dani as she moved about the store. She'd worked wonders with the decor in the cramped and crowded space. Each morning, it seemed, she arrived with another idea, another brilliant scheme. When he saw how well her ideas sold his inventory, John had given her free rein.

He swore she sold whatever she assembled as fast as she put it together. It started off with a formal dining room display her third day. She'd set the mahogany table with fine bone china and pink linen napkins. Next, she used an antique cut-crystal bowl and arranged a breathtaking centerpiece with silk flowers. With crystal goblets gleaming and silverware shining, it looked as if dinner guests were about to be escorted into the stately room and seated.

The entire room sold within two days, centerpiece and all.

"Admit it, John," Mamie coaxed. "She's terrific."

"She is," he said with some hesitation.

Mamie all but cooed. "I knew it. Her window displays are the talk of the bridge club. By the way, wherever did you find that lovely cradle?"

"It's been in the back room for several months." Now that his mother mentioned it, Dani had sold everything from that first display but that cradle. He wondered why. His price was fair, and it had certainly attracted enough attention.

"From what I understand, the newspaper's sending someone over to take a picture of the 1950s bedroom she made up," Mamie continued. "I understand it's very clever."

"It is." Who would have believed those old album covers and a lava lamp would cause such a commotion?

"You don't sound very enthused."

"On the contrary," John muttered. "I couldn't be more pleased with the increase in sales." Actually, he could use the additional space the extra sales had left him. The antiques he'd purchased in San Francisco would arrive within the next week and he'd need the room.

"I'll see you Saturday evening?"

John didn't know why his mother bothered to ask. He had dinner with her every Saturday night. "I'll be there."

"Great. I'll see you then." She ended the conversation on such a cheerful note that John half suspected his mother had something up her sleeve. John trusted that Mamie knew better.

He wouldn't allow his mother to meddle in his love life.

John replaced the receiver and watched as Dani handed a sales receipt to Mrs. Albertson. The seventy-year-old widow walked out of the shop and Dani turned to John, and it looked as if she was having trouble keeping a straight face.

"Something's amusing you?" John asked in the same practiced, cool tones he'd used with her from the beginning.

"Didn't you see?" Dani asked, gesturing toward the 1950s bedroom display. "Mrs. Albertson bought the lava lamp."

John had a difficult time disguising his surprise. "Mrs. *Albertson?*"

"Personally I find it a hoot."

John didn't say anything. He returned to the figures he was compiling before being interrupted by the phone. The silence seemed heavy, but he didn't look up. It was best not to encourage conversation with Dani. The less he knew about her the better, and he certainly didn't intend on anything more than a casual relationship between the two of them.

"You don't like me very much, do you?" she asked in a soft voice.

The question sounded as if it had hurt her to ask it. "I don't dislike you," John said evenly.

"That wasn't the question I asked. I said, you don't like me very much, and there's a significant difference between that and your response."

John sighed. It was just like a woman to involve him in a game of semantics. "Frankly, I don't see the problem."

"Why not?" she asked.

John wasn't accustomed to dealing with a woman who was so blunt. He stiffened. He might as well tell her the truth. "You're leaving."

"I am?" she asked, elevating her voice with surprise.

"I suspect you'll move back to Seattle before the end of the summer, October at the latest. Not that I'd blame you. You're very good at drumming up sales and I suspect you'll find the shop here won't be much of a challenge after a while."

"I love Ocean Shores."

"I'm sure you do," John said. "And why shouldn't you? The weather's been great the last couple of weeks. The tourists flood the store on the weekends, and there's lots to see and do. But that will all fade in time."

"*You* stay year after year."

"I'm different than you."

"How's that?"

John had a sneaking suspicion he was only making matters worse. He hoped to bridge any differences with honesty, but from the way her eyes flashed at him, one would think he'd purposely insulted her. All he'd done was answer her questions.

"You've been great, Dani. I appreciate everything you've done around the store, but you're young and attractive and you'll soon grow tired of living so far away from the city."

She frowned and he noted a weary sadness in her that had escaped him previously. "I don't think so."

"Time will tell, won't it?" Frankly, he was growing tired of these silly games.

"Yes, it will." She turned away, her shoulders stiff. Dani hadn't gone more than a couple of steps when she whirled back around. "Do you care to place a small wager on the fact?" she asked.

"About what?"

"My leaving?"

John shrugged. He had no intention of doing any such thing. "No," he said bluntly.

"Oh, sure," she said, tossing her arms into the air. "You can say what you will, insult me . . ."

He expelled his breath slowly. "I didn't mean to insult you."

"I was with Murphy's Department Store for seven years. What makes you think I'd leap from one job to the next?"

"You belong in the city."

"Who told you that?" she demanded.

John was at a loss as to how to answer her.

"I'll have you know," she returned, and braced her hands against her hips, "I was born and raised in a small town and I loved every minute of it."

"I thought you said—"

"It's true, we moved to Seattle when I was in high school, but I've always been a small-town girl at heart and don't you forget it."

She certainly felt strongly about the subject. "All right," John agreed, sorry now that he'd said anything at all. That had been his first mistake and he seemed intent on adding to the list.

"Great." She beamed him a smile that would dazzle the sun, and held out her right hand.

John stared at it. "What's that for?"

"Our bet."

"What bet?" He hated to be obtuse, but he hadn't a clue what she was talking about.

"That I'll stay on past the summer months."

John continued to stare at her hand. "Dani, listen . . ."

"That's an improvement," she said, smiling once more. She dropped her hand and relaxed. She sat on the edge of his desk, facing him. John couldn't have avoided her, had he tried.

"What's an improvement?"

"Calling me by my first name. You've avoided it for two weeks. Really, Ms. Beckman is much too formal, don't you think? Come on, John, it's time to loosen up a bit. It's only the two of us."

That was the problem. Just the two of them together, day after day. John bit down hard on his back teeth, unwilling to answer her. She was right, he had avoided using her first name, although he certainly thought of her as Dani.

"About the wager," she pressed.

"I don't think that's necessary."

"I do," she said with conviction. "You seem to think I'm the type of woman who goes after whatever is brightest and prettiest without a thought or a care. Frankly, I don't like the implication."

"I see."

"I want a chance to prove myself."

"All right," John said, surprising himself with his willingness to involve himself in this ridiculous wager. "I say you won't last much past October."

"I say I'll stay."

"If I'm right, then..." He couldn't think of anything he'd want from her.

"Then I'll agree to come back and do your window displays once a month for the next year, free."

It was difficult to disguise his delight. "Great."

"What are you offering me if I stay?" she continued, looking very much like a cat about to dip its tongue into a bowl of heavy cream.

"A raise?" he suggested.

"I'll be entitled to one by then. I want you to put something that matters to you on the line. You're so sure of yourself about this, John Osborn, make it worth my while to stay."

"Okay..." But even at that he couldn't think of anything that would induce her to remain in Ocean Shores, and quite honestly, on a personal note he wasn't sure it was a good idea.

"Would you like a few suggestions?" she asked.

"All right."

"How about offering to take me to dinner for a month of Sundays."

"Dinner? Thirty times?"

"Sounds good to me," she said, smiling as if she'd stumbled across a brilliant idea.

"No," he said automatically, shuffling the papers around the desk, straightening stacks that were already straight. He avoided eye contact.

"Why not?"

"First of all, it's not going to happen. . . ."

"Then you don't have anything to worry about."

"And secondly, I don't think it's a good idea for us . . ." he paused and cleared his throat ". . . to see each other socially. It's simply not a good business practice."

Her eyes widened as if the thought of the two of them as a couple had never occurred to her. "Of course . . ." A faint pink tint invaded her cheeks.

"Would you settle for thirty dinners, then," he offered, "with the companion of your choice?"

"All right," she agreed. "I didn't mean to suggest . . ."

"I realize that, Dani."

"I didn't want you getting the wrong idea."

"I didn't," he assured her quickly, uncomfortable with the subject.

"Then you agree to the terms of our wager?" she asked after a moment.

"You realize this is like taking candy from a baby."

"Do you or don't you agree?" she pressed.

"I agree," he muttered.

"Great." The smile was back in place and John had to force himself to look away. He found her far too attractive for his own sense of well-being.

She held out her hand, and John shook it. To the best of his knowledge, it was the first time they'd ever touched. Her skin was smooth and soft, but her handshake was firm and confident. Like the woman herself.

"I'll write everything down so there won't be any misunderstandings between us," she offered.

"That sounds like a good idea."

Dani glanced down at his hand and John realized his fingers continued to clasp hers. Embarrassed, he released her abruptly, and returned his attention to the ledgers.

"If you give me half a chance, you might learn I'm not so bad," she said softly.

"I didn't think that," he muttered, hating the way his heart and head reacted to a tiny slip of a woman who'd be in and out of his life in a matter of weeks. Already he'd started to lower his guard with her. What his instincts had told him in the beginning were true. Dani Beckman was a dangerous woman.

Dani wished now that she hadn't agreed to this dinner with John's mother, but Mamie had insisted. Saturdays were the busiest day of the week. The shop had been full of customers from the moment they opened the door until John turned over the Closed sign at six o'clock.

It amazed her that customers would purchase hundreds of miles from home.

She left the store at six-thirty and wondered how much longer John would end up staying. When she'd mentioned she had a dinner appointment, he frowned and all but escorted her out the door. For no reason she could decipher, Dani was left to feel she'd done something wrong. It had been on the tip of her tongue to inform him that her dinner engagement was with his mother, but she stopped herself in the nick of time.

Dani hurried back to her small rental home, showered and changed into a comfortable pair of jeans and a sweater.

Mamie Osborn greeted her as if she were a long-lost relative. "Welcome, welcome," Mamie said, hugging her. "I hope that son of mine isn't working you too hard."

"Not at all." The smells coming out of the kitchen were enough to make her stomach growl.

"I hope you're hungry."

Dani pressed her hands against her abdomen. "I'm famished." She walked around the ocean-front home, admiring the view. The sun cast pink-tinted shadows over the water. She envied Mamie, living on the beach. The shop had a wonderful view, but she'd been so busy that there was rarely an opportunity to admire it.

"I certainly hope John has been treating you well."

"He's loosening up a bit," Dani said, turning away from the window. "His main problem is that he seems to think I'm going to leave him high and dry come autumn."

"Really? One might think such a thing had happened in the past."

Mamie said it in such a way as to leave Dani wondering. "Has it?"

Her employer's mother hesitated. "Perhaps it would be best if John told you about Patricia himself."

"Patricia." Dani repeated the name softly under her breath. Was it possible John had experienced the kind of disappointment and pain she had? If so, he'd certainly never let on, never hinted, but then, there was no reason he should. Nor did he know about Bob.

"We all have reasons for the things we do," Dani said, surprised by her willingness to defend John. Especially when he'd been a thorn in her side from the very first day.

"And our excuses," Mamie added, bringing Dani a glass of white wine. "By the way, I passed the shop this morning and noticed that the cradle hasn't sold yet."

"Not yet." Dani looked down, hoping to hide her guilt. She'd done everything she could to keep customers distracted from the piece. Selling the cradle would be like letting go of part of her own dream. And as ridiculous as that sounded, Dani couldn't make herself do it.

A car door closed, the sound carried with the wind from outside. Dani looked to Mamie. "You're expecting someone?"

Mamie set her wineglass aside. "Excuse me a moment, I need to check on the roast."

"Mamie?" Dani called after the older woman.

The door opened, and before Dani could fully turn around she knew who the other guest would be. "Hello, John."

"Dani." He stood frozen, just inside the doorway. "What are you doing here?"

Chapter Three

It was apparent the moment John walked in the front door of his mother's house that he didn't want Dani there. "I'll leave," she offered. She could think of no reason for the two of them to spend an uncomfortable evening in each other's company.

It hurt. Dani was just beginning to think that she'd made some headway in her relationship with John, but it was clear that she'd misjudged the situation.

He looked appalled by the suggestion. "You'll do no such thing. Stay here." With that, he disappeared into the kitchen. Although she couldn't make out what was being said, it was obvious John wasn't happy.

After the first few words, Dani was able to make out a phrase now and again. It wasn't that she wanted to eavesdrop, but she found it impossible not to.

"I only thought..." This part came from Mamie.

"You're matchmaking again, Mother, and I won't stand for it." There was more, but John had apparently lowered his voice or had turned away.

Matchmaking? Her and John? Clearly the woman saw something Dani didn't. John was no more interested in her than the man in the moon. She definitely wasn't in the mood for another romance. Not after the last experience. It would be a good long while before she laid open her heart for another man to break.

". . . lovely girl," Mamie continued.

". . . not my type."

It was a good thing Dani's ego wasn't riding on John being romantically interested in her, because she was sure to be disappointed. Not that it hadn't happened before. Disappointment was a mild word for what had happened between her and Bob.

Gathering her resolve, Dani squared her shoulders and walked into the kitchen. Both Mamie and John abruptly stopped talking and stared at her as if she were the last person either one of them expected to see.

"I'm sorry to interrupt, but it's apparent my being here is causing a problem. I'll come for dinner another time, Mamie. Thank you for thinking of me."

Dani didn't stand around and wait for them to change her mind. She turned and was out the front door before they had a chance to react to her words, which was exactly the way she wanted it.

"Dani, wait." John caught up with her before she got inside her car. "Listen," he said, sounding breathless, "I behaved like a heel. Mom's gone through a good deal of trouble for this. If anyone should leave it's me."

The wind off the ocean buffeted against her, tossing her short hair against her cheek. They stood facing each other, and for the life of her Dani couldn't move. She was tired and her feet hurt and it seemed that everything she'd tried to do was for naught.

"Don't go," John added softly. It was as if he'd read her thoughts and knew how close she was to tears. It was as though he understood that it was tenderness and warmth that she needed just then.

"What about you?" she asked. The words had a difficult time working their way around the lump in her throat.

His eyes held hers for the longest moment and it seemed to her that something dark and deep showed itself there. Something she couldn't read or understand.

John sighed. "I'll stay."

She smiled briefly. "I take it your mother's plotting against us."

"Just be aware she's the world's worst matchmaker. Somewhere along the line she got the notion the two of us are perfect for one another. She'll make our lives miserable if we let her." He touched her elbow to guide her back to the house.

"Luckily we both know the truth," she reassured him.

John hesitated. "We aren't the least bit suited."

"Besides, according to you, I'm leaving," she reminded him.

"Precisely." The ghost of a smile formed brackets at the edges of his mouth. "As I recall, we've got a wager riding on this."

Mamie appeared in the doorway. "I certainly hope you two are going to listen to reason."

"Go inside, Mother," John called over his shoulder.

"Are you staying for dinner?" she demanded first.

"Yes." Again it was John who answered for the both of them.

Mamie clapped her hands. "Great. I'll get the roast on the table."

"Shall we?" John asked, offering Dani his arm.

John wasn't blind. He was all too aware of the attention Dani had generated among the single men in Ocean Shores. Nor was he fooled by Brent Anderson's sudden interest in antiques. The schoolteacher stopped by the shop and claimed he was looking for a birthday gift for his mother.

His mother! John nearly laughed out loud.

Brent wasn't the first man to develop an unforeseen curiosity in antiques, either. Charley Sooner and Doug Foster were making routine stops at the store with one questionable excuse or another.

Their purpose should have been obvious to Dani, but if it was, she never said a word. Not that she was likely to confide in him.

John didn't like all the attention she generated, either. Naturally he couldn't say anything. It was none of his damn business who Dani chose to date, but the subject occupied far more of his thoughts lately than it should. When he couldn't stand it any longer, he brought it into the open.

"That's Charley Sooner's third visit this week, isn't it?" he asked, doing his best to sound nonchalant and disinterested. He wandered over to where she was standing and leaned against the desk. He crossed his arms and met her gaze.

The Closed sign was in the window and this was the first time all day that they'd had the opportunity to speak without interruptions.

"Fourth," Dani corrected.

"What's he looking for?"

"He claims it's a crystal doorknob but..."

"But," he prodded when she hesitated.

"What he really wants is a dinner date."

Her directness surprised him once again. It shouldn't, he supposed; the woman said exactly what she was thinking and had from the first.

"Are you going out with him?" John could be just as blunt when the need arose, and frankly he was curious.

"No."

"Why not?"

"Laura Noble's had her eye on Charley for months now."

"Laura?" This was news to John. "The pharmacist?"

"Yes."

"But..."

"But she's shy and uncertain. We've been talking, and I gave her a few pointers. Charley's never going to notice her if she doesn't say something."

"Charley and Laura?" Personally John couldn't picture the lumberjack and the pharmacist as a couple. Charley was about as subtle as a Mack truck, while Laura was a quiet, delicate creature. If he'd been in the market for female companionship, John might have considered asking her out himself.

"What's so odd about the two of them?" Dani wanted to know. "They complement each other very nicely."

John scratched the side of his head. Frankly he didn't care who Charley Sooner dated as long as it wasn't Dani.

As soon as the thought formed, John realized how close he was to making a fool of himself over his assistant.

"What about Doug Foster?" he asked next. "Doug's a decent guy and as far as I know there aren't—"

"You want me to date Doug?"

"Sure," he said without conviction. "He's a great guy."

"Yes, I know."

Doug wasn't *that* great, but John couldn't very well claim otherwise now. "Are you going to date him?"

Dani looked away from him. "I don't think so."

"Why not?" John pressed.

"Well, for one thing, Doug hasn't asked."

It was downright ridiculous the way his heart reacted to that piece of information. "Is that a fact? I would have thought Doug would have been Johnny-on-the-spot by now."

"All right, Doug hasn't asked me recently."

John's hands tightened into fists before he realized what he was doing. "You should accept when he does," he said with a complete lack of enthusiasm.

"Frankly, John, I'm not interested in dating anyone at the moment," she said, and lowered her gaze. She stiffened slightly as if bracing herself against some pain, and when she spoke, her voice was lower by several decibels. "I... recently ended a rather painful relationship."

John hesitated, uncertain how to proceed. He was curious, but respectful, too. He knew what it was to have someone pry into a fresh wound on the pretext of helping, and almost always doing further damage.

"I'm sorry, Dani," he said with genuine caring. "I didn't know."

She shrugged, a gesture he'd done a hundred times himself after Patricia had walked out on him. It was supposed to say that it really didn't matter that his heart was broken. A shrug that said that everything would turn out for the best, when he didn't believe it himself. It was supposed to reassure everyone else, when he felt as if his future resembled a bottomless black pit where his dreams lay shriveled and dying.

"It's for the best," she said in a small voice. "I was in love with a man who didn't exist, building the future on a shaky foundation."

"That's why you moved here?"

She nodded, and looked up suddenly, her face tight. "Do you mind if we change the subject?"

"Of course, forgive me."

She glanced at her watch as if she had places to go and people to see all at once. "I'd better get home."

"Sure." As it was, he'd kept her an extra twenty minutes, but he found himself wishing he had an excuse for her to stay. She gathered together her purse and a sweater, and headed for the door.

John followed, intending to lock up for the night. "Dani," he said, stopping her.

She looked back, her eyes incredibly sad and round.

"I didn't mean to pry."

A soft smile touched her lips. "I know." She left him then and John stood for a long time at the window, watching her walk away.

As crazy as it sounded, he found it one hell of a temptation not to hurry after her, wrap his arms around her and pull her into his embrace.

Something was different about John. Dani couldn't put her finger on exactly what it was, other than the fact he was more friendly and open. She discovered, to her delight, that they worked well as a team.

It surprised her how often they laughed together. They talked often, too. Although there were plenty of subjects on which they agreed, there were more that set them at odds.

John always heard her out, even when he disagreed with her. He respected her opinions and wasn't averse to expressing his own. More often than not, at the end of the day they spent an hour or more after work just sitting and chatting. All on the pretext of closing the shop for the night.

When she'd first come to work for John, Dani had viewed him as unfriendly, dull and unimaginative. He'd defined the term "stuffed shirt." It wasn't that he'd changed into jeans and sneakers overnight, but he'd relaxed enough for them to become friends.

Dani liked it that way. A friend was safe and secure.

"Dani," John called from the other side of the store, disrupting her thoughts. "Could you give me a hand with this?"

"Of course." John had spent the better part of the day unloading the shipment of antiques he'd purchased on his buying trip to San Francisco. Dani had done what she could to help him between customers, but they'd both been so busy that neither had taken time to eat lunch.

"Hold this ladder steady for me, would you?" he asked.

Dani looked up. "What are you going to do?"

"The problem with this building is that I don't have enough space. These boxes are an eyesore and I want to store them in the attic."

"There aren't any stairs?"

"No. Just hold it steady and I'll be fine."

It took him three trips to get everything he wanted up into the high cupboard.

"I want to see what you have stored up there," she said after he'd climbed down. "Sometimes I'm convinced you haven't got a clue what's hidden away."

"Really?"

"Really," she teased, enjoying the way his eyes brightened when they became involved in these verbal sparring matches.

Not waiting for him to give her permission, Dani climbed up the first five rungs of the ladder.

"Dani, damn it all, be careful."

"Don't sound so worried," she berated him. "I've been climbing trees since I was a kid. This is a piece of cake." With her hands against the sides, she looked up, eager to discover what buried treasures lay tucked away in his attic.

It would have been, easy, too, if her foot hadn't slipped and she hadn't lost her balance.

With a small cry of fright, she lost her footing and her balance. Before she could catch herself, she went catapulting backward into the empty space. Dani was too shocked to scream.

How John managed to catch her she'd never know. One moment she was in the air and in the next she was tucked securely in his arms. Both were breathing hard, and John's eyes closed momentarily with what she suspected was relief that she hadn't hurt herself.

It was on the tip of her tongue to crack a joke about her usual lack of grace, to laugh off the entire incident and claim that for her next trick she'd leap over a tall building. But the words never made it past her lips.

John's gaze pinned hers and his eyes held a haunted look. Emotions flashed across his features, from fierce, burning anger to a relief so great it left him weak. Then his eyes softened to another emotion, one equally strong, equally potent, that she was sure she'd misread.

John wanted to kiss her.

Her feet remained several inches from the floor and still he didn't release her. She could feel the heavy thud of his heart and knew her own beat just as hard.

For several long seconds his eyes delved into hers, and all at once Dani was afraid. Frightened of what would happen if John did kiss her. Frightened it would change the hard-won camaraderie between them. Frightened it would disrupt a friendship that was coming to mean a good deal to her.

"Are you all right?" he asked in a voice that didn't sound anything like his own. He set her feet on the floor, but they didn't move away from each other.

She nodded, uncertain she could speak coherently.

"You're sure?" His thumb found her lip and brushed back and forth as if the action would appease the hunger between them. It didn't help. If anything, it created an even stronger desire to sample forbidden fruit.

John closed his eyes, fighting her so hard she could almost feel it. "Dani..." He must have read the doubt in her eyes because he hesitated.

It had been a long time since a man had held her. A long time since she'd felt this protected, this cherished, this desirable.

John cleared his throat. "Yes, well, I guess you're not hurt."

"I'm... fine. Thanks for catching me...."

"I don't think it's a good idea for you to be climbing any more ladders."

"John, it was a fluke. It won't happen again."

"I know, because you won't be going up any more ladders."

Dani knew from the tone of his voice that he wouldn't listen to reason, nor was she willing to argue with him. Not just then, not after he'd held her so close.

"About... what almost happened," he said uneasily.

"Don't," she whispered, pressing her hand against his hard chest.

His eyes widened as if he wasn't sure what to expect.

"Let's not confuse our relationship.... You said once, and I'm sure you're right, that it wasn't a good idea for two people working together to become...involved." She moistened her lips while she struggled with the words. "We're friends and I don't want anything to ruin that."

He frowned and looked away. "You're right, of course."

For two days following the incident on the ladder, John treated her like a polite stranger. If she hadn't known better, Dani would have thought he was afraid of her.

"You know what I miss more than anything about the city?" she announced one afternoon when Mamie was visiting. "Pizza. One with a thick crust and oodles of cheese."

"You can buy pizza in Ocean Shores," Mamie assured her.

"Not the thick, gooey kind that was available in the University District, with three different kinds of cheese melted across the top."

"I make a fabulous deep-dish pizza, don't I, son?" Mamie prodded John. "We had a neighbor once who was born and raised in Germany. I know it sounds nuts, but she made the best homemade pizza I ever ate."

Dani flattened her hands against her stomach. "You're making me hungry just talking about it."

"I have the recipe."

"You do?" Dani's eyes lit up at the mere thought.

"Come to dinner tonight and I'll bake us all a pepperoni pizza."

Dani was more than willing to agree. She wondered if John would show up, but guessed that he probably would.

"So you're already missing the city," he said, after his mother had left. "I thought you would." His eyes gleamed as if it gave him a great deal of pleasure to think he was right about her, after all.

"Don't be so quick. I didn't say anything about returning to Seattle."

"True," he was ready to admit. "But you're beginning to think along those lines."

"I most certainly am not."

"First it's insatiable hunger for pizza, then it'll be a sudden need to shop in a real department store, followed by the ever popular escape to a multiplex theater."

"Would you kindly stop?"

"Torturing you, am I?" He laughed as if victory were already his. "I can taste success."

Although he was teasing, and gaining a good deal of enjoyment doing so, a sudden thought hit Dani like a brick aimed square against her chest. "John," she said softly, "do you want me to leave?"

The laughter drained out of his eyes and for several moments he said nothing. "No," he whispered and having said that, he turned and walked away.

John stared at the chessboard and frowned. He should have known better than to agree to a match against Dani. She'd made it sound much too easy to outsmart her. That should have been the first clue that something was amiss. Four plays into the game and John knew he was facing an accomplished player.

"It's your move," she reminded him, sitting back, looking as smug as if she'd already won.

"I know whose move it is."

"There's no need to get testy."

John had been had, and he knew it.

"How's the game going?" Mamie asked as she strolled into the living room and plopped down on the arm of Dani's chair. It didn't escape John's notice the way women stuck together. The two had teamed up against him and he was lost.

"We're doing great," Dani answered, and nibbled on a handful of pretzels.

John reached for his wineglass and took a sip. He needed help. Big-time.

"Who's winning?" Mamie asked next.

"Me," Dani whispered, as if saying the words out loud would evoke his ire.

John kept his gaze lowered as he continued to study the chessboard, but he could still feel his mother's amused gaze watching him. He wasn't any slouch when it came to chess and she knew it.

"John won a trophy for chess."

This was the last thing he wanted his mother to tell Dani.

"Really?"

"He was quite interested in the game for a time."

"Mother," he said with limited patience. "You're breaking my concentration."

"He was quite good," Mamie continued in a whisper.

John ground his teeth. If the truth be known, he'd gotten the chess trophy because Mary Margaret Wilson was in the chess club.

"But I think he was more interested in Mary Margaret Wilson than he was chess."

"Mother," John said again, louder this time.

"Sorry," she said, not sounding the least bit contrite.

"Perhaps," Dani said with a smug smile, "he should have paid more attention to the game and less to Mary Margaret, then he might not be in this predicament."

"Predicament?" Mamie asked.

"We have a wager on this game," Dani whispered gleefully.

John would prefer it if she didn't remind him. In a moment of weakness, he'd agreed to go bicycling with her on Tuesday afternoon...on the off chance he lost the match. Worse, she'd insisted that they rent one of the tandem bikes that were so popular with the tourists.

"I was tricked," John muttered under his breath.

"How was that?" Dani asked with the innocence of a child.

He couldn't very well claim that she'd looked at him with those big, brown eyes of hers, and he was lost. He discovered, much to his chagrin, that he would agree to just about anything when she batted those long lashes of hers in his direction. Come to think of it, Mary Margaret Wilson had done the same damn thing.

"I was sucker punched," John said, repositioning his queen on the board.

Dani straightened and cast him a smile that would have melted an Alaskan glacier. She slapped her hands free of salt, and moved her bishop.

John groaned and closed his eyes. He was doomed. "Who tutored you, Bobby Fischer?" he asked sarcastically.

"No, my grandfather. We played every Sunday for years."

John frowned. "You might have warned me."

"Generally I do say something," she said, sounding marginally contrite. "But your ego's strong enough to accept a loss. Besides, I really wanted to try one of those tandems."

"And you figured the only way you could ever get me to agree was to casually involve me in a game of chess and then beat the pants off me."

"John!"

"It's an expression, Mother, it doesn't mean anything."

"I should hope not."

"It is an interesting thought, though," Dani said, wiggling her eyebrows suggestively. "Have you ever played strip chess?"

"Dani Beckman." Mamie laughed. "You amaze me."

His mother wasn't the only one who was surprised. If he wasn't careful, the salesclerk his mother had hired was about to wrap him around her little finger.

"Are you ready?" Dani asked, hurrying into the shop. She studied her watch. "I've got the bike reserved between three and four and it's almost three now."

"Is there any way I can buy my way out of this?" John asked, knowing even before she answered that she wasn't going to let him off the hook.

"No," she said and laughed.

"I'll give you a raise."

"John! A deal's a deal."

"I haven't been on a bike in years."

"This is great exercise. It's good for your heart."

He rolled his eyes. "I'd rather eat oat bran."

She laughed again. "Are you coming or not?"

"Do I have a choice?"

"No."

"That's what I thought." He followed her outside with a decided lack of enthusiasm.

"It'll be fun, I promise." Luckily the bicycle shop was little more than a block from the antiques store. The weather was postcard perfect. A light breeze blew off the ocean and the sun was warm and inviting.

"It looks like rain," John muttered, shading his eyes to look at the sky.

"There isn't a cloud in sight and you know it."

"Yes, well, I was hoping."

Jeff Dolittle operated the bicycle shop. He rolled out the tandem when he saw them approach. "Howdy, John."

"You say one word about this to the Rotary Club and I swear I'll find a way to get back at you," John warned without preamble.

"No problem," Jeff said, but it was apparent he was holding back a laugh.

"Now, boys," Dani said, chastising the pair.

"How'd you ever get him to agree to this?" Jeff asked, as she signed the final paperwork.

"Don't trust her, Jeff," John said before she could answer. "She looks sweet and guileless, but beneath those innocent brown eyes of hers lies a heart as black as coal."

"I beat him in a game of chess," Dani explained.

"Beat me. First off she misled me into thinking she barely knew the difference between a queen and a pawn and the next thing I know I'm the laughingstock of the entire town."

"No one will laugh at you, John," his friend promised. His eyes briefly met Dani's before he added, "At least not to your face."

"You're a great comfort."

"If he hadn't been so willing to polish his pride by beating me he wouldn't be trapped into doing this," Dani informed them both. "And I didn't sucker you into the game. If you recall, you're the one who asked me if I played."

"More fool me," John muttered, climbing onto the seat in the front. "Are you ready or not?"

"I'm ready." She positioned herself behind him, and slipped her feet onto the pedals. It felt a bit awkward to not have control of the handlebars and not see where they were riding, but she soon became accustomed.

"Come on and admit this is fun," she said to John after the first few moments.

"All right, it's fun."

"Oh, look, there's Laura." Dani waved and called to the woman who had become her friend. Laura brightened and returned her energetic wave.

"Doug Foster asked her out to dinner," she told John.

"Doug? But I thought it was Charley Sooner Laura liked best."

"It is. But dating Doug was the best way to get Charley to notice her."

John shook his head as if to say all this male-and-female intrigue was beyond him. "Has Charley noticed?"

"Not yet, but he will," she said confidently.

They rode down the main road that paralleled the ocean and back again, taking the route that placed them along the long list of shops that catered to the tourist traffic.

Several people came out of their shops and stopped and stared.

"What's so interesting?" Dani asked after a while.

"You and me," John told her.

"Why?" To Dani's way of thinking, they weren't any different than any other couple out having a good time.

He didn't answer her for several moments. "Riding a bike isn't something I would normally do. In case you haven't guessed, I'm known around here as something of a stuffed shirt."

"Not *you,*" she said, throwing back her head and laughing.

"You, my fair-haired assistant, have gone and ruined my reputation."

Chapter Four

"Was that you I saw riding a bike last week?" Mrs. Wenchel said to John on Wednesday morning as he opened the shop.

"Yes," he grumbled. He stood in front of the store and made polite conversation while he fiddled with the keys, wishing he could avoid the mayor's wife.

"That was Dani Beckman with you, wasn't it?"

John muttered another reply. He swore if one more person mentioned seeing him with Dani he wouldn't be held responsible for his response. First off, the woman had tricked him into a wager, and then she'd insisted he keep his word.

"Well, I'll let you get inside. It was good seeing you, John."

"You, too, Mrs. Wenchel."

A smile tugged at his mouth. Despite all the flack he'd gotten for the episode with the tandem, John had to admit it had been fun. Possibly the most fun he'd had in years. It came to him afterward that since his breakup with Patricia, he hadn't allowed himself much time to enjoy life. It was as though his quota of fun had been forever lost with the relationship. Funny, he hadn't realized that before now.

What John had learned in the last few weeks was that one couldn't help but laugh when Dani was around. Her joyous, fun-loving mood was infectious. No longer did the zany way she dressed disturb him, nor her complete lack of talent with anything having to do with numbers. The contributions to his life far outweighed the liabilities. He didn't like admitting that even to himself.

"'Morning," his mother said as she bustled in the front door a half hour later. "I'm sorry I'm late."

"No problem," John assured her. He was grateful that with the increase in business, his mother had agreed to work for him on Dani's days off.

"Have you been terribly busy?" Mamie asked, after she tucked her purse and sweater in the back room. She pressed her hand over her heart as if wishing it to slow down a bit.

"It's barely ten."

"It's just that you've been so preoccupied lately, and I had visions of you swamped with customers. Lena Phelps phoned just as I was about to leave. I should never have answered the phone and you know how Lena is when she wants something. I thought that woman would never let me off the phone."

"Mother, until recently there was only me."

"I know, but you've gotten so much new business since Dani started working for you."

John had no room to argue, not that he thought he should. "I'll admit Dani was a real find. I don't know how I got along without her."

Mamie looked well pleased with herself. "She's such a dear heart."

Even knowing his mother was looking for reasons to pair the two of them together, and would analyze his every response, John found he couldn't argue. "She is indeed that."

Mamie pressed her hands together and sighed with all the drama of a stage star. "You do like her, don't you?"

He stiffened. Much more of this and Mamie would soon be humming the "Wedding March." "It's impossible not to like Dani, but that doesn't mean we're... involved."

"But, John..."

"Mother," he warned and was saved from responding further when the door opened and his first customer of the day strolled inside.

It seemed to John that Wednesdays were the longest days of the week. By midmorning, he found himself glancing at the clock, wishing the time would pass quicker. He hated to admit how much he missed Dani on Wednesdays. He couldn't help speculating what she did on her time off. He wondered if she slept in late, then lazed in bed and read for an hour or two. That was doubtful. Knowing her, she was probably up at the crack of dawn and had jogged three or four miles before he ever thought about starting his day.

Business was slower than usual. John strolled through the store, admiring Dani's personal touch on a variety of floor displays.

"Mother," he asked abruptly, finding the original piece that had started Dani working on the window arrangements, "what's wrong with this cradle?"

"What's wrong with it?" she asked, gazing at him from above her reading glasses. "Why, nothing that I can see."

"Several people have shown interest in it, but I can't seem to sell it."

"That's odd."

John walked over to the corner where Dani had tucked the cradle and ran his hand over the top of it. He'd polished it until the wood gleamed and the grain showed clearly. "The price is fair," he said, thinking out loud.

"I agree."

"If I didn't know better," John said, "I'd think Dani didn't want it sold." There'd been any number of times that a customer had asked about it. As he recalled, she'd generally steer them in another direction.

"Why would Dani care one way or the other if the cradle sold or not?" Mamie asked.

"I don't know."

"If she wanted it, she would buy it herself, wouldn't she?"

"Of course," John murmured. He could think of no reason for Dani to want the cradle from yesteryear. If she were a collector, which she wasn't, or a young mother, that either, he could better understand what was happening.

"Isn't that Dani now?" Mamie said, looking out the large picture window in the front of the store. Situated on a corner, the antiques shop was granted a wide, unobstructed view of the ocean beach. "It looks as if she bought one of those kite kits and is assembling it."

Curiosity got the better of him and John joined his mother and gazed out the window. He found Dani almost immediately, sitting on top of a sand dune. Even from this distance he could read the perplexed look about her. Her shoulders were hunched against the wind and she had the instructions clenched between her teeth. It was apparent even at that distance that Part A was not fitting into Part B.

"Assembling those kites can be complicated," Mamie said, and eyed him. "What Dani really needs is someone with a functioning left brain."

"Give her time, she'll figure it out." John had every confidence in his assistant. If she could stomp him on a chessboard, then she could assemble a kite.

"Dani's so creative she thinks with her right brain, and when it comes to..."

"Mother, you are not suggesting I leave the store and go over and help her, are you?" The idea was ludicrous. For one thing, he didn't want Dani thinking he was spying on her. For another, he preferred not to have the good people of Ocean Shores linking them together.

Mamie looked up at him with wide eyes. "Yes, I think you should help her."

"I have a shop to run."

"It's been slow all morning. Besides, just how long will it take to assemble a silly kite? If Dani saw that you were having trouble, do you think she'd hesitate to lend you a helping hand?"

She had him there, and if the truth be known, he wanted to be with Dani, talk or no talk. "All right," he said as if she should appreciate the sacrifice he was making. "I'll be back in five minutes."

"Take your time," Mamie insisted.

John looked both ways before jogging across the street and onto the beach. He slowed his steps as he grew closer, uncertain exactly how to approach her.

John was only a few feet away when Dani groaned in abject frustration and fell backward onto the sand.

"Dani?" John decided playing innocent was the best approach. "Is something wrong?"

She opened her eyes, then sat up abruptly. "It's supposed to be so easy. The instructions on the kite said it was simple enough for a ten-year-old to assemble. Sure, one with an engineering degree!"

John chuckled and sank onto the sand next to her. "Do you want me to take a look at it for you?"

"Please." She bundled up the pieces and handed it to him. "I'll have you know this isn't one of the cheap ones, either. I paid nearly forty bucks for it."

He was grateful she didn't ask how he knew she was having troubles. "Where are the instructions?"

"Trust me, they're worthless. They might as well have been written in a foreign language."

"You don't have them?"

"I do, sort of." She leapt to her feet and raced over to the trash barrel, and returned a few moments later with a wadded-up piece of paper. "They won't help."

"Let me see." John smoothed out the crumpled instructions as best he could, and found no fault with them.

"This is Stick A," Dani said, identifying the narrow wooden strip. "According to what it says there, Stick A is supposed to fit into Section One. The key phrase here is *supposed to.* But it doesn't work. I've tried it ten times and no matter what I do, it won't slip in the way it should." She sounded exasperated and tired as she sank to her knees next to him.

John turned Stick A around and neatly slipped it into Section One.

"How'd you do that?" Dani cried, exasperated."

John didn't have the heart to tell her how easy it had been. Within minutes he had the box kite, with squares in red, blue, yellow and green, completely assembled.

Dani shook her head in marvel. "I can't believe this. You don't know how I struggled. Thank you, John. I didn't mean to disrupt your day."

"Let's see if we can get this airborne before you thank me, all right?"

She nodded eagerly.

John attached the giant roll of string and walked closer to the water's edge. Within minutes the kite was lofting toward the sky and Dani was clapping her hands with delight. It had been months since John had spent a day on the beach. Longer than he could remember. He lived in a resort town, but rarely enjoyed the delights the ocean had to offer.

John handed Dani the controls, and stood behind her, keeping a safe distance between their bodies while she learned to manipulate the kite. John enjoyed being close to her, probably more than he should. He regretted now not kissing her when he'd had the opportunity.

Dani brought sunshine and laughter into a world that had been dull and lifeless for longer than he cared to admit. She'd made him feel again, laugh again and think. Before she had come to work for him, he used to consider the store his life. The business was all he'd ever need. But recently, when he crawled into bed at night, it wasn't antiques that filled his thoughts, it was Dani.

"I'd better get back to the store," he said reluctantly.

Disappointment clouded her beautiful dark eyes. "Thanks for your help," she said and smiled at him. "I appreciate it more than you can know."

"No problem." He buried his hands in his pockets and walked backward a couple of steps before turning and racing across the street. He looked back only once and found Dani sitting in the sand, the brightly colored kite twirling cheerfully in the chaotic wind. His gaze lingered for several seconds before he turned and walked away.

His mother was standing just inside the doorway. John guessed she'd been watching him from the moment he'd left.

"I see you got her kite up for her."

John nodded and walked over to his desk and sat down. He didn't have anything particularly pressing that demanded his attention, but he felt the need to analyze what was happening between him and Dani. If anything.

"It's been slow here," Mamie said, following him. "One phone call," she announced. "A wrong number. It hardly seems worth staying open when the only business is a phone call the entire morning."

She hesitated and seemed to be waiting for something. The problem was, John didn't know what. His mother could hint from now until the twelfth of never and it would do no good.

"Are you suggesting we close the shop down for good?" he asked.

"Not for good," she said calmly, with a small, distinct smile. "But surely one day wouldn't hurt."

"One day," John repeated, not following her drift. "Listen, Mother, if you've got something more pressing to do, there isn't any reason for you to hang around here."

"I haven't got a thing."

"Then what was all that business about me closing down the store?"

"Just that. You could do with a day off yourself. Do you have any appointments this afternoon?"

John checked his engagement calendar, but he knew there wasn't anything there. "Not really."

"That's what I thought. It's a beautiful day."

"Mother, I can't afford to close up shop every time the sun makes an appearance."

Mamie sighed, losing patience with him. "John, for the love of heaven, would you stop and listen to me? Take the rest of the day off. I'll stay at the shop if you want. Actually, I'll be happy to do that."

"Mother..."

"Enjoy life. Let your hair down. How can you walk away from Dani like that? She looks so alone."

Involuntarily, John's gaze returned to the beach. The idea held a certain appeal. All right, it held a lot of appeal. There was nothing he'd enjoy more than spending the day lazing away on the beach with Dani. The last time... He didn't want to think about the last time because it had been with Patricia. Dani, however, was different.

And John knew it.

* * *

She was lonely, Dani decided, and feeling melancholy. That was why she'd purchased the kite, looking for something to relieve the blahs.

It hadn't. Not only had assembling the silly thing frustrated her no end, it had cost her forty of her hard-earned dollars. She could have used that money as layaway for the cradle. She wanted it, and had from the first moment she'd seen it tucked away in John's storeroom. Why it appealed to her so strongly, she didn't know. Heaven knew she had no earthly use for it.

The cradle.

The last thing she needed was a reminder of dreams lost. That was what the cradle would become, another trophy for her to dust that would remind her of all that she'd missed when she'd broken off her engagement. Severing the relationship with Bob was the right thing to do, but it hadn't been easy and certainly hadn't been painless.

She struggled not to feel sorry for herself. Life had fit into a comfortable package of late. Despite John's claims otherwise, Dani had adjusted to life in a small town. She'd made new friends and thoroughly enjoyed her job. Her window-dressing talent was recognized by the community. The local newspaper had done a piece on her, and several people had commented about her work. She'd never attained such notoriety in Seattle. It felt good to have her talent appreciated.

But filling up the lonely shadows of her life with work wasn't enough. Dani longed for all the things that had made marriage to Bob so attractive. A husband, a large home filled with children.

She'd loved him, trusted him and now she didn't know if she dared rely upon her own judgment ever again. She'd believed in Bob, believed in his love.

If she'd made so great an error assessing character once, then it stood to reason that it could happen a second time. Or heaven help her, a third. Panic filled her chest.

A sea gull had floated past just then, cawing for all it was worth. Dani watched the bird, effortlessly carried with the wind almost as if it, too, were attached by some unseen string. She felt like that bird, struggling against the wind, at a standstill despite her best efforts.

"Hello, again."

She turned her head and discovered John. She blinked, thinking he might be a figment of her imagination.

"You're back," she said, pleased to see him.

"I thought you might like some company."

It amazed her how easily he read her moods. She'd been close to tears when he'd found her on the beach earlier, angry with herself for spending a ridiculous amount of money on a kite Einstein couldn't assemble.

"I'd love company."

"I see the kite's still in the air."

"Thanks to you." She'd secured it to a log that had drifted onto the beach, and left it to soar on its own while her heart sang the blues.

John lowered himself onto the soft sand next to her, and bunched up his long legs. He studied the sky for several moments.

"What about the store?" Dani felt obliged to ask.

He glanced at her and grinned. "I closed it for the day."

It couldn't have surprised her more had he said he'd sold everything and was moving to the big city. John worked long and hard. His mother often lamented that he didn't take nearly enough time for himself. It must have been an old argument because whenever she raised it, his arguments were swift and fervent.

"It's a beautiful day," he said, as if that was excuse enough to close down the store. There was more than a trace of a smile in his voice. After all the times they'd been at odds, it felt good to know that John was her friend.

"Yes, it is a beautiful day," she agreed, but they both knew that wasn't the real reason he was there.

Neither said anything for a couple of moments.

"Listen..."

"Dani..." John said at the same time.

She paused, and gestured toward him. "You first."

His eyes met hers and in them she read a mixture of puzzlement and reluctance. In the weeks since she'd come to work for John she'd seen him at his cynical best; she'd tiptoed, first around his resentment of her, and then later, his pretended indifference. Somehow, with effort on both their parts, they'd become friends. Good friends.

John reached for her hand, lacing her fingers with his own. "I've never known anyone like you, Dani Beckman. You're like that kite up there, bright and cheerful. You're warm and generous, and you're hurting."

"Is it so obvious?" she asked.

He shook his head. "Not to others. I just happen to know you a little better. Can you tell me what's wrong?"

Dani looked away, fighting back tears. It did little good; they filled her eyes and she bit hard on to her lower lip in an effort to keep them from spilling onto her face. Knowing she wouldn't fool him, she brushed her hand over her cheeks. "I'm feeling sorry for myself is all. It's nothing, really."

"Let's talk about it."

She knew he wouldn't accept an excuse, and truthfully she was glad, because if anyone understood her feelings, it was John.

"I told you once briefly...the reason I moved here."

"Yes," John answered softly.

"But I didn't tell why I chose Ocean Shores."

"No."

"I came because I was looking for an escape." She swallowed once to keep from sobbing. "It sounds so simple to say I called off the wedding, but it was probably the most painful, agonizing decision I ever made."

His fingers tightened over hers, encouraging her to continue.

"In the beginning I used to walk along the beach or sit here on one of the sand dunes and listen to the surf pound against the shore. There was something soothing about being so close to the water, something freeing. All I know is that I could sit here and for those few hours it didn't hurt as much. I could almost pretend that my heart was whole again." She stopped and looked at him, her face tight with pain. "You think I'm running away from my problems, don't you?"

"I didn't say that," he refuted gently.

She bunched up her knees and pressed her forehead there. "Perhaps, in a way of thinking, I was running away, but it was necessary. It hurt too much to stay in Seattle and see Bob day in and day out. I couldn't have stood that. Bob seemed to think that all I needed was a little time and I'd come to my senses and everything would go back to the way it was before."

"And you were afraid that in time he'd wear you down." He spoke as if he was privileged to her fears.

She lifted her head to look at him. "Yes," she whispered. "How'd you know?"

John looked out over the water, and it was as if his features had been chiseled out of granite. "I was engaged myself once, and something similar happened with me. The woman I loved fell in love with someone else. It was painful enough that she'd deceived me, but she apparently felt the need to rationalize her actions." He hesitated and his jaw tightened. "She seemed to find it necessary to blame me."

"Blame you?"

His mouth twisted into a sarcastic smile. "It doesn't matter now."

But Dani had the impression it had mattered dearly at the time. His fiancée had walked away, but before she'd gone she'd stripped him of his pride, and crushed his ego. A swell of tenderness came over her and she placed her hand on his arm.

He looked out over the ocean and exhaled. "But it's over now, and has been for a long, long time."

"Is it ever really over?" Dani asked. "No one understands. Not really. Everyone keeps telling me how fortunate I am, but I don't feel fortunate."

"Cheated and angry summed up my emotions," John told her.

"I feel shortchanged and so terribly foolish. Why was it everyone could see what kind of person Bob was, but me? How could I have been so blind?" She didn't know when John had slipped his arm around her, but it felt good to have it there. She let her head rest against his shoulder.

"Do you sometimes wonder?" she asked after a moment.

"About what?"

"If you can trust your own judgment." John's heart felt strong and steady against her ear. "I mean, if I could give my heart to a man completely lacking in moral integrity once, what's to say it won't happen again?"

John was silent for a long time. Dani wished he would offer her reassurances. That was what she needed, what she wanted, but apparently he had none to give her.

"I've asked myself that same question a dozen times in the last five years," he admitted gruffly. "Unfortunately, I don't have the answer."

"Oh, great," she said, half crying and half laughing. "We're both doomed, then."

"Doomed?"

"If we can't trust anyone of the opposite sex ever again, what are we going to do? Spend the rest of our lives alone? Frankly, I'd like to marry someday and have children. Of course, I could always take potluck."

"What do you mean by that?"

She lifted one shoulder. Inexplicably, she felt better for having bared her soul to John. What had seemed overwhelming only moments earlier didn't feel nearly as horrible just then.

"I suppose I could answer one of those date-line ads in the newspaper," she explained. "I've read a hundred stories about how people meet through those. It might be worth my trouble, don't you think?"

John tensed. "Tell me you're joking."

"Well, haven't you ever been tempted to do that?"

"No. Never."

"Oh."

"Might I suggest something else?" John said.

"Of course." She was open to all suggestions.

"Date a friend. Someone you already know and trust."

"Friends," she said with a hefty sigh, "are in limited supply at the moment."

"What about me?" he asked. "I realize we've only known each other a short time, but it seems that we've come a long way since that first day. I deeply admire you, Dani."

"You? The two of us? But I thought... You once said..." Flustered, she couldn't seem to get the right words out, and when she noticed his frown, she wasn't sure if she should continue.

"All you need say is no," he told her, his voice stiff with pride.

"Yes," she said quickly before she made a bigger mess of this. "I'd enjoy dating you, John."

Although he'd been the one to issue the invitation, he didn't seem overly pleased with himself. A frown darkened his face.

"Have you changed your mind already?" she asked.

He chuckled. Dani loved the sound of his laughter and couldn't keep from smiling herself.

"How about dinner?"

"Really?" She twisted around in order to get a better look at him. "Would you mind terribly if I made it? I'm very good in the kitchen, but it isn't much fun when there's only yourself to cook for. And there's a new recipe I'm dying to try."

"Are you sure you wouldn't prefer a restaurant?"

"Next time, okay?"

He grinned and brought her back into his embrace. He rested his chin on the top of her head. "When would you like me to come?"

"Is Saturday all right?"

"It's perfect."

Dani was late getting to work Saturday morning, but she suspected John wouldn't mind, especially when she told him the reason. She'd stopped off at the grocery store and picked up the necessary ingredients for their dinner.

John had insisted they eat at his house and, because she was curious to see his home, she'd readily agreed. Taking the brown paper bag of perishables inside the store with her, she set it inside the compact refrigerator in the back room.

"I'm sorry I'm late," she said, joining him out front.

"Don't worry about it." His gaze held hers for several moments. Although they had yet to go out on an official date, they were the talk of the town. Rumors of a thriving romance between them made the rounds faster than a brushfire in August.

Townsfolk looked at Dani and smiled indulgently. John hadn't so much as kissed her and yet, if she listened to the gossip, they were days away from announcing their engagement. What people didn't understand and what neither John nor Dani would explain was that they were two wounded, lonely souls struggling to overcome their fears.

Mamie was in the height of her glory. She claimed she'd orchestrated everything. The last Dani heard, Mamie was handing out advice to a handful of other mothers on how to handpick their children's spouses.

"I picked up a few groceries for our dinner," she explained.

"Dani—" he hesitated "—there's something we need to discuss." He sounded dark and serious, almost the same way as in the beginning when she'd so often displeased him.

"Yes?" Her heart raced. She'd done something wrong. Her mind quickly reviewed the last few days and she couldn't think of what it might be.

John's gaze shifted about the room, his uneasiness palatable. "I fear there's been some talk about the two of us that you might find embarrassing. First we were seen riding the tandem and then Wednesday we were kite flying, and I'm afraid folks have put two and two together and come up with five."

"Are you referring to the news that we're about to become engaged?"

His eyebrows rose. "You heard?"

"It's all over town."

"It doesn't trouble you?"

"No." She was thinking that perhaps it should. People didn't know John one bit if they believed he'd marry anyone after so short an acquaintance. John Osborn was methodical and thorough, without an impulsive bone in his very fine body.

"All the talk will settle down soon enough," he assured her.

"I suspect it will."

Customers came in just then and their conversation was interrupted. John was helping the young couple looking for six shield-back chairs to match their dining room set, when the phone rang.

Dani answered it and was writing down the information when she happened to notice that the cradle was missing. Her hand froze.

"I'm sorry," she said, when she realized she hadn't heard the last bit of conversation. "I was momentarily distracted. Could you repeat the spelling of your name once more?"

It was an agonizing five minutes before John was free.

"Was that phone call for me?" he asked.

"Yes." She tore off the pink slip and handed it to him, but her gaze remained riveted on the spot where the handcrafted cradle had once rested.

"What happened to the cradle?" she asked. John's gaze followed hers. "Someone bought it this morning while you were shopping. I was beginning to wonder if I was ever going to get rid of that piece. You were rather fond of it, weren't you?"

"Yes," she said softly. "I hope it found a good home."

"I'm sure it did," John assured her.

Chapter Five

It was inevitable that John would sell the cradle, Dani knew, but it felt as if he'd let go of something that had personally belonged to her. Something she'd loved and treasured.

"Dani, what's wrong?"

"Nothing." She never had been able to lie easily. "I'm disappointed . . . I loved that cradle."

"If you wanted it for yourself, why didn't you say something?"

She shrugged. The argument was one she'd had with herself on a daily basis from the moment she'd discovered it hidden in the back room. "It was expensive."

"Had I known, we might have been able to work something out."

"I realize that."

"I hate to see you disappointed."

Dani had no one to blame but herself. "Really, John, I have no cause for complaint. I should have said something a long time ago."

He dropped it at that, and Dani preferred not to dwell on the subject. The cradle had sold, but John had assured her the people who bought it would cherish it. She couldn't ask for anything more than that.

The shop was busy. The population of Ocean Shores swelled to nearly ten times its size on weekends with the heavy tourist traffic of summer. Lunch was a few bites of salad between customers. Dani didn't know how John would ever have managed alone.

By six, Dani's feet hurt, and the small of her back ached, but nothing could put a damper on her enthusiasm for this first official dinner date with John. Rarely had she looked more forward to anything. It didn't feel like a date, her first since breaking up with Bob. John was her friend, and their spending time together was a natural extension of that friendship.

After locking up the store, John carried out the groceries for her and paused before placing them inside her vehicle. His brow folded into thick lines as he frowned.

"Is something wrong?" Dani asked.

"I can just imagine what people will say when they see you following me home," he muttered.

"Does it bother you? Because..."

"No," he reassured her and relaxed enough to smile. "I was afraid it would upset you. Let 'em talk to their hearts' content. We know the truth and that's all that matters."

Only, Dani was beginning to wonder exactly what the truth was when it came to her and John. What had once seemed crystal clear had clouded as the boundaries of their relationship expanded.

Dani liked John's house immediately. It was built on the water, but unlike his mother's home, he'd chosen to live on the other side of the peninsula. The tranquil waters of Gray's Harbor were a stark contrast to the tumultuous ocean that roared outside Mamie Osborn's back door.

To Dani's surprise, his house was furnished not in antiques, but with solid contemporary style. His leather sofa was a deep shade of brown, with two matching chairs. She found the kitchen to be spacious and modern. The man never ceased to amaze her.

He must have read the incredulity in her eyes. "I built the house for Patricia," he said starkly, holding her gaze. "After she left I had too damn much pride to sell it. I'm glad now I held on to it."

"It's lovely."

"Actually I think the house alone might have been enough to frighten her off," he admitted with a chuckle. "The original plans called for five bedrooms. I've turned one into a library and another into a media room, but the house was specifically designed with a large family in mind."

For reasons she couldn't hope to understand, Dani's heart tightened in her chest with joy. "You like children?" she asked excitedly.

"Very much."

"Did you have many brothers and sisters?" Dani couldn't remember Mamie mentioning any of John's siblings.

"No, there's only me. Perhaps that's the reason I was hoping for a houseful myself. My father died when I was young. I barely remember him, only that he loved my mother with all his heart and that she loved him.

"He was tall and his laughter was so loud it sounded like a freight train. It used to frighten me." He stopped suddenly as if he hadn't meant to say that much. "What about you?"

"I have one sister. Delia. She's intelligent and beautiful, but painfully shy."

"*Your* sister?"

"She stuttered as a child, and has overcome that except when she's under a lot of stress, but she prefers to keep to herself. I worry about her sometimes."

"Is she married?"

"No," Dani said, and added on a sad note, "I wonder if she ever will marry. It would be a shame if she doesn't. Delia has a lot of love to give."

"Eventually she'll find the right person."

Dani unloaded the grocery sack and hesitated, her hand inside the brown bag. "How confident you sound. It's almost as if you can read the future. If you're so good at it, take a look at my own, would you?"

John reached for her hand, turned it over and pretended to examine her palm. He rubbed the underside of his chin. "Now that's interesting."

"What?" She found herself studying her hand, expecting to find something that hadn't been there earlier.

"Look at the love line." He traced his index finger across the width of her palm, which caused a deep, sensual sensation to curl in her belly.

"Short and stubby, right?" she joked, wondering at the peculiar sensation.

"On the contrary, it's long, very long. I don't think you have anything to worry about when it comes to love."

How she wished she could believe him. "That certainly hasn't been the case thus far."

"Perhaps," he agreed. "But if your palm's to be believed, that's all going to change."

Embarrassed now with all this talk about love, Dani returned to the task at hand. She finished emptying the sack and set the ingredients she'd purchased that morning along the kitchen counter.

"You never did tell me what you were planning to fix."

"I didn't?" She glanced at him over her shoulder. "It's a casserole recipe made with tofu and..."

"Tofu?" John interrupted.

"I know it has a bad reputation, but it's really wonderful stuff, fat-free and..." She stopped when she noticed John open the sliding glass door and step onto the patio. "What are you doing?"

"Getting out the barbecue. I've got a couple of steaks in the freezer that the microwave can thaw. I'll toss a couple of potatoes in there while I'm at it."

"The barbecue?"

"No, the microwave."

"You mean to say you won't even taste my casserole?"

John looked as if he was of two minds on the subject. She was convinced he didn't wish to offend her, but at the same time tofu was a stretch for a man who subsisted on meat and potatoes. It didn't look as if he was willing to change his mind about her casserole, either.

"How about if we cook both?" he suggested as means of a compromise.

Dani nodded. "Okay, as long as you agree to taste my dish."

He made some diplomatic reply and smiled so warmly at her she didn't press him. Once he saw her concoction, he'd willingly taste it.

They worked side by side. Dani slipped out of her shoes and padded barefoot across the kitchen. He didn't own an apron so she tucked a linen dishcloth into her waistband. John turned on the stereo and played soft classical music.

"Do you have anything country?" she called out.

"I don't think so," he said, sorting through his CDs. "Next time we do this, leave the tofu at home and bring your own music."

"You're going to eat those words, John Osborn. This casserole is to die for."

"You mean it's going to kill me?" he teased.

She rolled her eyes and returned her attention to the cutting board, where she had chopped green peppers, mushrooms and an onion.

The evening was lovely, and once the casserole was in the oven, John poured them each a glass of white wine and gave her a tour of the house. The balcony off the master bedroom was her favorite spot.

"It's so beautiful here," she said, leaning her elbows against the edge. The view of the harbor was unobstructed, and the night sang a gentle melody.

"It's one of my favorite spots, as well." He stood beside her and placed his arm around her shoulders. Dani found herself leaning against him, not for any physical support. A need strong and profound drew her to his side. Their hips brushed against each other. She paused and, wondering if she was the only one experiencing this awareness, she glanced up at him.

John removed the wineglass from her unresisting fingers. He set it aside and then turned her so they were facing each other. Gently, his large hands cupped her face. His thumbs caressed her cheeks in a circular, catlike motion. He seemed to be studying her, reading her.

Dani knew he was going to kiss her, the same way she'd known he'd wanted to the day she'd slipped from the ladder. They'd both been afraid then of what would happen if they explored the sensation between them. Need overrode anxiety this night as John slowly lowered his mouth to hers.

The kiss was slow and thorough, as if giving them each time to assess what was happening. To give her time to pull away if that was what she wanted. Dani didn't.

He eased back and studied her, and it seemed to Dani that the air grew chilled. His gaze searched hers as if seeking some form of reassurance.

"John..." She didn't know who reached for whom, but within seconds she was back in his arms. His mouth was warm and moist and enticing. John moaned, and cupping the back of her head with his hand, he deepened the kiss until they were both breathless and weak.

A heavy, warm feeling filled her. "Is this something friends do frequently?"

"I wouldn't know," John answered. "I've never had a friend like you before."

"I should hope not." She flattened her hand over her heart. "It's pounding like crazy."

"Yours? Listen to mine." He pressed her hand over his chest and she felt the staccato thud of his heart racing against her palm.

A timer dinged in the distance and for the life of her, Dani had a difficult time making sense of why it had sounded. It came to her in a rush. "My casserole's done." Time had slipped by unnoticed and Dani was sorry for this new intimacy to end.

John seemed as reluctant to release her as she was to leave the warm shelter of his arms.

"I suppose I should go take it out of the oven," she whispered.

"I suppose," John agreed. But he didn't move and neither did she. A moment later, with what felt like supreme effort, Dani eased herself out of his arms and headed for the kitchen.

"I'd best get those steaks on the barbecue."

"Just remember that you promised to try my casserole," she reminded him.

John hesitated. "I did?"

"John! I'm going to be terribly disappointed if we end up cooking separate meals all because you're leery of a little bean curd."

"Any man with pride wouldn't ever admit to eating tofu."

"But you said you would," she reminded him.

"As I recall, I promised I'd sample your recipe. Sample, as in taste. Taste, as in one small nibble from the end of a fork, and nothing more."

Dani allowed a sigh to quiver through her lungs. "You're a sorry disappointment to me." She turned and was about to leave when John captured her hand.

"Am I?" he asked, his eyes dark and serious.

"What?"

"A sorry disappointment to you?"

"Ah..."

He brought her back into his arms and kissed her again and again and Dani's toes curled with the intensity of it.

"Am I a disappointment?" he asked her a second time, while he spread soft kisses along the delicate line of her chin.

"Not...really," she whispered, barely able to find her voice. "It's just that..."

"Yes?"

"You're sure about friends kissing like this? It feels much too good...much too right."

John hesitated. "To be fair, when it comes to you, I'm not sure about anything. Not anymore."

"Admit how good the tofu tasted," Dani insisted. They sat in the bowling alley with Laura and Charley.

"I believe the word I used was *interesting,*" John answered with a teasing light in his eyes. Dani noticed the way his gaze found Charley's, as if to suggest he was being a good sport about the whole thing.

"As I recall, you ate three helpings."

"Was it really three?" John asked.

"Tofu?" Even Charley seemed to have trouble believing it.

"It's not half as bad as we've been led to believe." John told him, "Especially when it's used in humble pie."

Everyone laughed.

"It's amazing what a man's willing to do for a woman," Charley said, standing up and reaching for the bowling ball. "I've never been bowling in my life. I was convinced I'd make a first-class idiot of myself. Yet, here I am wearing the most ridiculous-looking pair of shoes I've ever seen, tossing a ball at a few pins, hoping to impress Laura with what a great athlete I am." He walked up to the line and released the ball as if he'd been doing so twenty years or more, not bothering to see how many pins he knocked down.

Laura smiled broadly at Dani, her eyes bright with happiness.

Charley walked back and slumped into his seat. "I'm not the only one, either. Here's John," he said, picking up the conversation as though he'd never left, "eating tofu and swearing he likes the stuff."

"You didn't have to come bowling," Laura shyly insisted.

"Yes, I did," Charley countered with the hint of a frown. "It was either that or risk the chance you'd spend the evening with Doug instead of me."

Once more, Laura's smiling gaze drifted to Dani. It made Dani feel as if she were some sort of expert in the matter of love, when nothing could be farther from the truth. Her own life was evidence of that. She'd fallen flat on her face when it came to her relationship with Bob.

Bob.

It used to be, when she thought about her ex-fiancé, that her heart would involuntarily clench and a part of her soul ached. There'd been a time, in the not-so-distant past, when the mere mention of his name would produce a bout of spontaneous tears she'd struggled to hide.

No longer.

The cure had come in the form of a certain shop owner, another of the walking wounded. A man who'd trod the path of broken dreams and found his way through the maze of disappointments.

Working with John hadn't cured her broken heart, not exactly. But he'd helped her center her focus, not in the fog of her pain, but toward the future.

At one time Dani had loved Bob, truly loved him; at least, she'd convinced herself of that. Now she realized that what she'd fallen in love with was the dream. She hungered for a husband and children, and Bob had played nicely into the idyllic picture she'd created. He'd seemed so wonderful, so genuine and sincere. He'd insisted that her dreams had been his own. Perhaps they were, in some small way.

"How about coffee?" Charley suggested after the match. He tucked the bowling ball away, and casually draped his arm over Laura's shoulders.

"Not tonight, but thanks." John reached for Dani's hand and lightly squeezed it. As soon as their friends were out of earshot, he asked, "You don't mind, do you?"

"Not really." She didn't object, but she was curious. Charley and Laura had been the ones who'd suggested this outing. When Dani mentioned it to John, he'd readily agreed.

John seemed unusually quiet on the ride back to her small rental house. To her surprise, he drove past it.

"You just missed my house."

"I know," he answered, turning the corner, and heading for the beach. "I thought we might enjoy a walk along the ocean."

"That would be wonderful." And romantic. John hadn't kissed her since Saturday evening, but then, there hadn't been much opportunity, either. They hadn't been alone more than a few minutes at a stretch. It had disappointed her that they'd been so busy at the shop that there wasn't time for them.

Bowling was an excuse to be together and they'd both welcomed it. Or so she'd like to think. But in retrospect, she realized that although John had joked and laughed and given the appearance that he was having a good time, something was on his mind.

John parked the car at the beach. His hand gripped the steering wheel and he kept his face averted. "I've been wanting to talk to you." He turned and their eyes met. Even in the dark, with only the glow of a half-moon illuminating the night, Dani could read the intensity in his eyes.

"You have?" The temperature in the car seemed to heat up by several degrees.

John's hand lovingly cupped her face. He closed his eyes and Dani was convinced she heard him moan.

"Let's walk," he said, thrusting open the car door, and climbing out of the vehicle.

"All right."

His hand held hers as they strolled along the shore.

They'd gone for some time before she said, "I thought you wanted to talk."

"I do."

"We could have talked at my house, too, you know," she teased.

"I don't think so." His pace slowed and he stopped and stared down at her. "I'm afraid if we'd gone back to your house we'd have ended up making love."

Her face went pink. "Oh."

"I trust myself to behave while we're in public, but even that's becoming iffy. I'm not certain where this relationship is headed, but before matters go any further I need to be sure you want the same things I do."

"Oh . . ." Dani couldn't stop looking at the man bathed in moonlight. It didn't seem possible that it was the same one who'd grumbled and complained about her just a few weeks earlier. "Couldn't you just kiss me first?" she asked, wanting him so much it was difficult not to take the initiative herself. She struggled to keep from throwing her arms around him. "I promise we can talk later."

His kiss revealed the depth of his hunger. By the time he eased his lips from hers, Dani felt drained and exhilarated and desperate for more of the same.

"John . . . please," she whimpered when he outlined her mouth with the tip of his tongue.

He groaned and wrapped his arms around her, his grip viselike. "It wasn't supposed to happen like this."

"What wasn't?" she asked, spreading kisses along the underside of his jaw.

"It would be best if we stopped."

"Best for whom?" She leaned her body into his, loving the hard feel of him.

"Dani . . . I can't think straight when you're in my arms, and we need to talk."

Dani smiled to herself. She couldn't very well say she hadn't noticed, because she had. Knowing she was the reason produced a keen sense of satisfaction.

"You're sure you want to talk?" she asked, nibbling on his ear.

"Yes... no." He drew in his breath.

"There's no need to be so serious." It was in her mind that he would suggest that they take this attraction wherever it would lead them. It was in her heart that he might suggest that they think along the lines of making their relationship permanent.

"I was thinking..."

"Yes," she purred.

John cleared his throat and put some distance, very little, between them. "That it might be a good idea if you found another job."

Chapter Six

Dani didn't sleep all that night. She vacillated between outrage and tears. First, she would pace the compact bedroom, counting the hours before she could confront John and tell him exactly what she thought of him. Then she would tire and her anger would dissolve into a rough-edged pain.

To his credit, John claimed he had a list of excellent reasons why he'd come to this conclusion. Not that she'd given him the chance to list a single one. She'd been too hurt, too shocked, too furious for that.

In the end she'd insisted on walking back to her house. Alone. He hadn't allowed her even that one display of pride. She'd walked, all right, but he followed her in his car with his window rolled down, and attempted to reason with her. The man should have recognized she was in no mood for reason. He insisted that he'd talk to her in the morning, then had the audacity to park outside her home until he was assured she was safely inside.

Well, it was morning and she hadn't seen hide nor hair of John Osborn.

Dani sat at her kitchen table and covered her face with her hands. She didn't know how she would pay her bills. That wasn't entirely true. Since she'd started doing John's window displays, several shopkeepers had approached her at one time or another about doing displays for them. Dani knew without asking that no one shop could afford her full-time. It had occurred to her once before that it would be a simple enough task to form her own business.

She would, she decided.

She sipped her coffee, and wondered why she didn't feel any better. Financially she should be able to work everything out. It wasn't the lack of a job that plagued her, although that was what she'd centered her thoughts on during the long, sleepless night.

No, it was the feeling of betrayal she'd felt when John casually announced he was letting her go. To be fair, she hadn't stood around for him to explain. As far as she was concerned, she'd heard all she'd wanted. It had hurt and the pain had cut deep.

Dani studied the kitchen clock and wondered what John would do when she didn't show up for work that morning. He hadn't said if he intended for her termination to be effective immediately.

What she hoped, what she wanted, was for John to come for her. He apparently was patiently waiting for her to arrive at the shop.

In his dreams. It wasn't likely that he'd stop by and see her, either. If this morning was typical of the way business had been the last two weeks, John would be swamped the minute he opened.

By ten, Dani had changed her sheets, washed the kitchen floor and cleaned out the refrigerator. She'd worked up a sweat, venting her frustrations.

The doorbell chimed, and with her heart racing, she removed the yellow rubber gloves and headed for the front door.

So he'd come, after all. Good. She felt better already. Dani had worked matters out in her mind. The morning hadn't been a waste. If anything, it had helped her clear her thoughts so that she knew exactly what she planned to say to her employer. Ex-employer, she reminded herself.

Dani couldn't have been more prepared had she written out a speech. What she didn't anticipate was the man who stood on the other side of the door. It wasn't John.

It was Bob.

His smile was filled with boyish charm. "Aren't you going to invite me inside?" he asked.

He really was a handsome devil, Dani was willing to admit, but she realized how artificial good looks could be. It seemed impossible that she could have loved this man so intensely. She stared at him, wondering what it was that had fascinated her.

"Dani?"

"Hello, Bob," she said, recovering awkwardly. "I wasn't expecting you."

"Can I come inside?"

She lifted her shoulder in a halfhearted shrug. "If you want." Holding open the screen door for him, she allowed him to pass. To her way of thinking, he wouldn't be staying long, so she kept the door open.

"What can I do for you?" she asked stiffly, and folded her arms.

"You're looking great," he said with a wide grin. He made himself at home. He sat on her sofa and crossed his muscular legs, resting his ankle on top of his knee. "I don't suppose you have any coffee brewed."

"I don't."

"I could really use a cup."

"Then I suggest you go buy yourself one," she said without emotion. It surprised her how indifferent she felt toward him. In the beginning, she'd fantasized about such a meeting between the two of them. In her mind's eye she had the supreme pleasure of tossing him out of her home and out of her life. Now that he was actually with her, the only emotion she felt was pity and sadness for the time she'd wasted on him.

Bob's eyes widened as though her words had hurt him. "I'd hoped we could talk without the anger," he said gently, and held out his hand to her. "Sit down, please. There's so much to say... I don't know where to start."

She stood exactly where she was. "There's nothing left between us," she said, and if any emotion stirred within her, it was more sadness.

Bob briefly bowed his head as if seeking some greater wisdom. "I'd hoped that given time you'd come to your senses."

"Me?" she cried, flattening her hand across her chest.

"I gave you the space and the freedom I felt you needed," he continued. "Now I can't help wondering if I did the right thing." A pained look crossed his face. "No matter what you think, Dani, letting you out of my life hurt like hell."

It was all she could do to keep from rolling her eyes.

"When you settled out here, I decided to give you three or four months to mull everything over. I felt that in that time frame you might come to realize that what we had was too special, too wonderful, to throw out the window."

"I wasn't the one who blew it, Bob."

"True, true," he said, holding up both hands. "I accept full responsibility for what happened. I was a fool, and I'll be the first one to admit it. I made a mistake, Dani. Albeit, it was a doozy, but I've learned my lesson. I have, darling. I swear by everything I hold dear that it'll never happen again."

"It's too late." It gave her no degree of satisfaction in telling him this. "It's over, Bob."

He did an excellent job of looking as if her news had crushed him. "Is it because of John Osborn?"

Dani stiffened. "What do you know about John?"

Bob shifted uncomfortably in his seat and glanced away. "Nothing much.... I'd heard rumors about the two of you. Something completely ridiculous about you two becoming engaged."

He had people watching her, Dani realized, and fumed.

"I knew the minute I heard you were engaged that it couldn't possibly be true, but I came to check it out." He laughed lightly as if the notion made no sense whatsoever. "I met the man this morning and I'm here to tell you, there's no way the two of you..." He paused when he saw her fierce look.

"You saw John this morning?"

"Well, yes. I expected to find you at the antiques store."

"Did you introduce yourself?" she asked.

"Of course I did." He said this as if it was the only gentlemanly thing to do. Funny it never occurred to him that fidelity had honor, as well.

"What did John say?" Dani found this to be of far more concern than how the two reacted to each other.

Bob's shoulders stiffened. "In the beginning he wasn't going to tell me anything about you." He paused and straightened the knot of his tie. "But I set Osborn straight. Really, Dani, I can't imagine you with this kind of man."

"And why not?" She braced her fists against her hips.

"Well, he's . . . unsuitable."

"For whom?" she demanded. "John Osborn is worth ten of you. He's a man of character and honor. I can tell you right now that John would never think to cheat anyone. He's honest and fair and intelligent and kind. . . ."

Bob stared at her in horror. "You are in love with him?"

"Yes." She wasn't going to deny it.

"But . . ."

"I've decided I must never have loved you," Dani said, cutting him off. "I can only assume I was in love with the idea of being in love.

"I couldn't have fallen so quickly or so hard for John if I'd truly loved you," she admitted without malice. "I don't think I realized what it was to feel this strongly for a man until I met John." Even as she said the words, she recognized the truth of them.

"You can't be serious."

"Oh, Bob, don't you know me at all? Do you honestly think I would make something like this up?"

He stared at her as if he wasn't sure what to believe any longer. Finally he rubbed a hand down his face and stood. "I'd hoped..." He paused, his disappointment evident. "But I can see that you've made up your mind."

"Yes, I have."

His eyes met hers. "You could do better than Osborn."

"Better?" she cried, shaking her head in wonder. Bob was far more obtuse than she'd realized. "I don't know what John feels for me, but if he does love me, I'll go to my grave forever grateful that a man as wonderful as John would love someone like me."

Bob glared at her for several moments. "He loves you."

Dani's heart froze. "How can you be so sure?"

"Just take my word for it, Dani, the man's crazy about you. Crazy enough to release you from any obligation to him so you'd be free to leave with me if you so desired."

She hesitated. So that was the reason he'd fired her. It made an insane kind of sense now, not that she approved. In fact, she deeply disapproved.

"Perhaps you're right about there being no future for the two of us," Bob said and exhaled as though deeply hurt. "We had some good times, though, don't you think?"

She nodded, willing to grant him that much.

"I owe you this one. Just remember in the years to come that I was the one who told you that John loves you. Fact is, I went out of my way so you'd know how he felt." Bob hesitated and frowned. "It doesn't concern you that he's never told you how he feels?"

"No." After all, she hadn't told John her feelings, either.

Bob shrugged. "I'll leave, since that's what you seem to want." A sadness sneaked into his eyes once more. "I only want the best for you, Dani. You might not believe this, but I do love you."

Dani did believe it. In his own way, as much as he could, Bob did care for her.

The two briefly hugged and then he was gone.

Dani changed out of her shorts and sleeveless blouse as fast as her trembling hands would allow. Her mind was on John every minute of the drive over to the antiques store.

When she entered the shop, she noticed that he was with a customer. His gaze found hers, and it seemed as if everything faded from view but the man who stood no more than a few feet from her. John was reluctantly pulled back to the customer and the conversation. Fortunately, the man left two minutes later.

Without another word, John stepped into the back room and a moment later his mother appeared. Mamie's gaze found Dani and she broke into a wide grin.

John walked over to where Dani stood waiting. "Hello."

"Hi."

"Are you free for lunch?"

Eating was the last thing on her mind, but she nodded. "Sure."

They walked two doors down and bought thick deli sandwiches. John carried them to the beach and they sat next to each other in the sand. The sea gulls flew overhead and the ocean slapped the shore.

"I understand you had company this morning," he said.

Dani noticed that neither one of them appeared interested in their sandwich. "Yes. Bob stopped by. I take it you gave him my address."

John nodded. "So?" he said with a decided lack of composure. "Are the two of you getting back together?"

"Hardly. It seems grossly unfair to string Bob along when I'm head over heels in love with you."

It seemed in that moment that the wind ceased to blow, that the ocean no longer roared and that the sea gulls went still, frozen in their flight pattern against the backdrop of a dazzling blue sky.

John's gaze narrowed, as if testing the truth in her words. As if he was afraid to believe them.

"The craziest part of it was that Bob insisted you loved me." She tried to make light of it, and knew she wasn't any better at disguising her feelings than he was with her. "I was rather hoping that was the reason you'd decided to fire me... although I have to say your thinking is a bit twisted."

"I do love you." He paused and granted her a half smile. "Enough to give Bob your address and allow you to make your own decisions when it came to your ex-fiancé."

Just the way he said the words told her how difficult it had been for him to sit back and wait.

She smiled and leaned her head against him, and John wrapped his arm around her shoulders, bringing her closer. He gently kissed the top of her head.

"I thought you wanted me out of your life," she said, struggling, even now, to release the hurt his words had caused her.

"No, never that, but I wanted you to be free of any obligation to me should you decide to leave. I've never done anything more difficult in my life than release you."

"I wasn't going to leave."

"But you didn't know about Bob then."

"I knew everything I needed to know about him." She looped her arm around his. "Actually, several people had approached me in the last few weeks about doing their window displays and I thought . . . I hoped . . . I could make enough doing that to survive until you came to your senses."

"It's not such a bad idea."

"I could set up my own small company and work . . ."

"Part-time," he inserted, and at her questioning glance, he added, "Until the children are in school."

It felt as if the world were suddenly devoid of oxygen. "Children?"

"I'm praying like crazy that you'll agree to marry me."

Unable to find her voice, Dani eagerly nodded. "When?"

"Oh, I figured since we had something of a whirlwind courtship that we should wait a year or so to start our family. But basically, I'll leave the decision up to you."

"Wedding . . . when?" She waved her hand as if fanning a fire and hoped she was coherent enough for John to understand her question.

His eyes widened as if he found her inquisitiveness something of a surprise. "I'd prefer it if we could be married soon. Very soon. The sooner the better. Are you free next weekend?" At her stricken look, he amended, "You decide the date, just promise you won't keep me waiting much longer."

All at once she was in his arms. John's kiss was filled with a desperate kind of longing, one that matched her own. Dani groaned in welcome and opened her mouth to him. John's tongue eased forward, probing deeply, mating with hers in a frenzied erotic game. When he finally dragged his lips from hers, he gulped air into his lungs.

"You'd better make it quick," he urged in a rough whisper.

"Quick?"

"The wedding. It's getting to the point that even a public beach isn't safe. I want you so much I'm willing to be arrested."

"I don't think it'll come to that," she said with a lazy, happy smile.

"Don't be so sure, Dani. You don't have a clue how tempting you are."

"Temptation is good for the..." She wasn't allowed to finish because John was kissing her again; this time he tangled her hair with his fingers and dragged his lips over hers. The kiss was warm and moist. Warm and potent.

"Do you think we could arrange a wedding by next week?" She whispered the question when she could breathe.

He nodded. "We'll find a way." He braced his forehead against hers. "Mother is going to gloat."

"Let her," Dani said, more than willing to be generous with John's mother. "She deserves to, don't you think?"

She felt his smile against her skin. "I suppose you're right.

"Shall we tell her?" He stood and offered Dani his hand.

"Now?" Everything was happening so fast, her head was spinning. She accepted his help and reached for their untouched lunches.

"You object?"

"No...no, it isn't that. I've got so much to do. I need to call my parents and my sister and tell them. Delia will have to fly in and... Oh, good grief, you've never even met my parents. What will they think when we announce we're getting married so soon?"

"Well," John said, looping his arm around her waist. "Either they'll assume we're madly in love, or that you're pregnant."

Dani laughed, and covered her mouth with the tips of her fingers. "No doubt Dad will thank you for making an honest woman out of me."

"And your mother?"

"She'll ply us both with a thousand questions. She'll want to be assured we know what we're doing, rushing into marriage this way."

"Do we?" John asked.

"Probably not," Dani answered, wondering if he'd already changed his mind. She studied him, searching out his face, looking for telltale signs. John was a man who seldom acted impulsively.

"No, Dani love," he said and kissed her temple. "I haven't changed my mind. Nor will I. Now come back to the store because I have a gift for you."

"A gift?" Dani wasn't sure what to think.

John held her hand and together they trotted across the busy intersection back to Osborn Antiques. Mamie was occupied with a customer when they walked into the store. She stopped abruptly, said something to the client and looked to John and Dani.

"Well?" she asked expectantly.

"We're getting married," John announced.

Mamie folded her hands and raised her eyes skyward. "Praise be to the saints."

"Next week, Mother."

"Next week?" Mamie pulled out a chair and literally fell into it. "These youngsters think everything has to happen overnight. I can't believe this. I really can't. Do either of you realize how much is involved in arranging a wedding?"

"Not really," John said, smiling at Dani. "I guess we'll just have to wing it."

"I'll take care of the flowers and the music. Bertha Johnson does fabulous cakes, but I think you and Dani should be the ones to pick it out."

"We will, Mother," John promised.

"I've heard that before."

Dani wasn't sure who Mamie was speaking to, but it didn't matter. John walked over to his desk and took out a key. He led her to the storage room she'd discovered all those weeks ago. Dani didn't realize he kept it locked these days.

He unlatched the padlock and opened the door. Then he leaned into the compact room, and turned on the light. "This is for you," he said, with his back to her. When he turned around, Dani realized that he held the cradle she'd loved so dearly in his arms.

Tears leapt to her eyes, and she struggled within herself for a couple of moments. "You said you'd sold it."

"Not exactly. The gist of what I told you was that it was going to a good home. What I didn't say was that I sincerely hoped it would be our own. Whatever happens between us, I want you to have the cradle."

"I won't accept it," she said, and after a sufficient pause added, "Without you." Closing the storage room door, she walked over to the man she loved with all her being.

John set the cradle aside, and wrapped his arms around her. "You already have me, Dani. You have for a very long time." Their kiss was deep, slow and potent enough to weaken her knees.

"We're crazy," she whispered.

"But it's a wonderful kind of crazy," John added, and she couldn't agree with him more.

* * * * *

BEGINNINGS

Gina Ferris Wilkins

A Note from Gina Ferris Wilkins

I couldn't possibly write about motherhood without turning it into a tribute to my own mother, Beth Vaughan. From the time I was old enough to sound out letters, she put books in my hands. She encouraged my lifelong love of reading by introducing me to the childhood classics—*Little Women, Eight Cousins, The Five Little Peppers and How They Grew, The Bobbsey Twins*—and, as I grew older, she shared the contemporary and Regency romances she particularly enjoyed.

She guided my reading, but never restricted it, encouraging me to read a variety of books and make my own judgments about their contents. I strongly believe that the early development of literacy is the key to performance in school—which, to me, is illustrated by the fact that my mother was valedictorian of her class. I graduated with honors from both high school and college, and the two of my three children who are now in school have been A students from the beginning.

I have followed my mother's example—reading to my children when they were small, providing them with plenty of books as they grew, teaching them that reading is not a chore, but a pleasure to be shared. I speak frequently to students and to parents, talking to them about literacy as the key to opportunity. This I learned primarily from my mother.

My mother is an executive secretary. For most of my life, she worked outside the home, and as soon as I reached my teens and begged to go to work during the summers—greatly preferable, in my opinion, to staying at home with three pesky younger brothers—she helped me get a job with the company she had worked for for many years. She taught me about independence, competence and professional behavior. She taught me about working with others and respecting my employers. She taught me self-respect.

Even though she worked outside the home, my mother always stressed the value of family. A successful career was something I should strive for, but she urged me not to overlook the equal importance of marriage and children. The blessings I have received from my happy marriage and three wonderful children have richly rewarded me for listening to her wise advice.

Most of all, my mother stressed etiquette. She taught me about being an old-fashioned lady, as well as being a modern woman. She raised me in a rural community steeped in Southern tradition, and my childhood was a happy one. I was taught to "mind my manners," "respect my elders," and "never wear white shoes before Easter or after Labor Day."

I learned early that cursing is a sign of a limited vocabulary, that ladies stand up straight and dress modestly and wear clean, untorn underwear—in case of accidents, of course. I was raised to say "sir" and "ma'am" and "please" and "thank you." I'm raising my own children the same way, and whenever I am complimented on how well behaved they are, or how well they perform in school, I smile and silently thank my mother for providing me with such a wonderful example of motherhood.

Thank you, Mother. I love you. I dedicate this story to you.

Gina Ferris Wilkins

Chapter One

Margot hurried to the door in answer to an insistent summons from her doorbell. Her hair was still wet from her shower, her robe gathered hastily around her. "Who is it?"

"Delivery," a pleasant-sounding male voice replied. "I need a signature."

Made careless by her impatience to get ready for her date that evening, Margot opened the door without further question. Then froze. Her eyes widened in horror. Her terrified scream was swiftly, efficiently silenced by the slash of a...

The insistent buzz of her own doorbell brought Delia Beckman abruptly out of the mystery novel gripped tightly in her hands. Startled, she blinked, and looked toward her apartment door. She wasn't expecting anyone this afternoon. Who on earth...?

Still a bit unnerved by the passage she'd been reading, Delia clutched the paperback to her chest and rose from the blue, white and rose striped couch on which she'd been curled. She approached her door cautiously. "Who is it?"

"Are you Delia Beckman? If so, I have a package for you," a pleasant-sounding male voice replied.

Delia gulped. "A, um, package?" she repeated weakly.

"Yeah. It just arrived. And it's a big one," he added.

Keeping the chain securely fastened, Delia risked opening the door an inch to peek out. Standing in her hallway was an enormous cardboard box with bare brown legs and sneakered feet. At least, that was the way it appeared to her. The man holding the box was almost completely hidden by it.

As though to reassure her, the guy craned his neck around one side of the box and gave her a smile. "I was just coming back from a run when the delivery truck arrived," he explained. "When the driver found out that he was going to have to haul this thing up two flights of stairs, he refused. Said you'd have to come down and get it—this was his last delivery of the day and he was in a hurry to be on his way. I volunteered to bring it up to you."

He was young—late twenties or very early thirties—and dark, his eyes bright blue in contrast to his tanned skin and heavy mop of near-black hair. Delia recognized him immediately. She'd seen him often during the past few months—sometimes accompanied by an attractive woman, though rarely the same woman more than once. He lived on the first floor of this building. They'd shared a few polite nods, though they'd never actually spoken.

"Would you like me to bring this in for you?" he asked before she could speak, shifting his weight a bit awkwardly beneath his bulky burden. "It's sort of heavy."

Delia flushed and hurriedly released the safety chain. "Sorry," she murmured, opening the door. "I wasn't—um—you s-startled me," she explained, exasperated with herself for stammering like the awkward schoolgirl she'd once been.

"No problem." He crossed the threshold with the carefully measured steps of someone clinging to his balance. "Where do you want this?"

Still holding the book in her left hand, she motioned toward an empty patch of rose-colored carpeting with her right. "Just set it on the floor here," she said, stepping back.

He set the box down carefully, and with obvious relief. "Whew!" he said. "Feels like a load of bricks."

Delia had already noted the return address on the shipping label. "It's from my sister and brother-in-law," she mused aloud. "Must be a birthday present from their antiques store."

Her neighbor cocked his dark head. "Today's your birthday?"

Delia cleared her throat and glanced back down at the box to avoid looking at him. Something about his attractively windblown hair and the firm, tanned body intriguingly revealed by a gray half T and brief red running shorts made her feel plain and self-conscious.

Since she hadn't been expecting company on this Friday afternoon, she was dressed in worn jeans and a black camp shirt she hadn't even bothered to tuck in. Her sandy brown hair was loose around her shoulders, and the makeup she'd applied for the office that morning had long since faded. "Tomorrow's my birthday," she explained, resisting an impulse to run her hand through her hair.

"Then I'll be one of the first to wish you a happy one." His smile looked as though it belonged on a campaign poster.

"Thank you." Delia eyed him through her lashes, reluctantly impressed by the perfection of his features. She could easily picture him as the captain of the football team in high school, student government president in college, up-and-climbing junior executive now. The type of guy who'd ignored her through most of her adolescence, when they weren't teasing her about her stutter. The men Delia knew and dated tended to be more like herself, serious, quiet, average. This man, whatever his name was, looked like a mistake waiting to be made.

As though he'd read her thoughts—and Delia sincerely hoped that wasn't one of his talents—the man suddenly made a face and shook his head. "I haven't even introduced myself, have I? I'm Lane Conley. I live downstairs, first floor."

Masking her self-consciousness behind her habitual facade of cool composure, she nodded in response to his introduction. "And I'm Delia Beckman—as you've already ascertained from the mailing label on my package."

"It's very nice to finally meet you, Delia. I've been meaning to introduce myself, but you always seem to be in a hurry when I see you," he said, faintly chiding, though his smile was a teasing one.

She privately acknowledged that she *had* tended to hurry away on the few occasions when their paths had crossed. She couldn't have explained why, so she settled for a vague smile.

"Well." He shifted his weight, obviously groping for another conversational gambit. He glanced around her living room, and then his gaze fell on the large box at their feet. "Looks as though your sister intended that packing to survive a tornado. Think you'll need any help getting into it?"

Delia looked at the thick swathes of packing tape draped over every visible surface of the box. She smiled. "Dani tends to get carried away. But I'll manage to cut into it."

"Oh. Sure." He shifted again, then ran a hand through his disheveled, damp-tipped dark hair. "Guess I'd better head for the showers. It was nice meeting you, neighbor," he added with another charming smile.

She held firmly to her own smile and motioned toward the package. "Thank you again for bringing this up for me."

"No problem. Uh, see you around, okay?"

"Of course." She held the door for him, then closed it firmly behind him when he left. Her smile vanished with the click of the lock.

Well, wasn't that nice, Delia? You displayed all the sparkling personality of a plastic fern. Lane Conley is probably running downstairs as fast as his gorgeous legs will carry him.

She shook her head in accompaniment to her mental chiding and went into the kitchen for a sharp knife. The silent lecture continued as she began to hack her way through the mountain of packing tape on her birthday package. The box was big, *and* heavy. She would have had a tough time carrying it up the stairs by herself. It had been very nice of Lane to go out of his way to deliver it to her. The least she could have done was to have offered him a cold drink or something. Instead, she'd frozen, going tongue-tied and awkward the same way she had whenever she'd been confronted by an attractive male during her painful teen years.

She'd thought she'd long since outgrown that stage. Apparently, some men—or at least this particular man—still brought out the old reflexes.

Sawing doggedly at one particularly stubborn section of tape, Delia grinned at the thought of mentioning her meeting with Lane during her morning coffee break at work the next Monday. Her friends would get a kick out of hearing about him—and then they would most surely warn her not to waste her time with a man like that. Heartache-on-the-hoof, they called his sort. Most of them spoke from painful experience.

Almost a year ago, the Monday-morning coffee break had evolved into an informal support-group meeting of single women from the huge Seattle insurance-company office where Delia had worked for five years. The idea had been proposed by Sherry Cooper, a childless divorcée who'd just turned twenty-eight and was bemoaning her lack of a social life or prospects for a family. It turned out that most of Sherry's unmarried friends shared her frustration at not being able to find a suitable life partner, and sympathized with the ever-increasing demands of her biological clock.

Sherry had been the one who'd given a name to their mutual resolve to take positive steps toward personal fulfillment. She'd dubbed it the G.A.L.B.A.T. Plan. *Get A Life By Age Thirty.* Every Monday, she expected her friends to report on what they'd done to further their mission during the weekend. Joining singles groups, signing up for night-school classes, taking up new hobbies, all counted as positive steps. Staying home alone all weekend to read or watch television, going alone to theaters or movies or other noninteractive activities, or buying a cat for companionship were all on the firmly discouraged list.

The group included working women from every level of the company—clerical, supervisory, even one woman of twenty-nine who'd recently been named a junior vice president. Marriage wasn't the primary target—personal satisfaction was the goal. Still, of the original ten members of the loosely organized group, three had married during the past year and one was now expecting her first child. Delia was quite sure she wasn't the only one who secretly battled unbecoming twinges of envy.

The overwrapped package finally fell open beneath Delia's persistence to reveal the carefully wrapped gift inside. Delia lifted the carved box out with a murmur of pleasure. The antique music box was large, some thirty inches wide and eighteen inches deep, and heavy, made of several beautifully grained hardwoods stained to a soft luster. The accompanying note explained that it played three different tunes—"Greensleeves," Beethoven's "Moonlight Sonata" and "Für Elise."

Very carefully, Delia wound the key and pressed the button that activated the movement. Dozens of tiny raised bumps made contact with scrupulously measured strips of metal, resulting in full chords that resonated from inside the wooden box with a beauty that made Delia's breath catch in her throat. "Ooh," she whispered, resting one hand on the gently vibrating top of the music box. "How lovely."

Dani had been too generous—as always. The music box would have sold for a high price from the antiques store Dani operated with her husband, John Osborn, in the tourist-popular community of Ocean Shores, Washington. But Dani must have known how much Delia would truly love the gift.

Dani had slipped a recent photograph inside the cheerful birthday card packed with the music box. Delia smiled mistily as she studied the obviously happy trio in the photo, Dani, John and adorable two-year-old Johnny. Delia was delighted that her older sister was so blissfully happy, especially after Dani's first engagement had ended so awkwardly and painfully. Now, of course, Dani saw that breakup as a blessing in disguise.

Delia set the photograph aside with a wistful sigh. Her own biological clock had been clanging dementedly during the past year, and tomorrow she would turn twenty-seven. If she was going to get a life—and a family—before thirty, she was going to have to hurry. She'd come a long way during the years since high school, finally conquering a lifelong stutter and the almost debilitating shyness that had accompanied it. She liked her work in the personnel department of the insurance company, loved the apartment she'd furnished so carefully, had made several close, supportive friends, had enjoyed a few brief, but generally pleasant relationships with nice, respectable men. Now she wanted more. She wanted what Dani had found.

She thought of the date she'd made for dinner the next evening. Wayne Heslip was a nice guy, thirty-four, attractive in an average sort of way, one of the top salesmen in the insurance company's local district. He had a good future ahead of him in the company's management and he'd made it quite clear that he was ready to settle down. Delia tried to work up a sense of anticipation as she envisioned his pleasant face and friendly brown eyes. Instead, she found her mind filled with a picture of tousled near-black hair, a killer smile and a pair of bright blue eyes that glinted with temptation and potential heartbreak.

She shook her head in exasperation. Sexy Lane Conley didn't come close to fitting into Delia's plans. At this point in her life, she was looking for a lifelong commitment, not the passionate, ego-boosting temporary fling that might have tempted her a few years ago.

Some little voice inside her asked why she was automatically assuming that Lane was the love-'em-and-leave-'em type. Maybe he was really a nice, steady, dependable guy like Wayne, who was only waiting until he found the right woman to settle down and start his family.

His wicked smile flashed again in her thoughts, as clearly as though he were still standing in front of her, lean and tanned and damp from his run. She smiled ruefully and shook her head. Steady-and-dependable type?

"Not," she murmured with a chuckle.

She pushed him from her thoughts and closed her eyes, deliberately losing herself in the magic of Beethoven.

Chapter Two

Delia woke early Saturday. Her morning was filled with telephone calls from friends and family wishing her happy birthday. She dressed in comfortable khaki slacks and a bright red top, then met two of her friends for lunch at a popular deli in one of Seattle's older neighborhoods currently on an upswing of renewal and popularity. Her friends presented her with a gift they'd bought together—a pair of hammered silver earrings designed by a local artist.

Delia was delighted with the gift, and had a very nice time during the meal. It was a beautiful June afternoon—clear, warm, a rare day of cloudless skies and mercifully clean air. She couldn't have asked for a nicer birthday.

Still in a good mood from lunch, and with several hours ahead of her before her dinner date, she stopped by her favorite neighborhood bookstore on the way back to her apartment. She was never more comfortable or more at home than in a bookstore. Books had been her friends during her childhood, her escape. She'd lived through the characters in her favorite novels, reading them over and over, unencumbered by the embarrassing stutter or crippling shyness that marred her real life. She had actually substituted reading for living for a time, a habit she'd fought hard to overcome.

She still had to resist the temptation to spend too much time locked in her apartment with her books and her CD player. But that indolent, solitary behavior wouldn't have been at all compatible with the G.A.L.B.A.T. Plan, she reminded herself wryly. She managed to confine her reading to no more than two hours a day—less than most people spent staring at television screens.

Taking her time, she perused the newest titles in the romance and suspense sections, selecting a few intriguing paperbacks before moving to the mystery section. A newly released hardback by one of her favorite mystery writers caught her eye. She picked it up, studied it hungrily, then looked at the price. She sighed. It was tempting to splurge, using her birthday as an excuse for the extravagance, but rent was due this week and she'd overindulged in long-distance calls to her sister and a couple of other friends last month. She'd better wait a few weeks on the expensive hardback. She put it firmly back on the shelf.

"Happy birthday," she heard a man's voice say just as she reluctantly released the book.

She turned with a curiously lifted eyebrow. "Oh—hello," she said, her fingers tightening around the two paperbacks she held. She always seemed to be holding a book when she talked to this man, she thought incongruously.

Dressed in a dark blue pullover and faded jeans, Lane Conley was standing very close to her. And smiling. Delia couldn't help wondering whimsically if he'd registered that stunning smile of his as a potentially lethal weapon. In response to his birthday greeting, she returned the smile. "Thank you," she said.

"Having a nice one?"

"Yes, very nice."

He motioned toward the section of books beside them. "You like mysteries?"

"I do if they're well written and the characters are fully developed," she answered, listing her two top criteria.

He held up the luridly jacketed paperback loosely gripped in his left hand. "Have you read this one?"

"No, but I've read others by that author. She's good."

He nodded. "I'll try it, then. The premise sounds interesting."

"You like to read?" Delia was always pleased to find another book lover.

"Yeah. It's the way I wind down before bedtime. If I don't read, I can't seem to get my mind off work," he admitted.

Delia wondered what he did for a living. Male model? TV weatherman? Gynecologist? And then she chided herself for stereotyping again just because he had a pretty face. "I unwind with books, too," she volunteered. "I don't watch much TV."

"Other than the occasional news program, I don't, either."

"Oh." So much for that topic. Delia would have been willing to bet that reading for relaxation was just about all they had in common.

"So," Lane said. "How about if I buy you dinner tonight. You know, to celebrate your birthday."

Delia was surprised, but thought she managed to conceal it. "Thank you, but I already have plans for tonight."

He made a rueful face. "I expected that," he admitted. "But I thought it was worth a shot."

She couldn't help wondering why he didn't have plans, himself, for this Saturday evening. Last-minute cancellation, perhaps? "I'd better be going," she said, inching toward the register.

"Sure. Maybe we'll have dinner another night?" He watched her expectantly.

"Maybe," she said, taking another step backward. "'Bye, Lane."

He murmured something she didn't quite catch as she walked away.

Her group would be pleased with her should she report this Monday morning, she told herself. She'd had two—count them, two—invitations to dinner for one evening. Of course, one seemed to have been a spur-of-the-moment offer, probably because the guy had nothing better planned, but she wouldn't have to tell them that, would she?

As she dressed for the date she had accepted, she found herself trying to decide what she would have said to Lane had she not already had plans for the evening. And she couldn't help wondering whether he really would ask again.

Lane watched Delia Beckman leave the store with that graceful haste she always seemed to use when he was around. He shook his head, disgusted with his clumsy approach at asking her out. What was it about this woman that made him forget his usual conversational skills? It seemed to have started the first time he'd seen her, and noted the attraction of her wide-set hazel eyes and sweetly curved mouth. He'd wanted to introduce himself right then—and every time he'd run into her since—but the timing had never been quite right.

The arrival of the package for her had seemed like a sterling opportunity. And then he'd blown it by having his mind go inconveniently blank the minute she'd opened her door to him. He still cringed when he thought of his awkward attempts at making conversation with her.

Sighing in self-exasperation, he gave her plenty of time to leave the store before following. She wouldn't want him tagging at her heels back to their building. While he stalled, he picked up the book she'd been studying when he'd first seen her. He'd noticed the interest in her expression, and then the wince when she'd checked the price. He glanced at the tag and understood. It *was* sort of expensive. The author was a guaranteed bestseller with a huge, loyal following among mystery lovers. Still paying off student loans from law school, and currently working in the district attorney's office, Lane usually stuck to paperbacks, himself.

On an impulse he didn't stop to examine, he tucked the book under his arm with the paperback he'd already selected and headed for the register.

Wayne returned Delia to her apartment at eleven that evening. He lingered in the hallway until she felt obligated to ask him in for a nightcap, though she warned him that all she had to serve was an inexpensive bourbon left over from some baking she'd done for a Memorial Day cookout. Delia wasn't a drinker.

Wayne assured her that whatever she had would be fine. They sat side by side on her couch, sipping the bourbon and continuing the polite, relatively easy conversation they'd begun over dinner. At eleven-forty, Wayne glanced at his watch, set his empty tumbler on a coaster and rose. "It's getting late," he said. "I'd better be going."

Very gentlemanly—exactly what Delia had expected from a first date with this man. She smiled and saw him to the door. "I had a very nice evening, Wayne. Thank you for asking me."

"Perhaps we could do it again soon?" he suggested, smiling down at her. His smile was as pleasant and comfortable as Lane Conley's smile was wicked and lethal.

Delia hated herself for making the mental comparison. What was it with her lately, anyway? "That would be very nice," she assured him warmly.

"Good night."

She placed her hand on the doorknob. "Good night."

The parting kiss was brief, firm, as safe and pleasant as Wayne's smile. Delia closed the door behind him and sighed. What on earth was the matter with her? Wayne Heslip was attentive, amusing, successful. Available. So why wasn't her pulse racing? Why hadn't she been in the least tempted to ask him to stay a while longer?

Why hadn't she even mentioned to him that today was her birthday?

She really did want a life, she thought wistfully. She just wasn't sure she wanted Wayne's.

Utterly disgusted with herself, she threw up her hands, changed swiftly into a gown and robe and picked up one of the books she'd bought that afternoon. It was her birthday, she reminded herself, curling onto a corner of the couch with the book and a mug of hot chocolate. If she wanted to read the night away, she could. After all, it wasn't as if she had any more interesting alternatives. Though had she been out to dinner with Lane Conley, she wasn't at all sure she'd be at loose ends so early in the evening.

Scowling as the errant thought crossed her mind, Delia opened the book and plunged determinedly into it.

Chapter Three

Lane generally thrived on pandemonium—fortunately, since his workplace was usually chaotic. As it was on Monday afternoon, when he sat behind his scarred, cheap imitation-wood desk almost hidden behind a stack of files, telephone messages, lists of things to do before the day ended, law books, hastily typed depositions and some other things he wasn't ready to identify at the moment.

Noises swirled around him—telephones ringing, computer keyboards clattering, fax machines and copy machines whirring and buzzing, voices raised in laughter or anger. Business as usual in the D.A.'s office. Sometimes the turmoil got to him, made him long for just a few rare, blissful moments of peace. Silence.

At those times his stomach would clench and he'd reach automatically for a roll of antacids, to the sympathetic amusement of his more seasoned co-workers, who'd already moved on to the hard stuff—*liquid* antacids, guzzled straight from the bottle. He was only twenty-eight, they told him affectionately. Give it a year or two, and he'd become intimately acquainted with heartburn and ulcer pain.

He could feel the tension mounting as he looked at the pile of paperwork awaiting his attention before he could call it a day. He took a long, deep breath and closed his eyes. Using a standard relaxation technique, he tried to visualize someplace quiet and restful. Oddly enough, he found himself picturing Delia Beckman's apartment.

He'd been inside it for only a short time, but he could still clearly remember her blue, white and rose decor. The glossy woods, soft watercolor prints, plump, inviting pillows and thick rose-colored carpeting. The neat, but overflowing bookshelves had begged to be explored and enjoyed. Like the woman, herself, he couldn't help thinking.

He wasted another few minutes trying to analyze exactly what about her appealed so greatly to him. Maybe it was the way she looked. Heart-shaped face, widely spaced hazel eyes, nicely curved mouth. Not beautiful, exactly. Pretty.

Maybe it was the way she moved, with a quiet poise and dignity that made her stand out in a time when everyone always seemed to be in such a rush. Even though Delia Beckman—nice to finally know her name—usually seemed to speed up a bit when she'd caught him watching her, she'd always maintained her composure. He'd found an odd pleasure in just watching her walk away from him, her slender figure swaying gently, her steps graceful, unhurried. He found her fascinating.

Had he been the type to believe in auras, he would have said Delia Beckman's was the same soft blue she used in her decorating. Calm, peaceful, soothing. A very refreshing change from the tense, combative, hectic pace of his workplace.

He really would like to get to know her better. His one uncharacteristically awkward attempt at a dinner invitation hadn't gotten him far—but he should have known she would have plans on her birthday. Was she involved with someone else? If so, wouldn't she have said so when he'd hinted that he would be asking her again?

The muted "whump" of something landing on his desk brought his eyes open. One of the other young attorneys in the office, Cathy Haley, stood on the other side of the overladen desk, studying him with a quizzical smile. "Praying ain't going to put the bad guys behind bars, Conley," she teased in her Georgia drawl. "Much as we might wish it would."

He shook his head and reached resignedly for the fat, new file she'd tossed in front of him. He glanced at the rap sheet on top of the stack of paperwork and shuddered dramatically. "Praying can't hurt."

"Yeah, well, neither can a hell of a prosecution," Cathy replied prosaically. "Boss wants to talk to you about this one as soon as you've finished looking over the file."

Lane glanced at the stack of other files still awaiting his attention. "I'll get right to it," he murmured, pushing Delia Beckman out of his mind. For now, anyway, he thought, knowing he would think of her again before the day ended.

Delia stopped by the neighborhood supermarket on her way home from work Monday evening. She selected an assortment of healthy foods in servings-for-one packages, lingering for a long time at the bakery section before resolutely walking away from a Black Forest cake that looked like a big, thickly frosted chunk of sin. The cake was big enough to serve at least eight people. Unfortunately, if she bought it, she'd eat every bite herself, to her certain regret.

Her attention was captured in the cereal aisle by a chubby toddler in a shopping cart. He gave her a friendly, slobbery grin as his mother stood nearby, studying the dizzying variety of cereal boxes stretched out for yards in front of her. Delia couldn't help returning the tot's grin. "Hello," she said to him, pausing for a moment on her way past.

"Hi," the child promptly answered. Then said it again. "Hi!"

His mother glanced over her shoulder, gave Delia a quick once-over, then smiled. "He's the shy type," she said wryly.

"He's adorable," Delia replied, to the mother's obvious pleasure. Delia itched to stroke one soft, chubby little cheek. She resisted, because she knew how mothers felt about strangers and their children, but there was an oddly hollow feeling inside her as she continued with her shopping. She loved babies. She wished she could spend more time with her nephew, Johnny. And she hoped very much that she would someday have one or more of her own. Unfortunately, her immediate prospects didn't look particularly encouraging.

Her attention wandering, she rounded a corner and nearly collided with another cart. Jerking to a halt, she started to apologize, then nearly choked on her words when she recognized the other shopper. "Oh," she said. "Hello." *Very original, Delia. He's going to think that's all you know to say when you run into him.*

Lane Conley looked surprised to see her—and then pleased. He was wearing a suit, this time. A nicely cut, though off-the-rack, jacket and slacks in a dark blue that complemented his brighter blue eyes and dark hair. His shirt was white, wrinkled around the collar as though he'd tugged at it during the day. His tie was a muted geometric one, also slightly crumpled, the knot slipped down far enough to allow him to unfasten the top button of his shirt. He looked a bit worn, rather tired and slightly disheveled. He was still the best-looking man Delia had ever known.

"We meet again," he said, his voice slightly gravelly, as though he'd overused it that day.

Delia nodded. "We do live in the same neighborhood, and the same building," she pointed out. Surely he didn't think she was following him or anything like that!

"To my great fortune," he replied with mock gravity.

Flirting? She blinked, not quite sure how to respond. She'd never been particularly adept at flirtation, even when she'd gotten the nerve to try a few times.

She made a quick, surreptitious survey of his intended purchases. Typical bachelor fare—two large boxes of presweetened cereal, a pound of coffee, lunch meats and bread, a squeeze bottle of mustard, a couple of packages of frozen vegetables. And—darn it—one of the lovely Black Forest cakes Delia had so nobly resisted.

"I see you were out of dinner supplies, too," Lane commented, nodding toward her more nutritious selections.

"Yes. My cupboards were beginning to resemble Mother Hubbard's," she admitted.

"Her dog would probably turn up its nose at my cooking," Lane said with a chuckle. "But I grill a mean steak on my Jenn-Air. How about if I pick up a couple and we can share them this evening?"

Taken by surprise, Delia stalled. "I—um—"

"I've already gotten dessert," he added, patting the plastic cover that protected the cake.

She resisted an impulse to lick her lips. Definitely unfair, she thought. He couldn't possibly know how much she adored Black Forest cake. "I'll bring the salad," she heard herself saying.

Lane's smile kicked up a few kilowatts in voltage. "Great," he enthused. "I really wasn't looking forward to eating a cold sandwich by myself this evening."

She wasn't sure what she'd gotten herself into, but she figured it couldn't hurt to share a casual dinner with a neighbor. That was probably all he had in mind. If not, well, she'd handle that if and when it became necessary. "I'll see you at, um, seven-thirty?" she suggested, giving herself an hour to get home, put away her groceries, and change into something more comfortable than the gray-and-white-checked suit she'd worn to work.

"Sounds good. See you then." Lane turned his cart toward the meat counter, waving a farewell over his shoulder.

Delia tightened her hands on the cart handle, not at all surprised to find that they weren't quite steady. And then she headed rapidly toward the checkout stands. Before she lost her nerve and chased him down to tell him she'd changed her mind.

Lane's apartment was laid out exactly like Delia's. A large living room from which opened a short hallway leading to the bedroom and bath, a serviceable, U-shaped kitchen separated from the main room by an open, pass-through bar. Like hers, his one wall of built-in bookshelves had been put to good use, holding a small portable television, a stereo system and enough books to please even Delia. Well-read books, not the strictly-for-show leather-bound hardbacks some people considered impressive as a decorating feature.

Other than the crowded bookshelves and identical floor plans, their apartments couldn't have been more different. Delia had spent a great deal of time decorating her place, carefully choosing the accoutrements and furnishings. She'd been confined by a strict budget, but had always been secretly proud of the pulled-together results.

Lane's apartment looked as though it had been furnished with hand-me-down and secondhand store items, none of the same vintage. A brown-plaid couch, an oversize Boston rocker and a burgundy leather recliner made up the seating area. The tables were mismatched—oak end tables, a round mahogany coffee table—as were the two lamps, one of which was brass, the other porcelain. The walls were covered with framed posters, colorful, eclectic, attention claiming. A clutter of magazines, newspapers and scribbled-on legal pads covered most flat surfaces in the room. Spotting the toe of a dark sock sticking out from under the couch, Delia fought a smile as she pictured him hastily shoving things out of sight in preparation for her visit.

Lane, who'd changed into jeans and a short-sleeved gray sweatshirt, pushed a hand through his hair and motioned around him. "Um—I haven't had a chance to do much with the place," he admitted. "I've only been here a few months, and I don't have a lot of free time for furniture shopping."

"It looks very nice," she assured him, and discovered that she was telling the truth. True, his apartment was a decorator's nightmare, but it looked warm and welcoming and comfortable. A place where he could come home from work, kick back and relax. Probably all he required for now.

"Here, let me take that," Lane said, reaching for the large bowl of salad she held between her hands. "I was just about to put the steaks on. How do you like yours cooked?"

"Medium-well," she replied, then waited for the usual shudder of disapproval. For some reason she'd yet to fathom, most men tended to frown on anyone who didn't like their steaks served rare enough to get off the plate and make a run for it.

Lane surprised her by nodding and saying, "Yeah, so do I. I'll get them started." He turned toward the kitchen.

"Is there anything I can do to help?"

"You've already made the salad. That's help enough. How about something to drink while the steaks cook? Wine, cola, juice, mineral water? Beer?"

"Mineral water sounds good."

"Coming right up." He flipped the steaks onto the already heated grill, then opened the refrigerator.

Delia hung back, not wanting to get in his way, but reluctant to sit in the living room alone while he cooked. The eat-in kitchen was neat, clean, the round oak table already set for two. The dishes were inexpensive brown stoneware, the place mats plastic, but he'd set a small bouquet of fresh flowers in the center of the table. Delia suspected he'd purchased them in the floral department of the supermarket, and she was rather touched by the gesture.

He served her water over ice, with a twist of lemon. The glass sported colorful drawings of Fred Flintstone and Dino.

Seeming comfortable in his role as host, Lane kept the conversation going while he prepared the steaks. "How long have you lived here?" he asked. "In this building, I mean."

"Almost three years." Funny how fast the time had flown by since she'd moved from her first post-college apartment that she'd shared with two other recent graduates.

"Do you work close by?"

"Not far." She named the insurance company, and gave him a brief job description, then asked, "What do you do?"

"I'm an attorney. D.A.'s office," he added. "I've only been there six months. I spent four years in the navy after college, before entering law school."

She never would have pegged him as ex-military. But then, she really knew nothing about him. "Do you like your work?" she asked, gamely working to keep up her end of the conversation.

"Most of the time. It can be frustrating, but it has its rewards." He chuckled and motioned around him at the sparsely furnished kitchen. "Obviously, great wealth isn't one of them."

"Have you considered going into private practice?"

"Personal-injury stuff? Criminal defense? No. I've always intended to go into prosecution."

"The big money's in personal injury, isn't it?"

He shrugged. "Yeah, I guess it is. That isn't why I chose law."

"Why did you?"

He kept his eyes on the steaks. "I want to make a difference," he muttered. "I want to know that I did something to make the world safer. Better."

"You're an idealist."

To her surprise, he flushed. Then shrugged again. "I've been called that."

She found it touching that he was embarrassed.

Lane quickly changed the subject.

Delia was beginning to suspect that Lane Conley was a great deal more complex than she'd expected. So much for judging people on outward appearance, she lectured herself sternly.

She, of all people, should have known better.

Chapter Four

Lane enjoyed his simple steak and salad more than he'd enjoyed any meal in a long time. Maybe it was because he'd spent such a hectic day that there hadn't even been time for lunch. Maybe it felt so good because he was able to relax in the comfort of his own home, in his most comfortable clothes, without the bother of eating in a restaurant. Maybe it was just a pleasant change from cold cuts or TV dinners.

More likely his pleasure was entirely due to his dinner companion.

He was really starting to like Delia Beckman. As attractive as she was, she seemed wholly unconscious of her appearance, showing not the least bit of vanity or concern with her casual, yet still flattering, clothing. She didn't rush to freshen her lipstick after eating, and she ate with a delicate enthusiasm, making no attempt to pretend she wasn't interested in food. Particularly Black Forest cake, which she cut into with a sensual pleasure that he couldn't help but respond to.

She wasn't one to talk much, though she easily carried her side of the dinner conversation. She spoke slowly, clearly, taking time to organize her thoughts before verbalizing them. Her diction was so flawless that Lane found himself thinking of her as an Americanized Julie Andrews. He liked that.

He liked the signs of intelligence in her wide-set hazel eyes. The way the overhead lights gleamed in her glossy hair. The little habit she had of moistening her lower lip before she began to speak. The dimple at the right corner of her mouth. The tiny mole just above her left cheekbone.

Delia Beckman was seriously interesting.

"I'm glad I ran into you at the supermarket," he said as they finished clearing away the dishes. "This has been nice."

Delia returned his smile, and he was pleased to see that she was beginning to do so more easily. "It has been nice," she agreed.

"I have some of those flavored instant coffees in the cupboard. My mom loves them, so I keep several on hand for her visits. Or I could make a fresh pot of regular coffee."

"Instant's fine," Delia said. "I like the flavored brands, too."

He opened the cupboard and read the labels aloud. "French vanilla, mocha almond, amaretto?"

"French vanilla. My favorite," she admitted.

He filled a kettle with water and set it on a burner. "This will just take a few minutes," he promised.

"No hurry," she assured him.

He immediately decided that he liked that best. The restfulness about her. He could hardly imagine her rushing around in a frenzy, or pressuring him to hurry, hurry, hurry.

"Why don't you have a seat in the living room. Make yourself comfortable," he urged. "I'll bring this in as soon as it's ready. Would you like anything to eat to go with it?"

She laughed. "You must be joking. I couldn't eat another bite."

"Right," he said rather sheepishly. "Me, either."

He'd left the paperback mystery novel he'd purchased during the weekend lying open on one oak end table. Delia was looking at it when he joined her with the coffee. "Is it good?" she asked, setting it aside, careful not to lose his place.

"It's not bad. I think I've already figured out 'who done it,' though."

"That's the fun part of reading mysteries, isn't it? Trying to race through the clues and then feeling very smug and superior when you solve the mystery before the characters."

"Yeah. But not too soon," he said, sitting a proper distance away from her on the couch, despite his temptation to scoot a bit closer. "A really good mystery keeps me guessing through most of the book."

She nodded and they spent a few minutes sipping their coffee, discussing favorite authors, finding that they shared several favorite books. Lane mentioned a particularly funny scene from one of the books they'd both read, and they laughed together as they reminisced. She seemed quite comfortable with him now. The observation gave him the nerve to take a slight risk.

He picked up a package from the top of one crowded bookshelf. "I—um—got you a birthday present," he said, handing her the bag bearing the neighborhood bookstore's logo. "I didn't have any wrapping paper."

Delia stared at the package for a moment, then looked up at him. He couldn't read her expression, except to note that she was startled. He sat on the edge of the couch, trying to look relaxed even as he worried about her reaction. Had he moved too fast? Presumed too much? Had he just totally blown everything?

"I don't know what to say," she murmured, looking back down at the bag in her lap. "This is . . . unexpected."

"I know. It's not all that much, really," he said, deliberately downplaying the gift. "Just a little something to mark the reason we finally had a chance to meet—your birthday." When she continued to stare at the package as though waiting for it to do something, he cleared his throat and urged, "Go ahead. Open it."

Very slowly, she opened the bag and pulled out the hardcover novel he'd found her examining on Saturday. Her eyes widened. "Oh. This is—" Her voice trailed off.

"I saw you looking at it Saturday," he confessed when the pause threatened to grow awkward. "I thought you might like it."

"Thank you, but you really sh-shouldn't have," she said, and for the first time since they'd met, Lane thought she looked flustered.

He'd noticed the slight stammer, attributed it to her surprise. But he also noticed that she didn't look entirely displeased with him. Thank God, he thought, beginning to relax. He kept his smile casual, his pose relaxed. "You're welcome," he said simply.

She moistened her lips. He was growing increasingly aware of a desire to taste those lips for himself, but cautioned himself that he didn't want to frighten her away by moving too quickly. He'd have to be content with the progress he'd made thus far. If nothing else, they'd gotten a nice start on a friendship.

Delia still couldn't believe Lane had bought her a birthday present. She'd managed to interpret his dinner invitation as a spur-of-the-moment thing, one neighbor getting to know another, a nice alternative to eating alone. But a gift—especially one so obviously intended to please her—made her wonder what, exactly, Lane Conley had in mind.

Several hours after she and Lane had parted politely at his door, she paced her apartment, her gaze straying often to the hardback book lying on her coffee table. Though she wasn't a vain woman, Delia was experienced enough to know when a man was attracted to her. There was definitely an attraction between her and Lane—but she wasn't at all sure where she wanted it to lead. He seemed very nice, more so than she'd expected, actually. They had a surprising number of things in common.

He puzzled her in several ways. She'd seen him with several attractive women, and yet, he'd seemed rather at loose ends when she'd run into him lately. He didn't behave like a man who took women's attentions for granted; there were times when he even seemed a bit shy, uncertain. And, yet, he had to know how good-looking he was. The man had mirrors in his apartment.

She'd been surprisingly comfortable with him during the evening. Only once had she been betrayed by a stammer, and that after he'd startled her with the book. The hated stutter reappeared these days only when she was under stress, extremely tired—or caught by surprise. He hadn't seemed to notice. It wasn't that she was ashamed of her youthful affliction, but she didn't particularly like to talk about it. And she tended to avoid situations that caused her stress or extreme self-consciousness.

Delia was happy with her life now. She had a good job, good friends, a nice home and the self-esteem she'd worked so many years to build. She still wanted a family, longed for the happiness her sister and several of her friends had found, but when she thought of the type of man with whom she could find that future, she pictured someone like Wayne. Never mind that Wayne hadn't excited her, and that Lane made her pulse race. A racing pulse was not one of her top criteria for a lifelong relationship. Security, dependability, reliability, similar goals and values—all were more important to her than metabolism.

But it really had been sweet of Lane to buy her the book.

* * *

He called her at work the next day, late in the afternoon. "Are you free to talk?" he asked.

"Yes, briefly," she replied, wishing her pulse would settle back to normal. Who'd have thought that even the sound of Lane's voice could do this to her?

"Yeah, I'm pretty well snowed under, myself. I was taking a quick break and I thought about you, and I wanted to let you know that I really enjoyed last night."

"So did I," she admitted.

"So, could we do it again? Maybe go out someplace next time? Friday?"

Delia half expected Wayne to ask her out again for Friday. She'd been trying to decide what to do if he should. But he hadn't asked, yet, if he planned to do so, and she was free for Friday. Given a choice, she knew which of the two men she'd rather spend the evening with, caution notwithstanding. "All right," she said on a sudden rash impulse. "That sounds nice. Thank you."

"You will?" Lane sounded pleased—and maybe just a bit surprised at the ease with which she'd accepted.

"Yes. What time?"

"Eight?"

"Sounds good. Shall I meet you downstairs?"

"Of course not. I'll come up to your place. See you then."

"Fine."

"Delia?"

Her name sounded different when Lane said it. She didn't stop just then to analyze it. "Yes?"

"I'm really looking forward to it."

"So am I," she replied—and it was mostly true. Anticipation did seem to be outweighing apprehension at the moment.

"I guess I'd better let you get back to work."

She bade him a polite goodbye, carefully cradled the receiver, then buried her face in her hands and groaned. She couldn't help wondering what, exactly, she was getting into.

Lane was smiling broadly when he hung up his own phone. He laced his fingers behind his head and leaned back in his chair, ignoring the paperwork for a few more precious moments.

Delia was going out with him. On a real date this time.

He hadn't blown it, after all.

"Hey, Conley. You going to sit there all afternoon grinning at the ceiling, or are you going to get your butt down to the briefing room for the meeting?" the gruff voice of one of his associates demanded from the hallway.

Lane sighed, dropped his hands and shoved himself out of his chair. "I'm on my way," he said. But the smile lingered as he scooped up his pen and legal pad and headed down the hallway.

Chapter Five

"Delia, when are you going to tell us about this new man in your life?" Sherry Cooper demanded during coffee break one Monday morning. "Everyone knows you're seeing someone—and everyone knows it isn't Wayne Heslip. So...who is he?"

Delia lifted an eyebrow and lowered her foam coffee cup to the plastic tabletop. "What makes you think I'm seeing anyone in particular?" she asked, rather amused by the gleam of curiosity in Sherry's dark eyes.

Sherry lifted one hand and began to count off the clues on red-tipped fingers. "Wayne says you've politely turned him down twice for dinner. Nicki saw you at La Château with someone tall, dark and gorgeous. Molly swears it was you she saw with a to-die-for guy at the symphony performance last weekend. But the most conclusive evidence," she concluded dramatically, "is the sparkle you've had in your eyes for the past month or so."

Delia flushed a bit, but laughed and shook her head. "You're impossible," she accused, her gaze drifting around the group of six sheepishly nosy friends. "All of you."

"So," Sherry prodded, leaning forward with an infectious grin. "Are you going to tell us about him or not?"

"Is this your idea of getting a life?" Delia demanded good-naturedly. "Snooping into mine?"

Sherry drummed her fingers impatiently on the table. "Didn't I just tell you about the bozo I went out with because my mother begged me to? Didn't Arlene tell us about the new guy she met at the newsstand last week? Hasn't Cathy been keeping us up-to-date on her relationship with Greg? Fair's fair, Beckman. It's your turn to come clean."

Delia gave a dramatic sigh, in keeping with the teasing, but privately she wondered just how much, if anything, she should tell her friends about Lane. Everything was still so tentative. She'd been trying so hard to be cautious, to keep a level head about him, not to get carried away to the extent that she would be hurt if it didn't work out.

It had been three weeks since that impromptu steak dinner in his apartment. During those weeks, they'd been out six times. To dinner, to an art gallery opening, to a movie and to the symphony performance at which she'd apparently been spotted by a co-worker. During those outings, Lane had been charming, attentive, amusing. The perfect date. He'd picked her up and walked her to her door each time, which wasn't really necessary, since they lived in the same building, but he'd insisted and she'd found herself flattered by his attentions.

Maybe it was his old-fashioned courtesy that made Delia think in old-fashioned terms when she tried to mentally define their budding relationship. She felt almost as though she were being courted. Properly, politely... determinedly.

It wasn't as though Lane had said anything to make her think he was considering a long-term relationship. He hadn't even kissed her, yet, though he seemed to enjoy touching her—placing a hand at her waist, brushing a strand of hair away from her cheek, holding her hand as they'd crossed a busy street. Every time he touched her, her heart rate went into overdrive. She could only imagine how she would react when he finally got around to kissing her. Not *if,* she noted, but *when.* His desire to do so had been increasingly apparent in his eyes when they'd parted at her door. She suspected that he was only waiting for a sign from her that she was ready.

It was nice to be treated with such rare respect, but Delia was beginning to grow impatient, herself. She wanted very much to know what it would be like to be held in Lane's arms, to feel his mouth on hers. She looked forward to the experience almost as much as she feared it. Something told her that, once they'd crossed that invisible line, neither she nor their so-far-unthreatening relationship would ever be quite the same.

"Earth to Delia. We're still here, you know." Sherry's voice was rich with affectionate amusement.

Delia's flush deepened as the others laughed. "Yes, I know you're still here," she said. "And you aren't going to let this go until I come clean, are you?"

All six of her companions cheerfully shook their heads.

Delia groaned, then sighed in resignation. "All right, I'll tell you. His name is Vinnie. He's gorgeous and sexy and rich."

Six pairs of eyes widened. Six chairs shifted closer to Delia's end of the table.

Keeping her face straight, Delia continued. "He's married and he has six children, but his wife doesn't understand him. He hasn't told me exactly what he does for a living, but I think it has something to do with organized crime. He said something about making offers that no one is brave enough to ref—"

Six crumpled napkins pelted her from all directions amid a chorus of reproval.

Delia laughed and fended off the barrage with one hand.

"Honestly, Delia," Sherry said with a frown. "If you want us to butt out, just say so."

Delia smiled in apology for impulsively stringing them along. "Sorry. I couldn't resist. The truth is, his name is Lane, he's an attorney in the D.A.'s office, he lives downstairs from my apartment and he's very nice. But that's really all there is to it at this point. I've only been out with him a few times."

"How many times?" Cathy asked, wanting all the juicy details.

"Six," Delia replied. "Well, seven, I guess," she corrected, thinking of that steak dinner. Did that count as a date? She supposed it did. It had certainly led to everything else.

"I'd call that more than a 'few times,'" Nicki commented with a touch of envy. "That's longer than some of my entire relationships lasted."

"Lane and I are just friends," Delia insisted, toying nervously with her coffee cup.

Six knowing looks were exchanged around the table.

Delia sighed again, fully aware that the privacy she'd so enjoyed during the past three weeks had just been lost for good. And that changed things, too. Lane was starting to encroach on her real life. Which made it even harder to guard against getting too deeply involved with him.

* * *

They had dinner again that evening, at a quiet restaurant not far from their building. As always, Lane walked Delia to her door afterward. Since it was fairly early, Delia asked, "Would you like to come in for coffee? Or I have some ice cream, if you'd like, since we skipped dessert."

"Ice cream sounds good," Lane agreed immediately, then smiled. "But you should know by now that ice cream always sounds good to me."

She did, actually. She'd bought the brand and flavor he'd named as his favorites. Funny, the number of little things she was coming to know about him in such a short time. She knew that he was the only son of Neal Conley, a Portland, Oregon, dentist, and Betha Conley, a schoolteacher with a passion for genealogy. That he had two older sisters, both of whom were married and had children. That he had once thought of becoming a school administrator before he'd decided on a law career. That he'd mostly enjoyed his stint in the navy, but had been ready to get back to civilian life.

She knew that he'd once been a Boy Scout and that he loved fudge-ripple ice cream. That he was an odd mixture of idealist and political conservative, hard-line on crime, softhearted when it came to kids. She knew his religion, his educational background and that he was beginning to suspect he needed reading glasses.

She didn't have a clue how he felt about her.

Attraction, yes. Enjoyment of her company, yes. Plans for the future? She had no idea.

Not that they'd known each other long enough to be making any plans, she assured herself hastily as she scooped ice cream into two soda-fountain-style tulip dishes. But he'd spent so much time with her during the past few weeks, didn't appear to be dating anyone else, seemed to take it for granted that they would be spending more time together. And, yet, he hadn't even kissed her. What did that mean?

"Here you are," she said cheerily, joining him in the living room. He reached eagerly for his ice-cream dish, motioning for her to sit beside him on the couch.

"Fudge ripple," he said with a smile. "My favorite."

She returned the smile, and then hastily turned her attention to her dessert.

The ice cream had been eaten, the dishes put away and the evening news was wrapping up on the TV when Lane finally glanced at his watch and made a regretful murmur. "It's getting late," he said. "I'd better head downstairs."

Reluctant as she was to see him leave—it had been such a pleasant, peaceful evening—Delia didn't argue. It *was* getting late, and they had to work the next day.

Still seated beside her on the couch, he turned to face her. "I've been invited to a cocktail party Friday evening. It's a fund-raiser for a new substance-abuse program for teenagers. Senator and Mrs. McCain are the hosts. Will you go with me?"

Delia instantly tensed. Thus far, her dates with Lane had been quite private—just the two of them, even when they had been in public. A cocktail party would be different. He'd have friends there, business associates. She would be introduced, appraised, probably the subject of speculation. She knew how gossip went—look at the way her own friends had been talking about her and Lane! "I don't know, Lane. Cocktail parties aren't really my thing," she demurred.

He made a sympathetic face. "I know," he agreed. "They can be incredibly boring. But I'm sort of committed to this one. My boss has made it clear that he expects to see me there."

Again, he seemed to take for granted that his plans should include her. She moistened her lips. "I—um—"

Lane took her hand. "I'd really like for you to go with me," he said quietly. "I'd like to introduce you to some of my friends."

She searched his face. "Why?" she asked simply.

"Because," he murmured, his face very close to hers. "You have become very special to me. And I'm getting impatient to show you off."

"Sh-show me off?" she repeated, and then winced at the betraying stammer. Talk about being under stress.

"Maybe I shouldn't have worded it quite that way," he admitted. "But I really would like for you to go with me. Will you?"

She truly dreaded it. She'd always hated glitzy society affairs. She didn't know what to wear, what to say. She'd spent several years assiduously avoiding situations that made her uncomfortable. And, yet...Lane had said she was special to him. "If it's that important to you, I'll go," she said.

His eyes gleamed with pleasure. He closed the few inches between them and kissed her for the first time.

Delia had been right. Now that Lane Conley had kissed her, she would never be the same. Would never again be content with safe, gentle, *ordinary* kisses. Lane's kiss fit none of those descriptions.

The kiss was explosive. Hungry. Shattering. By the time it finally ended—and Delia couldn't have said whether it lasted minutes or hours—both of them were trembling, breathless. Lane pulled back slowly. Delia could only stare at him.

His eyes burned a brighter blue than usual, a warm flush darkened his evening-roughened cheeks. He attempted a smile, but the somewhat crooked result held little resemblance to his usual high-voltage grin. "I—um...*wow*," he said finally, shakily.

She could think of absolutely nothing to say in response.

With unsteady fingers, he brushed a strand of hair away from her kiss-moist lips. "That's why I haven't kissed you before," he admitted. "I knew it would be like that between us. And I didn't want to scare you off."

"You haven't sc-scared me off," she murmured.

His eyes narrowed, and he studied her with his head cocked. "It happens when you're startled, doesn't it?"

"What?" she asked warily, though she thought she knew.

"You stutter—just a little. Have you always?"

She looked down at her tangled, white-knuckled hands. "Yes," she said, speaking slowly, carefully. "It used to be much worse. I st-stuttered very badly as a child. It was . . . difficult for me."

"I'm sorry. I didn't know."

"I don't like to talk about it," she replied, gaining slight confidence in her speech as her pulse rate slowly settled.

"I want to know everything about you," he assured her. "The problems you had as a child are part of what has made you the way you are now. And, in case you haven't noticed, I like the way you are now. Very much."

She bit her lower lip.

"Delia." Lane reached out to touch her chin, lifting her face to his. "You have a lovely voice. It has taken me this long to even notice the slight stammer, and only because I've been paying such very close attention to everything about you. Don't be embarrassed."

"I'm not embarrassed," she said, then had to correct herself. "Well, maybe a little. I was teased so badly when I was growing up that I'm still rather sensitive." She was pleased that she managed the sentence clearly, flawlessly.

"Surely you don't think I'd tease you."

"No, of course not."

"Is that why you don't want to go to the cocktail party? Because you'll be self-conscious?"

Delia didn't like the implication that she never left her apartment. "I know how to socialize, Lane," she assured him. "I've attended fancy parties before. It's just not something I particularly enjoy."

He nodded to concede her point. "Then how about if we make an appearance just so the boss will know I was there, and then cut out early and go out for a late dinner?" he suggested. "Would that be okay with you?"

She twisted her fingers more tightly in her lap. "Lane—isn't there someone else you'd like to take? Someone who wouldn't mind staying for the whole evening? Someone who—"

He hushed her with a brief, tender kiss. "There is no one else," he murmured firmly. "Not since I delivered a package to a beautiful neighbor a month ago."

Her heart tripped. He said those things so easily. Could he possibly mean them? Was she a fool to want so badly to start believing? "All right," she said. "We'll go to your party. And we'll impress the socks off your boss."

He laughed and kissed her one last, lingering time before rising from the couch. "If I don't go now, I won't want to leave at all."

She didn't ask him to stay any longer. He didn't seem disappointed.

Somehow she knew it wouldn't have taken much to convince him.

Chapter Six

The cocktail party was very much as Delia had expected it to be. Glittering. Shallow. Why couldn't people just ask for donations for their pet projects instead of using the charities for an excuse to don fifteen-hundred-dollar dresses and have their photos taken for the society pages? Clad in her own considerably-less-than-fifteen-hundred-dollar black cocktail dress, Delia supposed she fit in well enough. She'd smiled, she'd mingled, she hadn't stuttered. It was just that she did not consider this a good time.

"I know," Lane murmured, slipping an arm around her waist an hour into the event. "I'm ready to get out of here, too. We'll cut out as soon as we can, okay?"

Delia smiled ruefully. "If I look that bored, then I should apologize for my bad manners."

"You don't owe anyone an apology," he assured her. "You've been great tonight. I can tell my friends are all quite taken with you. The only reason I suspect you're bored is because I am—thoroughly."

An older man with a receding hairline and protruding waistline appeared from somewhere and slapped Lane heartily on the shoulder. "How you doing, Conley?"

Lane managed a smile. He introduced Delia to the state district attorney. Delia murmured a polite greeting.

"Better get used to this sort of thing," the older man informed Lane with a grimace. "It's all part of the routine when you get into the political arena. God knows I end up at enough of these dos."

He didn't linger long enough for Lane to answer, his attention already caught by someone across the crowded hotel ballroom.

A bit impressed that the well-known political figure had recognized Lane, Delia asked, "What did he mean, you should get used to this sort of thing? I didn't realize being with the D.A.'s office was considered part of the 'political arena.'"

Lane cleared his throat and looked a bit uncomfortable. "That wasn't exactly what he meant."

"What did he mean?" she asked, narrowing her eyes as she noted his sheepish expression.

"Some people—the attorney general among them—have been trying to persuade me to go into politics," he explained, keeping his tone light. "They say there's a growing need for young conservatives with a strong stand on law and order. They seem to believe I fit that description."

"Politics," Delia repeated hollowly, her mind filling with images in connection with the word. Intense public scrutiny. Life in a fishbowl. Unscrupulous opponents. An endless procession of glittering, shallow events just like this one, filled with glittering, shallow people who were just as likely to stab backs as empty pocketbooks. The intrusive obsession of admirers, the vicious rumor-mongering of detractors. Even knowing that she was exaggerating—at least a little—she shuddered.

Lane didn't miss her reaction. "I didn't say I was going to do it," he reminded her quickly. "It's just something that has been discussed."

Delia suddenly discovered that she didn't want to talk about this. Didn't even want to think about it. Flashing him a bright, fake smile, she pressed a hand to her stomach. "I'm getting hungry," she said, deliberately changing the subject. "Are you?"

"Starving," he confessed, following her lead, though his eyes were still uncomfortably watchful. "Let's get out of here and go find some real food instead of these wussy little canapés."

"Sounds good to me." She slipped a hand through his arm and allowed him to hustle her through the crowded room, adroitly avoiding potential conversational delays.

There was no further mention of politics that evening. In fact, they both deliberately avoided mentioning it as they chatted over dinner.

It was quite late when Lane walked Delia to her apartment. He waited until she'd unlocked the door before pulling her into his arms. He kissed her slowly, thoroughly, and Delia discovered that this kiss was every bit as exciting and arousing as their first had been.

"I was so proud to be with you tonight," Lane murmured when he raised his head just far enough to speak. "Thank you for going with me."

Lane had been proud of her? Definitely flattering. He kissed her again before she could think of anything to say. And then again, until her heart was racing, her breath ragged, her body heavy with a dull ache of desire.

Lane was breathing rapidly when he finally pulled away. His smile was decidedly crooked. "I'd better go," he murmured, his voice husky. "While I still can."

It took quite an effort for her to release his jacket. She hadn't realized until then that her fingers had clenched so tightly in his lapels, almost as though she'd been afraid he'd slip away during their kisses. She was so tempted to ask him in—for coffee, conversation, any excuse to keep him with her a little longer. But she knew there was a chance he wouldn't be leaving at all should he come in now. And that was a step she wasn't quite ready for.

She was still taking this relationship with Lane very slowly. Very carefully. No matter how badly she might want to throw caution to the wind and throw herself wholeheartedly into the fire.

Delia discovered during the next month that it was becoming increasingly more difficult to think cautiously or logically where Lane was concerned. She saw him often, nearly every day now. Her friends at work had stopped teasing her about him and had started matter-of-factly referring to her and Lane as an established couple, no matter how often Delia reminded them that she and Lane were still "just friends." It was quite obvious that not a one of them believed her.

They still hadn't gotten around to meeting families. Delia had cautiously mentioned Lane to her sister, but downplayed the seriousness of her growing feelings. She wasn't quite sure why. Lane seemed eager for Delia to meet his parents and sisters, but Delia put him off. She wasn't quite ready, she said, and he reluctantly refrained from pushing her. She was glad he didn't ask what she was waiting for. She couldn't have told him.

Their courtship, as she continued to think of it in weak moments, was still very proper, very discreet.

Lane kissed her often, but they had yet to go beyond long, heated kisses and carefully restrained caresses. Delia still wasn't quite sure why Lane held back—and there were plenty of times when she wished he wouldn't be quite so noble—but deep inside, she was relieved.

When it came right down to it, she was no more ready to make love with Lane than she was to meet his parents, and she didn't know how to explain her reticence about either. Perhaps he sensed her confusion. He didn't ask about it, but she caught him watching her often with an expression she couldn't quite read.

He wanted her. He'd made that clear, in his own gentle way. But he'd made it just as clear that he would wait until she was ready. She didn't know how long his patience would last. No matter how much she tried to convince herself that she still hadn't completely lost her heart to him, she couldn't even bear to think of ending their relationship. Which meant that all her caution had probably been in vain from the beginning.

They'd been dating for nearly two months when Lane had to go out of town for several days on a business trip. A fact-finding mission, he called it when she asked. "I'll miss you," he said, holding her in his arms as he prepared to leave.

"I'll miss you, too," she admitted, and was dismayed by how true her words were. She was going to miss him terribly.

"Aren't you worried that he'll run around on you while he's gone?" one of her friends, who'd recently broken up with a habitually unfaithful lover, asked her at work the next day. "After all, a man who looks like that, alone for several days in a big city... well, you know what usually happens."

"Not with this man," Delia replied. If there was one thing she'd learned about Lane Conley during the past weeks, it was that he wasn't the sort of man who was interested in fleeting pleasures or irresponsible behavior.

"You really think he's going to be faithful to you?" her friend asked skeptically—and with a touch of envy.

"Yes," Delia replied confidently. "I do."

So much for trying to pretend, even to herself, that she and Lane were only friends. It was time, she decided during one long, lonely evening without him, that she admitted how much a part of her life Lane had become.

How much he'd come to mean to her. The shiver of fear that went through her was almost overpowered by the wave of relief that accompanied her long-overdue admission. Almost.

* * *

Delia welcomed Lane back with a smile and opened arms. He responded with an embrace that nearly compressed her rib cage and depleted all her oxygen reserves. She never even considered complaining.

"I've missed you," he said, kicking her apartment door closed behind him.

"I've missed you, too," she whispered, lifting her face to his again.

He groaned and pulled her even closer. "Delia." And then he kissed her again.

Delia hadn't consciously come to any decisions during the week that he'd been gone. She hadn't made any specific plans for his return. She hadn't come to terms with her feelings about him, her hopes or fears about their future. But when he lifted his head and looked at her with such raw, unmistakable hunger in his beautiful eyes, it seemed completely natural to step back, offer him her hand, and lead him toward her bedroom.

Lane followed slowly at first—as though he wasn't quite sure what she was offering—and then his steps quickened as her meaning became clear. The smiles they shared spoke more than any words could have conveyed.

They didn't bother with the lights. Enough illumination spilled through the open doorway for them to see their way to the bed. The room was quiet, dim. Utterly private. Delia would not have chosen any different setting in which to take this momentous step with Lane. She turned to him with a dizzying combination of fear, excitement, eagerness and shyness. Softened by shadows, his expression revealed almost as many emotions as she felt.

This wasn't a casual development, for either of them.

There was no reason to hurry, nowhere else either of them would rather be. They lingered. Savored. Took time to explore, to appreciate, to thoroughly enthrall. Delia had never felt more thoroughly seduced, more deliciously seductive.

Patience finally burned away in a flare of passion. Their movements became hurried, hands and mouths avid. Hearts raced, pulses pounded, breathing grew rough, interlaced with low moans and husky murmurs. They cried out together when the flames consumed them, searing away the last remnants of control.

They lay together for a long time afterward, faces close, limbs entwined, hearts drumming in unison. Delia's eyes were closed as she reveled in the feelings, unable to think beyond the moment. Unwilling to even try.

Lane was the first to speak. "I love you," he said, the words only a breath of sound in the darkness. And then he nestled her more closely and fell silent, apparently content.

He didn't seem to expect a reply. At least, not just then. Delia was relieved.

She wasn't at all sure she could speak coherently. The words she wanted so badly to say were locked behind a barrier of old fears and insecurities.

She only hoped Lane's love—and his patience—would outlast her own misgivings.

Chapter Seven

"Delia." Lane's voice was grave, his expression serious, his eyes glinting with determination. "We have to talk."

She'd been dreading the words for days—ever since Lane had returned from his business trip and they'd become lovers. Somehow during those days, she'd managed to avoid a serious discussion of their future, or of her feelings for him, though Lane had made his own quite clear. He loved her, he'd said. He wanted a lifetime with her. He had seemed content to give her time to come to the same decision.

Now it looked like her time was running out.

Hands clenched in her lap, she faced him across the breakfast table in her apartment. It was Saturday morning, and they had just spent a long, blissful night in each other's arms. She regretted that the idyll had to end. "What do you want to talk about, Lane?" she asked, deliberately obtuse.

"About us, obviously," he replied, giving her a look that held a mixture of reproval and sympathy. "We can't keep putting it off, Delia. We have to talk about this."

She swallowed a sigh. "All right," she murmured, then fell silent, waiting for him to take the lead.

Now that the subject had been broached, Lane didn't quite seem to know how to begin. He took a deep breath and toyed with the half-empty coffee cup he held loosely between his hands. "You know I love you?" he said, his tone making it a question.

Delia bit her lip for a moment before answering carefully, "You've said that you do."

"Do you believe me?"

Again she hesitated. "I want to believe you."

"But *do* you?"

She studied his face across the table, searching his eyes for the slightest indication of doubt. She found none. He looked so confident, so sincere—could he really be so sure of his feelings? "I...yes," she said, tentatively. "I think so."

He didn't look particularly reassured by her vacillation. "Believe it," he told her a bit curtly. "It happens to be true."

She bit her lip again, uncertain how to respond. She wanted to tell him she loved him, too. She did, of course. With all her heart. But something held her back.

"It's the political thing holding you back, isn't it?"

Delia wondered how it was that Lane knew what she was thinking even before she did. "That's not all of it," she said. "But," she had to add, "it's a big part of it."

She'd wrestled with this question for so many lonely hours. Even though Lane had told her he hadn't made a decision about going into politics, she knew it was still an option. Something he would be encouraged to pursue. There was just something about Lane, about his enthusiasm, his commitment, his charisma and deeply ingrained beliefs, that made her believe he would someday feel the need to pursue the changes he so passionately believed in.

Lane looked troubled. "I still haven't made any sweeping decisions about a political future," he assured her. "But I'm not sure I completely rule it out at this point. There's a whole network of people out there who want to make a difference, Delia. Young men and women from several political parties who are ready to get involved, ready to fight to change the system."

"And they want you to join them," Delia said quietly.

He shrugged. "Some of them do. You know how I feel about professional 'politicians' whose only commitment is to their own wealth and influence," he added with distaste. "And I know you consider me an idealist, but I'm not, entirely. I know that a perfect society will never exist, that corruption and power will always go hand in hand to an extent. I know how quickly idealists and 'do-gooders' get lost in the ugly reality of power and money and the established bureaucracy. I don't want to sound like one of those wide-eyed innocents who go to Washington with the belief that they can single-handedly change the world, but I believe with every part of me that change *is* possible. That it has to start somewhere."

"I agree with you."

"I don't have to be involved in that part of it," he continued, still watching her closely. "I can stay where I am, make my mark on the world one case at a time. Make my corner of the country a better place because I've helped put away the scum. I can continue to be involved with the early-intervention programs and crime-prevention projects I believe in so strongly. Maybe that's where I belong—in the trenches, rather than the foreground."

"Your decisions have to come from your own heart, Lane," Delia told him bravely.

"You are in my heart," he countered. "The decisions have to come from both of us."

She shook her head. "I would never want to hold you back from anything you want to do. I happen to think you would be a brilliant congressman or senator or governor—or president. Whatever you choose to do, whatever path you choose to follow. But..."

"But?" he urged gently.

"I don't know if I can follow that path with you." She said the words sadly, almost as if they were already standing at that imaginary crossroads.

"Because you stuttered as a child?" He seemed to be struggling to understand.

Delia squirmed uncomfortably in her chair. "Not just that," she argued, though she didn't like to admit—even to herself—how deeply that impediment had affected her confidence.

"I live a quiet life, Lane," she said, forcing her fears into words. "I've kept it that way by choice. I enjoy my privacy. My anonymity. Neither of those is possible in a political life. I've seen what happens to politicians—to their families. You're young, attractive, personable. The press will love you. Every detail of your life and your family life will become fodder for the tabloids. You know I want a family, and I don't want them subjected to that kind of scrutiny."

"It doesn't have to be that way," he argued, but she could see the doubt in his expression.

"Doesn't it?"

"Other people survive it. There are plenty of politicians who manage to keep their private lives relatively private. Their spouses choose to stay out of the spotlight, and are successful, to an extent."

"It happens," she agreed. "But there are no guarantees."

"No," he conceded. "No guarantees."

He was silent for a moment before speaking again. "And if I give you my promise that I will never go into politics? Will that remove all your doubts about us?"

"I would never accept that," she said flatly. "I refuse to place any limitations on your future. If I...if we decide to commit to a permanent relationship, it would be with the agreement that all options are still open. If you ever have any desire to pursue an elected position, you must be free to do so."

"Delia, I love you. I want to marry you. I want to spend the rest of my life with you—however I earn my living. Please don't turn me down just because of something that may never even happen."

"It isn't just politics, Lane," Delia said, her heart twisting. "It's...I..."

"What, sweetheart? Tell me what you feel," he urged, leaning forward intently.

Her throat was so tight she could hardly speak. "I'm sc-scared," she whispered, regretting the revealing stammer.

He rounded the table and knelt beside her chair, taking her icy hands in his own larger, warmer ones. "What are you afraid of, Delia?"

"Of being hurt," she murmured, avoiding his eyes. "Of disappointing you. Of having you ch-change your mind about your feelings for me. Of trying and failing. Before I became involved with you, the life I led might have been a bit lonely, but it was safe. C-comfortable."

"You could never disappoint me," Lane said with a gruff determination that sounded utterly, heatedly sincere. "And my feelings for you will never change. I want you to have so much more than a life that's safe and comfortable—and lonely. I want you to have love and laughter and excitement and children. I want to experience those things with you. I will pledge my life to making you happy, Delia. Even if it means signing a blood oath that I will never even consider a political career."

His face seemed to float in front of her, an illusion caused by a film of unshed tears. "Will you give me time?" she asked, her voice shaky. "Please?"

"All the time you need," he promised. "I love you."

He silenced her reply with a long, passionate kiss. By the time he released her, she had lost the nerve to tell him that she loved him, too. She wasn't sure whether she was more relieved or disappointed that he didn't press for the words.

Delia was finally forced into a confrontation with her own feelings. Unfortunately, it wasn't within the quiet privacy of her own home. The awkward moment of awareness occurred at a barbecue given at the home of one of Lane's co-workers, in front of a large group of his friends.

She'd been a little uncomfortable ever since they'd arrived over an hour earlier. So many people were introduced to her, so many names and faces she had to struggle to remember. The atmosphere was different from what she'd become accustomed to within her own social circle. Delia's friends tended to seek quiet, amiable entertainment. They gathered for games of Trivial Pursuit or charades or—on a really wild night—Pictionary. They wore old jeans and college sweatshirts, talked about books and films and discussed current events with objective, dispassionate interest.

Lane's friends, on the other hand, were noisy and energetic, seemed to be constantly chattering and laughing and moving. Simultaneous games of volleyball and touch football were conducted at opposite sides of the lush, acre-and-a-half back lawn. The games seemed good-natured enough, but the competition was obviously fierce. Politics and world affairs were discussed with a passion that sometimes led to raised voices. Everyone seemed to have a very strong opinion about every topic.

The invitations had specified casual clothing, but Delia was glad she hadn't donned jeans and a sweatshirt, opting for a jungle-print blouse over a khaki T-shirt with crisp khaki slacks, instead. The rest of the crowd could have posed for an L.L. Bean catalog. Expensive walking shorts, chinos, summer sweaters. Deceptively simple-looking T-shirts that probably cost more than Delia's entire ensemble, including her shoes.

Though Lane wore his favorite combination of comfortable jeans and a brightly striped polo shirt, he blended well with the crowd, Delia couldn't help noticing. His dark good looks and lazy charm served him well in this young, attractive, upwardly mobile setting. Delia could feel her hard-won self-confidence slipping from the moment they'd arrived, though she clung to it fiercely. She was sure Lane's friends were very nice people on the whole, she reminded herself sternly, though there were a few she didn't particularly like. It was stupid to allow herself to be intimidated by any of them.

She told herself that it was only natural that she'd feel somewhat jealous when a gorgeous redhead in a halter top and beautifully tailored shorts all but climbed into Lane's lap at one point. She forced herself to note that he responded with good-natured humor, but nothing more.

She couldn't fault Lane for his behavior toward her. Even surrounded by his friends, he stayed close beside Delia, making sure she was never alone, never bored or uncomfortable. She encouraged him to join one of the games; he declined with a smile and an explanation that he wasn't really in the mood for sports that afternoon. She suspected that he might have been in the mood had she not been with him, or had she been more at ease with his friends.

She tried. She really did. And she was privately pleased with her success. Until a heated political discussion suddenly broke out over burgers and barbecued chicken wings. Again, it seemed that everyone had a deeply felt opinion and a well-worded argument to support each position. Lane was right in the middle of the debate, arguing his own beliefs with the articulate skill he'd developed in his budding law career.

Wide-eyed and silent, Delia watched the group—their flashing eyes, flailing hands, firmly shaking heads. There seemed to be little real anger, but a great deal of heat. They *believed.* They were willing to go toe-to-toe, if necessary, to back those beliefs. And Lane's eyes glowed with the same intensity, the same passion, as his friends'.

It was inevitable that someone would finally turn to Delia. "Do you have any influence with this guy?" the woman who was on the opposite side of Lane in the controversy demanded. "Can't you make him listen to reason?"

"I—I—"

"What makes you think Delia doesn't agree with me?" Lane countered, facing the woman in grinning challenge.

Several pairs of eyes turned to Delia. "Well?" someone else asked. "*Do* you agree with him?"

Delia's face flooded with heat. "I'm s-sure Lane has st-studied this issue at great length," she hedged. The hated stammer made her insides tighten, took her back several years to a time when so many mocking eyes had been on her as she'd tried desperately to get through an oral book report an unsympathetic teacher had insisted she deliver, despite her pleas to be exempted. She shook off the ugly memory and lifted her chin, determined not to embarrass Lane—or herself—in front of his friends.

"But what do *you* believe?" the first woman asked.

Delia realized the woman wasn't trying to be cruel. She was simply trying to encourage Delia to join in the discussion. Probably on the assumption that Delia had an opinion as deeply entrenched as the ones the others were arguing, but had simply been too shy, or too polite, to voice them among near-strangers.

And that's when Delia understood one of the main reasons she'd been unable to commit to Lane. She chewed her lower lip as the realization hit her with almost staggering force.

Lane slipped an arm around Delia's shoulders. "Delia," he said smoothly, "believes in the right to remain silent if she so chooses. Now didn't I hear someone mention that Karen had brought a triple batch of her famous caramel-pecan brownies for dessert?"

That quickly, the conversation turned to food—chocolate, in particular. A trim and muscular young man decried the fat and calories in brownies, but was immediately drowned out by a chorus of voices—mostly women's—who insisted that there was absolutely nothing wrong with indulging in chocolate brownies on occasion. Everyone else descended greedily on the dessert table, leaving Lane and Delia behind.

"Sorry," he said quietly, his arm still tight around her shoulders. "I forgot to warn you that this group thrives on political arguments."

"It wasn't necessary for you to rescue me, Lane," Delia said, studying her clasped hands. "I would have thought of something to say."

"I know," he assured her. "But since I was the one who neglected to prepare you, I felt I owed you one."

Delia stood, smoothly dislodging his arm. "If we don't get over there soon, there won't be any brownies left," she warned. "And I, for one, don't want to miss out on caramel-pecan brownies."

"Me, either," he agreed, pushing himself to his feet. He was smiling, but Delia knew that he watched her with a probing intensity that told her he knew the incident had bothered her much more than she had indicated to him.

They would talk about it again later, when they were alone. And Delia dreaded that talk.

Chapter Eight

"You're very quiet tonight," Lane commented later, as he and Delia sat in her living room, sipping coffee. "Tired?"

She nodded. "A little."

Lane set his coffee cup on a table and turned to face her. "Delia, about what happened this afternoon. It's still bothering you, isn't it?"

This was it. Delia drew a deep breath and set her cup beside Lane's. "What, exactly, do you think is bothering me, Lane?"

He made a vague gesture with one hand. "I assume you're upset because you stuttered when Sharilyn put you on the spot. I'm sorry, I should have—"

Delia interrupted with a quick shake of her head. "That isn't it."

He stopped, surprised. "It's not?"

"No. My occasional stutter annoys me, of course. I hate it. But I've learned to live with it, for the most part. I manage to do so by reminding myself that I've almost completely conquered it during the past few years."

"And I admire you for that," he assured her, taking her hand. "Very much."

She left her hand lying still in his. "Thank you. But I'm not asking for compliments. I'm simply trying to explain."

His fingers tightened rather convulsively. "All right. I'm listening. What *is* bothering you? Do you resent that I interceded for you? If so, I'm sorry. I was trying to help."

"I know you were. And, yes, I do resent it a bit. I prefer to do my own talking, Lane, even if it means there's a chance I might stutter." That was another conclusion she'd reached sometime during the afternoon. One she wanted to make quite clear.

Lane nodded, looking properly chastened. "I'm sorry," he repeated. "It won't happen again."

"But it *will* happen again," she argued, sitting very still, very straight. Knowing this had to be said, no matter what the consequences. "At least, the same circumstances will happen again. You're a very deeply committed person, Lane. Your friends are activists and policymakers—as you are. Your beliefs are very strong, your dedication absolute. You would never be content to live as an observer, staying in the background, keeping your opinions to yourself and choosing to ignore situations you don't particularly approve of."

He started to speak, hesitated, then shook his head. "No," he admitted. "That isn't me. When I see an injustice being committed, even if it's only in my own opinion, I have to do something about it. I can't just stand back and look the other way."

"I know you can't. That's one of the things I admire most about you," she conceded. "You have a big heart and a great deal of courage. You want to make a difference."

"But?" he prodded quietly, visibly braced for the rest.

"But—I've never been like that, Lane. I'm afraid I've been one of the observers. Content to try to deal with my own problems and let others do the same."

Lane frowned. "You're saying you don't care about the problems our country is facing? That you really aren't interested in doing anything about them?"

"I didn't say that, exactly. Only that I can't seem to get as passionate about it as you and your friends are. At least, not yet. I'm very traditional in some ways, Lane. I'd like to be secure—emotionally and financially—and self-sufficient. I want a family, children. And I know myself well enough to realize that those children, my own family, would always come first for me. I'm not going to leave them with nannies while I'm out picketing polluters or chaining myself to trees."

He laughed at her imagery, then sobered quickly when she only looked at him without smiling. "Delia, I understand," he said, taking both her hands in his. "You're a very private person. Committed in your own quiet way. I know you want the world to be a better place for those children you want, and I know you would be willing to work to make it so—but I also know that you prefer to do so out of the spotlights. Behind the scenes."

She nodded. "Yes."

"That's all I would ever ask of you. Oh, if I go into politics—and that's still a very big *if*—there would be times I'd want you beside me. Parties, fund-raisers, whatever. But I would never ask you to neglect our children to support me. I give you my word on that."

The thought of Lane's children made her heart quiver, but Delia knew there was one more problem she had to broach. "Lane, you know that discussion you were having this afternoon?"

"Yes. I'm afraid you're right, sweetheart. Discussions like that will be inevitable around me."

"And I can handle them. But..." She moistened her lips.

"But?"

She took a deep breath. "I didn't entirely agree with you this afternoon," she admitted. "I understood your position, but I think some of the others were right about taking a different approach to the solution."

Lane frowned at her for a moment—and then a light of understanding dawned in his eyes. "You didn't agree with me?"

Biting her lip, she shook her head. "Not entirely," she added.

He suddenly smiled, and his fingers tightened around hers. "That's why you were reluctant to speak? Because you didn't think I would like what you would have said?"

"I didn't want to embarrass you in front of your friends. And I would never want to be a handicap to you in a political arena. I agree with you most of the time, Lane—but not always. And I simply don't think I can lie, or constantly prevaricate, whenever anyone asks my opinion, even if it contradicts yours."

"Delia." He tugged her into his arms for a hug. "Sweetheart, I really thought you knew me better than that," he said, his voice chiding even as he brushed a kiss across her temple. "Have I *ever* said anything to make you believe I wanted you to be a prop for me? That I wanted you to be a pretty, brainless ornament to dangle from my arm?"

She flushed. "I'm well aware that I'm not the type for that, even if you *were* interested."

He smiled. "If you mean you aren't ornamental enough, you're wrong. You're a beautiful woman, Delia Beckman. I'm always proud to be seen with you. But more than that, I'm proud of who you are. You are intelligent, capable and self-sufficient. You've successfully overcome a childhood problem that could have left you introverted and defensive. But you aren't. You know what you want—and what you believe. And I would never ask you to change on either count."

"Even when I disagree with you?" she asked, unable to hide a faint ripple of skepticism.

"Even then," he answered firmly. "I'm not saying I'm always going to like it. I'm only human, Delia, and I get mad sometimes. Don't you?"

"Of course, but—"

"Don't you expect to get mad at me sometimes?"

"I'm sure I will, but—"

"I may try to change your mind occasionally—in fact, I'm sure I will," he added wryly. "But I will always accept your right to your own opinion, regardless of whether it coincides with mine. I would certainly expect you to feel the same way about me—and I will try to always be open-minded about your opinions. In fact, I'm eager to hear your arguments about the discussion we were having at the party this afternoon. I always value a fresh outlook on things.''

''You really don't mind that I can't get as excited as you do about politics and philosophies?'' Delia couldn't help asking him, searching his face.

His smile was the one that had made her heart stop from the first time she'd seen it. ''I love you, Delia. Exactly the way you are. Your serenity, your quiet contentment—I was drawn to that from the beginning. Sometimes my entire life feels like one big argument, one never-ending battle. I love coming home to you, relaxing with you, sharing the peace and calm you surround yourself with. You can't know what it means to me to know that's waiting for me at the end of a horrible day.''

She frowned. ''You make me sound like one of those zombie wives from old television sitcoms. You know, wearing pearls and making brownies with a fixed smile, waiting at home with your slippers and your drink when you return from doing truly important things.''

''Don't be ridiculous. You have your own career, your own pursuits. I'd like to think there will be times when *you'll* come home from a hard day at work to find me waiting with your slippers and your drink. Whether you choose to advance your career or become a full-time homemaker, I know you will always be your own person with your own needs. I want us to be a team, Delia. Full partners. Two separate individuals who are fully committed to each other even as we pursue our own goals."

"That sounds almost too good to be true," she whispered, wanting so desperately to believe.

"I didn't say it would be easy," he acknowledged. "But I think it's possible. What do you think?"

He watched her steadily as he waited for her answer. Delia knew this was the moment that she had to stop stalling. It was time to stop waffling and to make a decision. Time to stop being afraid. When she spoke, she was rather surprised at how obvious the decision suddenly seemed. "I think you're right," she said, her head held high. "I think we can do it."

She was willing to work as hard as necessary at making their relationship last a lifetime. It was comforting to know that Lane would approach the commitment with the same passionate dedication with which he pursued everything else.

His eyes flared, but he held back. He seemed to be expecting something else.

She smiled. "I love you, Lane," she said, knowing what he wanted—needed?—to hear. "And whether I say it clearly, or with a stutter, I've never meant anything more."

He pulled her close to his heart and buried his face in her hair. "That was all I needed to hear," he murmured.

And then it was no longer necessary for either of them to say more.

Epilogue

Delia was reading when the doorbell rang. She looked up from her book with a frown. She wasn't expecting anyone. It was time for Lane to get home, but he wouldn't ring the bell. Unless he'd forgotten his house key again, she thought with a smile and a slight shake of her head.

She set the childbirth book aside and pushed herself off the couch, one hand pressed absently to her enlarged stomach. She and Lane had been married almost two years now. They hadn't wanted to wait any longer to start their family.

It had been a blissful two years, she mused as she waddled across the living room of their modest, but lovely, Seattle home. They were very happy. Lane worked hard—and she knew his hours would be even longer if he won the state senate race he'd recently been persuaded to enter—but he never gave her reason to doubt his love for her, or his commitment to their marriage.

Delia had left her old job at the insurance company when she'd learned that she was pregnant. This was what she'd always wanted, she'd told Lane at the time. A family. A home. Love.

She had already become more active than she'd anticipated in Lane's campaign. She spent several hours a day at his campaign headquarters, working side by side with dedicated volunteers. She'd found it impossible not to get involved—after all, it was so clearly obvious that Lane was the best candidate for the position. How could anyone not see that? she'd found herself wondering—completely objectively, of course.

She didn't always agree with him, and she'd found herself learning to argue her own positions with more conviction than she'd ever expected. There were a few times when he'd even changed his mind after being swayed by her arguments. Just as he'd won her over to his side a time or two. On the whole, however, their beliefs were very similar, which was nice.

The doorbell rang again. "Who is it?" Delia called out as she approached the door, cautious as always.

"It's me," Lane's voice replied. "My hands are full."

She opened the door quickly, then smiled at a sudden memory of their first meeting.

A large box with feet stood on the doorstep of her home. She held the door wide and stepped out of the way as Lane staggered through.

"Whew!" he said, setting the box on the floor with a look of relief. "Your sister's sent another incredibly heavy package. I pulled into the drive-way just as the delivery truck arrived."

"I bet it's something for the baby," Delia said, eagerly bending over the intriguing package.

"Well, let's find out." He pulled a penknife out of his pocket and began to hack at the thick layers of packing tape. It took some persistence on his part—and a few muttered curses—but the box finally opened.

Delia caught her breath when Lane lifted the wooden item out of its wrappings. "It's the cradle Dani used when Johnny was a baby," she exclaimed, reaching out to stroke the glossy ponderosa pine. She was deeply touched by the gift. She knew the cradle was an antique, and that it held special meaning for Dani and John. What a loving, generous gesture!

"She wishes us the same happiness she has found with her family," Lane said, reading from the card Dani had enclosed for both of them. His voice was a bit husky, proving he was as touched as Delia by the surprise.

Delia swiped quickly at a tear that trickled down her right cheek as she pictured her baby nestled in the cradle. "This is so special," she murmured. "Isn't it beautiful, Lane?"

He was examining the woodwork appreciatively. "It's really old, isn't it?"

"Over a hundred years old," Delia agreed, remembering what her sister had told her. "It's handmade."

Lane ran a hand over the snug joinings, the worn-smooth carvings. "You certainly can't find workmanship like this in the department stores."

He rocked it gently, then turned it over to examine it more closely. "There's something carved on the bottom," he announced, bending to peer through the lenses of the new glasses Delia liked so much on him.

She'd seen the cradle before, but had never studied it this closely. "What does it say?" she asked, leaning over Lane's shoulder.

" 'Made By Adam Stroud For His Wife, Sarah. Washington Territory—1857,' " Lane read aloud. *" 'For a new life and new beginnings.' "*

Delia was enchanted. Her mind filled with images of that man who'd created this cradle with such love and optimism. She hoped he and his Sarah had lived full, happy lives with the children they'd tended in this cradle. "That's so sweet," she murmured, her eyes filling again.

Lane had gone very still. "Delia," he said, something odd in his voice. "Didn't you hear those names?"

She'd been too overwhelmed with emotion to pay much attention. "What about them?"

"Stroud—my mother's maiden name," he reminded her.

She smiled. "A nice coincidence."

Lane slowly shook his dark head. "I think it's more than that. You know what a nut Mother is about genealogy."

Thinking of her delightful mother-in-law's well-known passion for the subject, Delia nodded. "Of course."

"She's been even more wound up about our background since I entered the senate race. She thinks I should make it well-known that my family has been in this area for many generations, that I have strong ties to this state and the people in it."

"It's not a bad campaign angle," Delia murmured, momentarily distracted.

Impatiently, Lane tapped the faded carvings. "Delia, one of my ancestors was named Adam Stroud. He was a trapper who married a woman named Sarah, a white captive he purchased from the Nez Percé in the mid eighteen hundreds. Mother was fascinated when she learned about that. She must have told me the story a dozen times or more. I'm surprised she hasn't mentioned it to you."

"But she has!" Delia exclaimed, slapping a hand to her forehead. "Last Christmas. I thought it was a wonderful story, but I'd forgotten the names—Lane, do you really think this was made by your own ancestor?"

"I think it might well have been," he said with a baffled laugh. "Isn't that weird? Wait until I tell Mother. She'll flip."

Delia was wiping her cheeks again—something she tended to do quite a bit lately. She smiled through the happy tears. "It's fate," she declared. "The cradle was meant to be brought back into the family."

"I don't know if it's fate or one of those bizarre coincidences," Lane said, reaching out to take her hand. "I only know I'm glad we're the ones who have it now. For our baby." He stood and rested his free hand on her stomach, his love shining from his gorgeous blue eyes.

Delia lifted her face for his kiss. She told herself she was being fanciful to feel as though she and Lane were being watched with warm approval.

But then again . . . maybe they were.

* * * * *

If you loved Beginnings,
then don't miss Gina Ferris Wilkins's
wonderful Silhouette Special Edition,
A Man For Mom—*available now*
wherever Silhouette Books are sold!